EVERY TIME I HEAR OF SCHRODINGER'S CAT I REACH FOR A GUN

Stephen Hawking

CROWLEY

AND THE CHEMICAL WEDDING OF SCIENCE AND MAGIC

JULIAN DOYLE
BRUCE DICKINSON

Matador
Troubador Publishing Ltd
9 De Montfort Mews
Leicester LE1 7FW, UK
Tel: (+44) 116 255 9311 / 9312
Email: books@troubador.co.uk
Web: www.troubador.co.uk/matador

ISBN 978 1848761 339

A CIP catalogue record for this book
is available from the British Library

Typeset in 11pt Book Antiqua by Troubador Publishing Ltd, Leicester, UK

Matador is an imprint of Troubador Publishing Ltd

To Simon and Jud
who made me laugh
and
'Whispering' Paul McDowell
who did the same.

Contents

Acknowledgements

Thanks to Patricia Alderidge, Archivist at Bedlam who put me on to Richard Dadd. The quest to understand his father's murder took me to Egypt and years of research into his God, Osiris and the occult knowledge that emanates from him. Thanks to all the writers of the books mentioned in the Bibliography, whether I agree or disagree with their theories they have all advanced my research. And thanks to Perrine Moran and Sandy Robertson for proof reading our work.

i

PROLOGUE

KANGCHENJUNGA MOUNTAIN 1905

The jagged peaks of Nepal rise out of a sea of cloud. Swooping down through the clouds into the darkness a raging blizzard bellows. Miniscule ant-like figures stagger up the grey snowfield. Raw hands clutch the frozen lifeline linking them. The wind rips at their frostbitten faces, their primitive defence of balaclavas, dark linen jackets and high leather boots are scant protection. A Sherpa stumbles and collapses, his impossibly heavy burden falls in the snow. In front, the leader jerks on the rope in frustration. He pivots revealing his nametag 'CROWLEY'. Furious he cuts through the deep snow until he stands over the man.

"Up!" he demands with the authority of an English Public schoolboy. The other climbers pause for breath in astonishment.

"Get UP!"

Without warning Crowley raises his silver handed walking stick and savagely brings it down on the hapless Sherpa.

"Do what I say you feeble excuse..."

He raises the stick again. The rest suddenly stunned into action push Crowley off and huddle around the groaning Sherpa.

Mitchell shouts through the wind, "For God's sake... his leg's gone."

"If he doesn't walk on it then he'll die."

"We can carry him."

"No!" orders Crowley. "I am the leader of this expedition, if he doesn't get up we will leave him."

The decomposing group regards Crowley with obvious disgust.

"You are out of your mind, we will do no such thing."

Crowley looks down on them with loathing and announces with utter certainty, "Then you will all die."

He pulls out a knife and severs the frozen hemp rope from around his middle. The slack drops at Mitchell's feet like a lifeless serpent; when he looks back up he is stunned to see Crowley trudging off into the grey blizzard, above.

Slowly the determined figure disappears into the storm.

A raging night of tempestuous winds and whipping snow descends on the peaks. A tent, impossibly situated 20,000 feet high on a precipitous ledge, withstands the screaming torment's attempt to dislodge it. An oil lamp vainly glows through the canvas. Within the cramped confines, Aleister Crowley shivers and rasps in the grip of an asthma attack. Glimpses flash through his tortured mind, ghosts of young Crowley's viscious past.

Images of Hell – as portrayed by his Plymouth Brethren parents from the Darbyite creed, who believed literally in the truth of every word of the Holy Book and chosen by God himself as the only worthy community to inhabit Heaven.

Images of Death – the final convulsive throes of his eccentric father leaving the eleven year old in the grip of a bigoted mother.

"You beast! You Beast!" she screams at the evil child.

Her death elicits his poem:

In her hospital bed she lay
Rotting away!
Cursing by night and cursing by day,
Rotting away!
The lupus is over her face and head,
Filthy and foul and horrid and dead,
And her shrieks they would almost wake the dead;

Rotting away!
In her horrible grave she lay,
Rotting away!
Rotting by night, and rotting by day,
Rotting away!
In the place of her face is a gory hole,
And the worms are gnawing the tissues foul,
And the Devil is gloating over her soul,
Rotting away!

Images of sadism - thwack! The perverted headmaster of Malvern school viciously thrashes his naked bottom.

Images of lust - the creatures of the night, stripped and thrusting vampires who gave the youth the naked sores that erupted from his illicit pleasure.

Alone as the violent winds thrash the tent, in a mad frenzy the Apostate is locked in a perilous struggle with self. For three long hours God and Satan fight for Aleister Crowley's eternal soul. Then as the howling winds calm, God finally conquers. Now the only doubt left in Crowley's tortured mind is, which of the two is God.

The tormented night gives way to a bright, blinding day. The precarious tent flaps open and the *Chosen One*, Aleister Crowley, crawls bleary eyed into the snowy glare. He accepts the Lords have chosen him even from birth as he bore on his body, the three most important distinguishing marks of the Buddha. He was tongue-tied and on the second day of his incarnation a surgeon cut the fraenum linguae. He also had phimosis, the membrane of his foreskin of the penis could not be fully retracted and necessitated an operation some three lusters later. Lastly, he had upon the centre of his heart four hairs curling from left to right in the exact form of a Swastika.

Leaving behind His belongings He trudges the last hundred feet towards the peak, oblivious that the thin air was tearing at His lungs. With each breathless step He pants rhythmically - couplets from Richard the Third.

"Go Gentlemen, every man to his charge.
Let not our babbling dreams affright our souls.
For conscience is a word that cowards use,
Devised at first to keep the strong in awe.
Let strong arms be our conscience sword our law.
March on join bravely let us to it pell-mell.
If not to heaven then hand in hand to HELL."

At length He stands triumphantly high above the forgotten world. Exhilarated He tears off His goggles and gloves then strips to the waist, falling on His knees in the snow before the rising sun. The Son of the sun always knew the Universe was invented for Him to suck. Now He grows delirious as He contemplates the delicious horrors that are to unfold His life. Passionately His croaking voice calls out in ecstatic impudence.

"Do what thou wilt shall be the whole of the law."

In the stratospheric stillness, an echo returns across the astral plane.

"Love is the law, love under will."

This glorious Son raises His arms and shouts back. "I am the beast – the beast incarnate! My laws alone will govern my life and all the lives before me. Stab your demoniac smile to my brain; Soak me in cognac, love and cocaine."

Below, beneath the veil of storm clouds, obscene shapes of bodies are scattered in the agony of death. Mitchell, his mouth frozen open, the icy rope connecting the others, all frozen, all dead.

20,000 feet below them the inhabitants having just finished one world war mercilessly, murder each other a second time.

ii

EPILOGUE

HASTINGS 1947

Grey bleached sky over dormant fields, gnarled trees scratch the winter skyline. Suddenly flapping black shapes scare into the air. The sound of a car, revving fast, the speedo trembles at 65 mph, a gloved hand turns the wheel, a foot pressed down hard on the pedal and a Cambridge scarf flaps violently to the speed. The sports car forks suddenly down towards the grey sea and white seaside houses of Hastings. The two pubescent Cambridge students drive towards the first landing place of their ancient ancestors.

Norman forefathers of both Alex and Symons disembarked at Hastings in 1066, defeated the English Troops (Angles Saxon and Jutes) and conquered this fertile realm decisively. These French, Lords and their Squires ruled over the Germanic English, who had 500 years earlier defeated the British, pushing them westward into Wales. The Norman Lords exploited the English mercilessly starving them with impossible work schedules and outlawing hunting. For their gratification they imposed the right to rape their peasants' newly married maidens. During this time the modern English language was fashioned from the Norman, French and the peasant Germanic. The food on the table is in the Lords language - Beef, Mutton and Pork and the food in the field in the Peasant Germanic - cow, sheep, pig. When the Germanic peasants attempted to use French words when pleading for clemency, they would wrongly use the word 'Mercy', giving it new meaning from its original French 'thank you'.

Alex and Symons in their expensive sports car are natural inheritors of the privileges of this deep-seated Norman Class system that would soon be threatened by the rise of the meritocracy, triggered by the reforms encapsulated in the 1944 Education Act.

The empty roads will also be threatened by the rise of mass production manufacturing but now the roads are their racing circuit with only the odd hop wagon trundling on.

Close to the outskirts of Hastings, Symons spins the wheel and veers up 'The Ridge' that circles to the east of the town. After a mile the car slows and turns on to a gravel drive, pulling up outside Netherwood House, a large sombre building shaded by a massive oak. The hot, vibrating engine is finally silenced and the young students stretch out and crunch across the gravel to the boarding house.

"I can't wait to meet the wickedest man in the world," quips Alex.

"Alex, you promised to behave yourself," warns Symons.

"Does that mean I have to be good or bad?"

"Don't play games Alex. He's powerful and dangerous if you cross him."

Alex rolls his eyes in mock fear as Symons pulls the bell. The door is opened by the landlord in carpet slippers, the racing post under his arm and his glasses perched on his head.

"Ah, Master Symons, he's upstairs in his room."

He opens the door further to allow them to enter.

The hallway is as cold and gloomy as a funeral parlour. The landlord picks up a couple of letters from the sideboard. "Take his post up will you, my legs..."

He is interrupted by the radio suddenly announcing 'they're off' at 12 o'clock at Aintree and the slippers race back towards the light, warmth and excitement of the back kitchen.

On the stairs a black cat watches the youths climb the stairs to the landing dominated by a large stiff aspidistra. The dark brown wallpaper is rather tattered and the paintwork peeling, reflecting the shortages and rationing of post war Britain.

Alex looks around disparagingly. "Come on Symons, look at this dump. He's the forgotten man of magic."

"Not so forgotten." Symons shows Alex one of the letters with a US post-mark. "He still gets post from followers in America."

Alex dismisses this with a sniff and glances at a framed sign that reads: 'Guests are requested not to tease the ghosts.' And another, 'Breakfast will be served at 9am to survivors of the night."

Alex makes a silly ghost impression. Symons shakes his head disapprovingly.

"You can't really take this stuff seriously?" huffs Alex.

"Those signs are jokes," says Symons. "Jokes and ridicule are used against the ignorant because the truth is complicated."

"Complicated, I see," says Alex sarcastically.

"Look Alex, you have no idea what you are dealing with here..."

Symons gives up as he reaches the door on the upper landing and knocks. Silence. They look at each other; he knocks again. A thin voice responds, 'It's open'. Symons turns the handle slowly.

The light from the window hardly penetrates the room, which is cluttered with books, paintings and an unkempt bed in the corner. Sitting alone in a tattered, winged armchair by the glow of the smoky coal fire is a frail old man. His skin like yellowed parchment, his hair, thin grey wisps, across a fragile skull, his eyes yellowed by life's impurities. This is the aging shell of the once notorious occultist, Aleister Crowley, now nearing the end of his existence. In the corner is his magic wand, which has been idle for years.

His voice croaks ritualistically. "Do what thou wilt shall be the whole of the law."

Symons responds, "Love is the law. Love under will."

Crowley takes out a gold pocket watch, flicks it open and checks the time.

"Midday."

The aging Aleister Crowley with his Magic Wand

"I had to speed a bit to be on time, Sir."

"Good; time is important. So Symons, how goes the studies?"

"I'm re-reading the Bible in the light of what you said. It's most interesting."

"Yes, unfortunately it is the last remaining source of primeval magic. And who is this?" says Crowley without looking at the other student behind him.

Alex replies, "Alex Lepard, Sir, I'm at Trinity too."

"Reading theology, like Symons here?" asks Crowley.

"No, reading science, Sir."

Crowley's eyes light up, "Ah, the new magic?" For Crowley is totally familiar with the latest astonishing theories of quantum physics,

Alex does not comprehend his meaning. "I don't think so, we are taught a healthy degree of scepticism."

Crowley searches deep into Alex's eyes then abruptly pronounces, "Scientist! Bah, you ooze disbelief! A good ritualized fuck would expand your consciousness not to mention your constricted orifices."

Alex tries to smile but his embarrassment shows.

"He doesn't understand yet," helps Symons.

Crowley keeps his eyes fixed on Alex and intones, "I see you in my wizard's spy-glass, on a lee shore with your masts all gone by the board and the Union Jack upside down flying from a stump. Your form forlorn and lost."

And with that Crowley turns back to Symons and speaks normally.

"Well, my winged messenger, what have you got for me?"

"Nothing special, Sir," answered Symons. "The newspaper. Oh, your post."

Symons hands over the letters and glances at the newspaper headlines,

'DEAD SEA SCROLLS WILL REVEAL TRUTH OF JESUS'.

"This could help with my studies."

Crowley glances up at him with pity, for he seems to know that Papal conspirators will conceal this 1947 find till Symons is well into his own old age.

Crowley checks the address on the first envelope and scowls.

"That stupid woman!"

He screws it up and throws it dismissively into the fire. He sees the US stamp on the second and smiles in recognition then settles back in his chair.

"Now Symons, time is of the essence, I'm not feeling any younger."

"Yes sir, I mean no sir. I do want to learn."

Crowley flares suddenly. "No, no, that won't do, it won't work unless you believe – believe in me right down to your very soul."

"I do sir but there's just three weeks and I still don't understand?"

Crowley calms, "Of course not, Lets start at the beginning." He strains up to open the glass door of a bookcase and take down a well worn leather bound volume. While his back is turned, Alex glances round the room. Among several photos is one of mountain climbers on Kangchenjunga.

"Wasn't there some sort of accident?"

"Have you ever climbed, young man?"

"No sir," admits Alex.

"Then let me tell you that only exceptional men retain their normal reasoning powers in the presence of mountains. And don't think it's just the panic of the peasant who loses his head and calls on all the Saints. I have seen scientifically trained minds frequently lose all sense of judgement and logic. In the case of Kangchenjunga the catastrophe was a direct result of mutinous disobedience to my orders."

He sits back down. "If you want to know your true self, young man, climb a mountain."

Climbers on Kangchenjunga (Crowley seated middle right)

Crowley opens the book and announces the title, 'The Book of Thoth'.

Alex glances from the picture across the desk to a thick notebook on which is written, in Crowley's spidery handwriting, *'The Secret Masters'*. He turns a page. Without turning Crowley feels the incursion and yells.

"Put that down! My Magical Diaries are not for blind eyes. They contain every rite, every sacrament of sexual magic that..."

He breaks off into a raking cough and nods from Symons to a glass and on to a bottle of Scotch. Symons grabs the dirty glass and pours a measure. Crowley snatches it and slobbers it down. The drink sooths the cough and he turns back to the pages of the ancient tome.

"The oldest and most powerful ritual, comes to us from Ancient Egypt. It is contained in the legend of Isis and Osiris. Plato himself said the story could be understood on twenty different levels and was true on all of them."

Crowley points out the detail from a pyramid text. "It tells of the betrayal and murder of Osiris by his brother Seth. Seth cut the body into fifteen parts and scattered them over the land of Egypt. His wife, Isis found most of the pieces and using her magic she fused them together in resurrection. But she was missing the phallus. She pleaded with the Lord of Measures, Thoth, to help her. Using his measuring reed as a substitute phallus she performed a wedding rite with Osiris, and brought forth a powerful son, Horus.

Symons puzzles, "It's a non-carnal union - a virgin birth."

"Exactly and of course Osiris is the original death and resurrection God. Only four magnificent times has the rite been performed; Joshua with the Magdalene and Abelard and Eloise are the two you know. "

"Who were the others?" asks Symons.

Crowley shakes his head towards Alex.

"On Friday when you return alone we will begin your initiation."

Symons hesitantly begins to explain. "I'm not sure I can afford..."

Crowley dismisses this and tears open the American envelope.

"Don't worry about money this will make…"

He takes out a letter and looks for something else.

"Where's the money damn him?"

He glances over the letter impatiently then bursts out. "What a fool! An ignorant, stupid fool! Don't they understand how little time..?"

He reads on getting more and more furious. "No! No! NO!"

The outburst frightens the youths. Crowley crushes the letter and thrusts it at Symons.

"Look at this. The head of our California brethren has fallen under the spell of a writer of science fiction. Of science fiction no less! You see what they use my ritual for?"

Symons un-crumples the letter and reads with astonishment.

Crowley angrily sips at the whiskey remembering the letter he received four months earlier from Jack Parsons, which introduced this L. Ron Hubbard as…

> '..a gentleman, red hair, green eyes, honest and intelligent. Although he has no formal training in magic he has an extraordinary amount of experience and understanding in the field. Ron appears to have some sort of highly developed astral vision. He describes his angel as a beautiful winged woman with red hair whom he calls the Empress who has guided him through his life and saved him many times. He is in complete accord with our own principles. I have found a staunch companion and comrade in Ron. L Hubbard.'

Crowley had immediately suspected Hubbard would tap Parsons' money the way he himself had been doing for years. For Jack Parsons was rich. He was a successful propulsion chemist and associate of the famous scientific institution, Cal Tech. Crowley who was a skilled Chemist in his own right, suspected Parsons had accidentally sniffed some concoction of chemicals in his lab that had turned his mind, for in his crazy way he had become Crowley's loyal disciple. Crowley made him the head of the OTO in America and charged him a regular fee for the honour. But now all this looked like it was coming to an end till a second letter arrived which pleased Crowley no end. Hubbard had stolen Parsons' yacht, his money and Betty, his girlfriend and set off into the open sea. The letter from Parsons explained…

> 'Hubbard attempted to escape, setting sail on my yacht. I performed a full invocation to the Bartzabel within the circle and at that moment, the ship was struck by a sudden squall off the coast, which, ripped off his sails and forced him back to port where I took the boat in custody. Here I am in Miami pursuing the children of my folly. I have them well tied up. They cannot move without going to jail. However, I am afraid that most of the money has already been spent. I will be lucky to salvage 3,000 to 5,000 dollars.'

'Hooray,' thought Crowley, but now the third letter announced astonishingly that Parsons had forgiven the two escapees and together – using Crowley's rites, they were in the process of producing…

"A moonchild!" exclaims Symons. Crowley snatches the letter back.

"That idiot Parsons claims a 'miraculous illumination' from this 'Lafayette Ron Hubbard'. He's given away the money due to me and now evokes my scarlet ritual to produce a Moonchild."

"God! What are you going to do?"

"Do! Do..." Crowley breaks off coughing. Finally clearing the phlegm he continues croakingly, "By dawn I will invoke such a 'miraculous illumination' that Jack Parsons will wonder..."

His voice cracks again as he is racked by cough. He spits out blood on the carpet. "Can I get you anything, sir?"

"No. No," he squeaks with difficulty. "You'll just have to excuse me a moment. I need medication." He smiles at Symons, who nods. Alex looks confused.

"Come on Alex," says Symons ushering Alex out and reverently closing the door behind them.

Once outside Alex turns to Symons, "What the hell is a Moonchild?"

"A Moonchild is an elemental – a reincarnated soul in a body created by ritual."

Alex bursts out laughing Symons tries to hush him.

"By sexual magic I suppose? It's elemental, my dear Symons, the fellow's a perverted nut."

"Alex, you're mad. He's traced back nine previous lives. It's all in his diaries."

"Previous lives?"

"Yes, Ko Hsuen, Count Cagliostro, Eliphas Levi," Symons explains. "Each one fixed by the wedding rite – what he calls the Chemical Wedding."

"The Chemical Wedding."

A crash comes from the room, the cat darts for it. Symons listens at the door.

"Mr. Crowley?"

There is a groan from inside. Symons taps his fingers in a faint knock then slowly opens the door and looks in.

"Oh my God!"

A collapsed Crowley lies on the floor. His dressing gown belt tied around his withered arm where a syringe hangs out of the vein.

"Alex, stay here," demands Symons as he runs for help.

Alex watches him go then turns to the body on the floor. He moves closer and bends down enquiringly. "Mr. Crowley?"

Crowley looks very dead, the eyes frozen, the lips drawn back, a dribble of saliva coming from the mouth. Alex gingerly pulls the syringe out and places it on the table. He shivers with disgust then pulls himself together and looks around the room. The magical diary catches his eye. 'What could be written in there that Crowley was so protective,' he wonders as he crosses over to the desk. 'Some mumbo jumbo, no doubt.' He checks the body then opens the exercise book and glances through the pages. Hundreds of symbols and numbers are annotated with tiny scrawled written notes. He brings the book close to read.

'The two equilateral triangles the upper spiritual one and the lower earthly come together to form the seal of Solomon.'

Alex studies it and can see it is actually made up of a triangle pointing upwards and one pointing downwards.

The symbol drawn is the Star of David

Interesting, curious, not quite what he expected.

He reads on 'An upper and lower circle has a similar meaning, the upper spiritual the lower, earthly. Where the upper and the lower cross over they form what Archimedes called the *'visica piscis'* this is because the intersecting circles form the shape of a fish.'

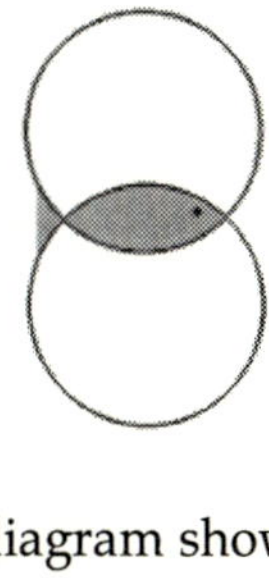

The 'Visica Piscis'

Alex can see that the diagram showing the intersecting circles does form a fish shape. He reads more. 'The *'visica piscis'* comes in fact from the mystic, Pythagoras and is referred to in the parable of Pythagoras observing the fishermen bringing in their catch. 'If I can guess the exact number of fish you caught' said Pythagoras, 'Then you must give me the catch.' He then states the number as 153 which being correct demanded the fishermen to return the fish to the sea. Pythagoras being a vegetarian believed that no animal should be killed. The parable is in fact a mathematical story that gives the mystic ratio of the *'visica piscis'* 153:265. As with most stories about Pythagoras, like walking on water and virgin births, this one is also reproduced in the bible...'

Alex looks round, he can hear them dialling for an ambulance from the phone by the front door. He is intrigued and tries to read on quickly.

> '..where the parable is slightly changed. John chapter 21 reads, 'He asked the fishermen to cast there nets on the other side of the boat. They do so and pull in a full catch. They are amazed especially when Jesus claims that they have caught exactly 153. He then announces that only those who are initiated will understand this parable. Of course Christians have no clue what he is talking about. But the visica piscis became a Christian symbol mainly to fit Jesus into the chosen one of the new age of Pisces this of course fits Plato's...'

Alex breaks off in stunned surprise. 'Is this true? What was the reference?' He looks back, *'John 21'*. He must remember to look it up in a bible. Maybe there are more revelations, he glances over to the dead body then an inexplicable sudden impulse makes him close the book and stuff it in the carrier bag. He had never stolen anything in his life and he breathes out with nervous guilt as he waits by the door for the others. Then he notices on the floor Crowley's gold pocket watch, ticking. Alex is unaccountably drawn towards it, now with the distinct compulsion to commit the crime. The ticking gets louder. Filled with evil thoughts he reaches down and picks up the watch. Suddenly the dead man's hand springs up and grabs his wrist. Shocked, Alex tries to step back. Crowley still looks dead, but his claw hangs on. His magic ring with the hieroglyphic inscription, 'Ankh-f-n-Khonsu', digs in painfully. Inexorably, it starts to drag Alex down, closer and closer. Alex struggles. Crowley's eyes suddenly flick wide open.

"I curse the hand that steals my time."

A bright stream of blood explodes from his mouth across Alex's hand and the watch. The claw lets go and Alex staggers back in horror. Crowley crumbles down croaking his final word. "Moonchild."

Alex spins round, from nowhere a baby cries out to take its first breath.

Symons and the Landlord hurry up the stairs. Suddenly Alex hurtles past startling them.

"What the? Alex. Alex!"

Alex flees on downwards in panic. The cat squeals as the foot catches him and Alex falls landing badly on his arm in the hall. He scrambles to his feet, flings open the door and runs out holding the wrist that is still covered in blood.

Once away he turns and looks back at the sombre building in white-faced horror.

The black dressed file follow the coffin into the Brighton Crematorium. The brass plate on the lid reads: 'Aleister Crowley. 1875-1947'. Inside the smell of polished wood and lilies pervades the Chapel.

The outer doors are pressed close and many disciples have to stand.

The impressive turnout of followers is somewhat bewildering since Crowley himself never attended funerals.

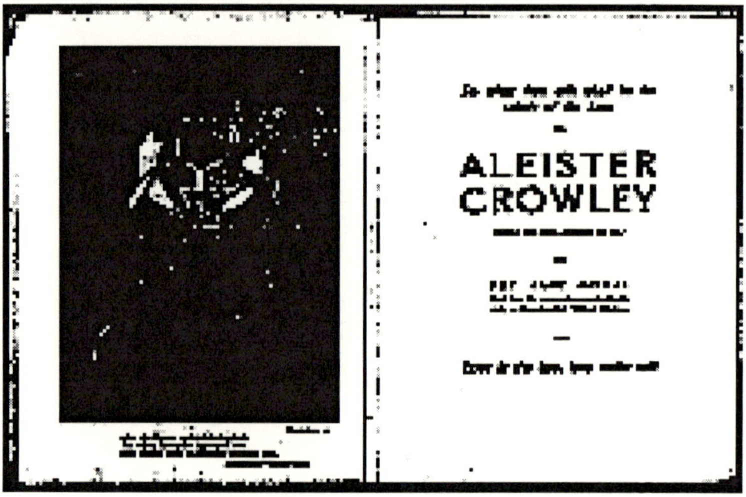

The Order of Service Pamphlet

He had a curious attitude to the deceased ever since as a boy he was dragged to see the dead body of his sister, Grace Mary Elizabeth, who had only survived five hours. 'I did not see why I should be disturbed so uselessly,' wrote Crowley. 'I couldn't do any good, the child was dead; it was none of my business.'

This attitude continued through his life.

> 'I have never attended any funeral but that of my father which I did not mind since I felt myself to be the real centre of interest. But when others have died, though in two cases at least my heart was torn as if by a wild beast and my life blighted for months and years by the catastrophe, I have always turned away from the necrological facts and the customary orgies. It may be that I have a deep-seated, innate conviction that the connection of a person with his body is purely symbolic. But there is also the feeling that the fact of death destroys all possible interest; the disaster is irreparable, it should be forgotten

as soon as possible. I would not even join the search party after the Kangchenjunga accident. It's not that dead bodies repel me in any way but what object was there in digging frozen corpses from under the snow.'

His followers seem to have missed the whole point and crammed in, either in respect of the Magus or for the spectacle of his concluding ritual.

The ceremony opens with the novelist, Louis Marlow reading from Crowley's 'Book of the Law'.

"Every man and every woman is a star.
Every number is infinite; there is no difference.
Help me, o warrior lord of Thebes,
in my unveiling before the Children of men!
Be thou Hadit, my secret centre, my heart and my tongue!
Worship then the Khabs, and behold my light shed over you!
Let my servants be few and secret:
They shall rule the many and the known.
These are fools that men adore;
Both their Gods and their men are fools.
Come forth, o children, under the stars, and take your fill of love!
I am above you and in you. My ecstasy is in yours.
My joy is to see your joy. "

The young students Symons and Alex sit in the congregation. Symons shakes his head sadly.

"If only he'd survived till the ceremony, what knowledge..."

Alex pulls out Crowley's pocket watch and puts it into his right hand, which is heavily bandaged.

"At least I can show my grandchildren, the watch from the wickedest man in the world."

"Damn you Alex, you'd tempt the devil himself."

"Don't be daft?"

"Daft? Is the curse of your hand not enough?"

"You're crazy. That was an accident."

"Was it? You were scared stiff."

"Disgusted, more like."

"You're making one big mistake here."

"What's your problem Symons? You still think he might resurrect. Or is it Jack Parsons's Moonchild who's coming to get me?"

Symons angrily snatches the watch, knocking the broken wrist.

Alex gives a pained gasp then looks around to see if anyone has noticed. A couple of neighbours frown disapprovingly. Alex gives a smiled apology.

The reading from the Book of the Law continues.

"The embrace of him intense on every centre of pain and pleasure. Flung down the precipice of being, even to the abyss, annihilation, Choronzon. Till the next coming."

Elgar's 'Nimrod' begins and as it reaches its climax the lever is pulled and doors open. The coffin of the Magus slides towards the gaping hole. Symons winds the watch nervously as the coffin disappears into the darkness.

The doors close. Blackness.

Suddenly with a roar a burst of red flames surrounds the casket. The brass plate melts as the coffin disintegrates in the scorching heat.

Ashes to ashes, dust to dust.

The roaring sound of the flames dissolves to a roar of engines...

iii

TRANSIT

The engines roar as the doors open and out of the blackness into the light of a new world comes a modern, shiny steel coffin-like sarcophagus. Following the steel sarcophagus on the conveyor-belt is a heavy wooden crate and a large cardboard box. The conveyor-belt stops the steel sarcophagus in front of a United States customs official with a clipboard who checks the labels, 'CAMBRIDGE UNIVERSITY DEPARTMENT OF PHYSICS'. He slaps on a LONDON HEATHROW sticker and the conveyor belt moves it on through clear plastic bendy doors. A forklift truck jerks it up into the air and wheels it out to a flood lit area beneath a giant Cargo Jet. The mechanical noises crunch above the drone of the jet engines as the sarcophagus slowly rises higher and higher on the arm till it is level with the black Cargo hole. The box disappears into the yellowy darkness and nestles in beside its crate companions.

The huge engines whine up, sucking air into their massive rotating blades and thrusting it out again with such force that the enormous cargo jet is thrown along the runway. When the speed reaches 180 miles per hour the air is deflected high over the oval wings creating a vacuum immediately above them, magically this draws the heavily laden jet up into the air. It soars higher and higher till at thirty thousand feet it begins its journey across the Atlantic Ocean.

The pilot, a well-read, freethinking young man, had cut his long hair to be sanctioned to indulge his love of flying huge jet planes. He looks down and contemplates the expanse of blue ocean. Who named this ocean Atlantic? He had read enough to know the Ancient Greeks already knew the name and Plato in his Timaeus claims that the Ancient Egyptians had recorded the existence of an Island in the centre called Atlantis. As the plane passes high over the underwater Atlantic ridge he remembers, that Atl is neither a Greek nor an Egyptian prefix. It is in fact from the Ancient Indigenous people of South America where the Atl prefix means water. Europeans employing this Indian prefix thousands of years before America was discovered? There must have been contact between Europe and the Americas? Unthinkable by Archaeologists but so was the discovery by forensic scientist Dr. Balabanova of substantial traces of cocaine in 3000-year-old Egyptian Mummies. This all left the young Pilot with the joy of more unfathomable questions relating to one of his favourite subjects, the ancient knowledge of antediluvian civilizations.

After eleven night hours traveling with the spin of the earth the rolling green hills of what the Romans called, 'the Mystery Isles' appears ahead. Within ten minutes the plane is traveling over the highest concentration of Neolithic structures in the world. Thousands of Stone Circles, hundreds of massive Standing Stones and numerous complex underground Burrows aligned to Venus, all built by six foot Giants long before the Trojan, Brutus, arrived to settle the land and call it Britain.

The jet screams lower, the noise is distressing and as the cross-shaped shadow passes ominously over the horses in a field, they snort and paw the ground before bolting.

The young pilot gently settles the steel sarcophagus back down to Earth and immediately reverses the thrust of the planes engines attempting to slow the huge momentum, but the sarcophagus and its accompanying crates attempt to maintain their 150 miles per hour velocity, pushing energetically forward into each other.

Finally plane and cargo come to a silent halt and the crew descend leaving their lifeless passengers alone in the darkness. Waiting.

> 'And what rough beast, it's hour come round at last,
> slouches towards Bethlehem to be born again.'

iv

ARRIVAL

CAMBRIDGE January 2001

Heavy clouds chase their shadows over the flat lands of the marshy fens. A river slowly meanders its way till it suddenly arrives at the impressive buildings and jutting spires of Cambridge.

The Ancient Romans built the town, as a convenient crossing point of the river, which was at that time called the Granta. The town became a prosperous port, since it was the head of the navigation of the Granta. The area by Magdalene Bridge is still known as Quayside, although now it only harbours pleasure punts.

In Anglo Saxon times, the city was called Grantabrycge. It was the Normans who built a castle on Castle Hill in 1068 to counteract the rebellious local hero Hereward the Wake. All that remains of that castle is Castle Mound the highest point of Cambridge, and allegedly, if you travel north in a straight line, there is no higher ground until you reach the North Pole.

Cantebrigge eventually became Cambridge. However, the river was still called the Granta. Someone thought 'Cambridge must be the bridge over the Cam, and the river should be called the Cam' and so the river's name was changed. However upstream, where it flows through Grantchester, it still maintains its original name the Granta.

Cambridge University dates back to 1209, when a number of Oxford students moved to Cambridge. The first college Peterhouse, was founded in 1284 and from then, numerous colleges sprouted sending their famous dreaming spires high into the air. It was Trinity College where Aleister Crowley spent his formative years.

In the town centre is the Church of the Holy Sepulchre, an unusual round church built by the Knights Templars, the Ancient Secret order allegedly founded in 1117 to help Crusaders in the Holy Land. In truth the original nine Knights housed themselves in the ruins of the Jerusalem Temple to excavate the labyrinth of tunnels below. They knew from surviving members of the Jewish Royal family, who fled the Roman destruction of Jerusalem, that documents and relics had been secreted there. As the Roman legions advanced on Israel copies of these parchments were also stored for safekeeping in the caves by the Dead Sea where they were rediscovered in 1947

Presumably the Templar Knights found what they were looking for because on their return from Jerusalem the organization developed into one of the richest and most powerful sects in the medieval world, having a large network of preceptories throughout Europe. They owned huge tracts of land including 'Temple' in the city of London and the area round 'Rue du Temple' in Paris as well as large sections of Cambridge.

After 200 years Pope Clement V issued the papal bull, which finally suppressed the Order. The initial event was sudden and brutal. In the early hours of Friday, 13th October 1307 the Templars were arrested by officials of King Philip IV in the name of the Inquisition and their property was confiscated. The event gave rise to the superstition concerning Friday the 13th.

The Templars were brutally tortured, charged with serious heresies and sentenced to perpetual imprisonment. Grand Master Jacques de Molay and Geoffroi de Charney, the Preceptor were ordered by King Philip IV to be tortured then burned at the stake.

As the Templars denied Jesus' passion on the cross, de Molay was tortured by being crucified to a door and then cut down and allowed to recover – covered with a Templar shroud, before being burnt at the stake alongside Geoffroi de Charney. The Turin shroud first appeared as a possession of the de Charney family and was carbon dated to that exact time. The image on the shroud is an exact resemblance of the tall bearded Templar leader Jaques de Molay and very dissimilar to the Roman charge sheet description of Jesus as short and hunchbacked. There is one reference in the Bible to Jesus height where it says that Nicodemus the tax collector climbed a tree to catch a sight of Jesus because he was short of stature. The Roman church decided to misinterpret this as Nicodemus being the one who was short of stature. But the truth makes it clear that the image on the Turin Shroud is not of the diminutive Jesus but of the tall Jacques deMolay.

As the smoke from his braising feet curled up and the flames blackened and blistered his buttocks and sexual organs, Jaques de Molay called out vengefully for the death of King Phillip and Pope Clement. When the fire burnt itself out the united charcoal body and stake was struck with a spear and they crumbled together into black ash.

Within the year the Pope and the King were dead.

The secrets and rituals of the Knights Templars though have survived into modern times in secret Societies. One member is standing by a large ornate Tudor Window of the University watching the passing clouds and winding Crowley's old pocket watch. It is Symons, now an old man his large head of grey hair suggesting the most profound capacity for reflection. His eyes are deeply cut by experience and shaded by bushy iron-grey eyebrows. His voice has mellowed as he recounts his story.

"Forty years I kept his watch ticking away the seconds of my life. It marked triumphs and failures, loves and loss and the long painful path to self knowledge. Ticking away reminding me that the only constant thing in life is change. In that time Lafayette Ron Hubbard moved on from Crowley's rites to inventing his own successful scientology ritual. Jack Parsons blew himself up in his laboratory after inventing the rocket fuel that in July 1969 put a man on the moon. And Crowley's image appears everywhere, staring out at me from the front of the Beatles Album or pinned up in Charles Manson's bedroom."

Symons turns to a figure seated in the shadows of his study and continues his story.

"Then four days ago he arrived from Cal Tech. The remarkable Joshua Mathers: who could know, let alone understand, exactly what happened over those four days. Four days that changed the course of our planet."

CHAPTER 1

DAY ONE

Tuesday 5th January

Across the fens a clammy and intensely cold mist made its slow way, like an evil spirit through the air in ripples that visibly followed and overspread one another like the waves of an unwholesome sea might do. It was dense enough to make tangled ghosts of isolated trees, their naked branches reaching up to the hidden sun. Silence, then the parallel iron rails that cut through the flat fields suddenly buzzed into life. The noise grew louder and louder till the mist parted and the London Express emerged and headed towards the misty spires of Cambridge.

Waiting on platform two of Cambridge Station was Leah Robinson, a pretty redhead, wearing a duffle jacket, sweater and black tights ending in soft, suede black boots that she stomped against the cold. As she saw the train approach she checked the Station clock and her watch which both showed the train was irritatingly late. The train slowed with a screech as it turned onto platform two. Turned because there is actually no platform two at Cambridge; just one long platform divided into sections called one to four; a curiosity that Leah thought must cause confusion and accidents but somehow never has. Once the train had stopped at the, so-called, platform two Leah watched the passengers fumble their way off. Only the regular travelers knew the way to open their carriage doors was to drop the windows and turn the outside handles. As those who had achieved this archaic task approached, Leah held up a card, felt penned with the name 'Prof. Joshua Mathers'. She studied the approaching passengers. A bearded academic with glasses, hat and weathered leather briefcase strode towards her.

"Professor Mathers?" she asked.

But he walked blankly past: then a voice behind.

"Hi."

Carrying a suitcase, an armoured briefcase and a shoulder bag was Joshua Mathers. Much younger than she expected, he wore a long raincoat and a blue scarf that accentuated the healthy LA tan that separated him from the pasty winter English.

Leah was stunned, "Professor Mathers?" she said taken aback by his good looks.

"Thanks for the promotion but just Doctor."

"Oh, sorry," she stuttered, "Um, welcome to Cambridge."

"Thank you."

Mathers handed over his shoulder bag; which buckled her under the weight and headed off down the platform.

On a bench on the opposite platform old Symons sat waiting. He glanced up from his Guardian newspaper as the London Express pulled out and revealed the two walking towards the exit; Mathers striding first, she following awkwardly under the weight. It hardly registered then but later Symons would remember this moment as his first glimpse of the remarkable man who would, in just four days, sacrifice his life for the red headed girl.

Mathers turned into the station building.

"You the welcoming party?"

"Well, no, not exactly," replied Leah hesitantly. "I'm Leah Robinson, I was hoping for an interview."

"An interview?"

"For Granta."

"Granta?"

She struggled to pull out a press pass. "The college newspaper."

"Oh, right," he said dismissively striding on.

Leah launched into her prepared speech while struggling to keep up with him.

"If you could spare me a few minutes to talk about your work and it's practical uses and how your theories relate to the holistic view of the earth as one organism and whether science is an adequate medium to fully explain this."

She paused then remembered the last bit. "Oh, but without reference to the spiritual dimension."

He stopped, "A few minutes?"

"Yes," she smiled hopefully

"You've got to be joking?" he declared and marched on. She followed him desperately.

"But I just skipped my English tutorial."

"Sorry about that."

Outside the station he found a waiting chauffeur holding up his name card. Mathers handed over his case and tried to retrieve his shoulder bag from Leah. She held it back, "Please."

He screwed up his face and shook his head, "Look, my work is... well it's just not the right stuff for a magazine."

"Why not? I read your 'Mysteries of Chaos' – it's fascinating and I know I could write an interesting piece."

"Really?" He thought for a moment. "If you're in a speeding train and you jump straight up in the air, do you land in the same spot?"

Leah puzzled "What? Yes…"

The chauffeur shook his head and Leah changed her mind.

"No. You'd land further back."

Mathers looked at her. "Leah Robinson?"

"From Granta," she added.

Mathers smiled. "Well, Leah... – You've got your interview."

Leah smiled. "Really?"

Mathers managed to take his bag from her and got into the car.

"I should be free by five. Okay?"

"Yes, great, thanks. Five. Was I right about the train?"

"No, and that's only Newtonian physics," he said and closed the door of the car.

As the chauffeur pulled away he checked the position of his mirror and gave a breathy whistle adding, "the stuff that dreams are made of."

Mathers looked up at him. "What?"

The chauffeur nodded at the image in his mirror. "The girl."

Mathers, turned and looked out the back window at Leah, registering her natural beauty as if for the first time and smiled to himself, 'The stuff that dreams are made of.' Then a thought struck him about the photons of light from the girl moving towards him while the cab moved away and he turned, pulled out a notepad and started jotting down equations based on Einstein's special theory of relativity.

In the road Leah was scratching her head still puzzling. 'If the train was traveling at sixty miles per hour then so am I. That's why you'd land in the same place. Wait he said Newtonian physics - of course there is another correct answer thinking relatively. To the man on the platform watching the train speed by then you would have jumped and landed further forward. Land in the same spot or land further forward are both correct. The only wrong answer is the one I gave - you would land further back.' She smiled then her face changed with alarm.

"Where?" she shouted. "Where at five?"

Too late, the car disappeared into the swirling fog. Leah pondered her own ineptitude. 'Am I stupid or what?' It's a question she had often asked herself without coming to any clear conclusion. She went over to the mass of bikes that clutter the square opposite the station and somehow picked out her own and began pedalling back along Station Road towards the town centre pondering again about her own capabilities.

She must be clever, she passed the exams to Cambridge. But then she knew full well, that just required repetitive learning and exam-passing technique. Make sure you answer every question – pick up the easy marks before you waste too much time on the extras – check previous papers to see what's liable to come up. A trained parrot could do it. She knew she was not quick. In fact sometimes she felt ponderously slow. How she would love to be fast witted like Jonesy who enjoyed making her look stupid with some trick question or another.

'Some months have 31 days how many have 28?" Of course she would answer one – February. And he would reply – "no – 12. All of them have 28 days." Or, "is it legal for a man to marry his widow's sister." "Yes'" she would reply. "No stupid because he's dead."

She laughed but deep down she felt slow. She was even a slow reader but then she would not let any word or idea pass without understanding it. And in discussion she found others who may be faster readers had not understood the concepts. 'So I am clever.' The thought made her pedal faster till doubt again settled on her. 'Doesn't everybody think they are clever?' In the heat of an argument nobody admits they are wrong. Her late father had once told her that even scientists do not admit they are wrong when some new theory clashed with their traditional one. No, they just slowly die away and the new theory eventually replaced the old.

The cold wind made a tear run down her face or perhaps it was the thought of her father. Her final sad memory of him was at the open door, with the morning light behind him, carrying his ever-present shoulder bag and waving goodbye. Her first memory of him was when lemon juice squirted into her baby eyes. As there was no water available he licked her tearful eyes and healed them. The bittersweet thoughts passed and as she turned into the High Street, her internal demons returned: 'You can not even say you are a good writer.' It was true there were many in her class who were far better wordsmiths than her. They wrote good stuff straight off. She struggled exceptionally slowly. But Daddy said the best drawers who go to art school do not make the best artists. Maybe doubt and suffering were what was really needed to make…

At that moment a speeding car swung dangerously close into Canon Street and she wobbled almost catching the kerb with her front wheel. She regained her balance and pedalled on realizing she had not been paying much attention to the road. In fact she could not remember any of the journey from the station or what she had been thinking.

The sun found a chink in the clouds and glistened off the icy waters of the river Cam fulfilling the scene's beautiful potential just as Mather's car crossed over the bridge and headed between the neat line of plain trees with the green fields beyond. His tiring journey had not dimmed his senses and he drunk in the scene unfolding before his eyes. Heading down a quaint cobbled street the car rounded an ivy-clad building and stopped before an ornate stone arched doorway. An enormous sense of awe struck Mathers as he stepped out and looked up at the tower over the doorway. In a central niche was a statue of King Henry the Eighth of England.

For this college was founded by Henry the Eighth and claimed as undergraduates many of Joshua Mathers all time heroes. From the 16th century philosopher, Francis Bacon, to the greatest of all physical scientists, Isaac Newton and right up to the present day James Clerk Maxwell, of the theory of electro-magnetism and Ernest Rutherford, pioneer of atomic physics. The college could also boast thirty-one Nobel Prize winners since they were first awarded in 1901. Two of these prize winners made Mathers smile. In 1906 J. J.Thompson had received the Nobel Prize for proving that electrons were particles. Then in 1937 he saw his son George Thompson awarded the Nobel Prize for proving that electrons were waves. The apparent anomaly was not a problem to Mathers who knew that both father and son were correct and both awards were fully merited. Electrons are particles and electrons are waves however impossible this may seem to those unacquainted with quantum physics.

Mathers took his bags from the car boot and was directed by the chauffeur towards the stone gateway. He walked into the darkened gatehouse, which opened through a second door onto the expansive, green-lawned quadrangle. It was like something from Alice in Wonderland, through the door to an alien, mystical world. The sun shone brighter, the grass was greener and the sound of modern bustle was gone. He stood there on the same hallowed ground that Sir Isaac Newton had once walked upon and looked across to the central fountain and the magnificent ornate Clock Tower to his right. Here 300 years ago Isaac Newton invented Physics - invented Physics! - when he wrote his three laws of motion which defined matter, energy and everything up to the orbit of the planets. Not that Newton would understand the way Mathers now saw the Universe but then even Albert Einstein found quantum mechanics incomprehensible. He was sure the equations simply represented some mathematical trick and although they were useful the true underlying reality would one day be found. But what Quantum mechanics went on to demonstrate was that nothing is real and that we cannot say anything about what things are doing when we are not looking at them. Even Schrodinger's mythical experiment, where the cat in the box is neither dead nor alive until we look at it, was invoked by him to dismiss the uncertainty principal - but instead it simply exposed the difference between the quantum world and the everyday world apparent. But all this did not prevent Mathers bowing in reverence to the man who set it all in motion in these tranquil College surroundings.

Observing Mathers arrival from an upper window, framed in ivy, was Dr Oliver Haddo, his robust frame shrouded in a black academic gown, his greying hair, hanging in long wisps over his collar. Dr. Haddo was from the other tradition of the College. Poets like George Herbert, Andrew Marvell and John Dryden not to mention Byron, Thackeray, and the novelist Vladimir Nabokov.

Behind him was his study where books covered the walls and filled four revolving walnut bookcases. They were largely on English literature with a modest selection on philosophy. There was also a large collection of Greek and Latin classics and a sprinkling of French and Russian novels. On one shelf shone the black and gold book of the 'Arabian Nights' of Richard Burton. Below a collection of old and middle English classics including the complete works of Chaucer. Valuable first editions of British poets stood beside extravagantly bound volumes issued by Isidor Liseux. On a card table was a chessboard with leaded Staunton chessmen in mid battle. The mantelpiece was full of Christmas cards and a small Christmas tree was shedding its pine needles in the corner.

Scattered silently on easy chairs were a number of students waiting patiently to begin the tutorial. Haddo however remained motionless at the window his rounded body an indication of a lazy man who enjoyed his puddings. But his mind was far from lazy. He was an expert on Shakespeare from whom he could quote profusely. His book 'Hidden Shakespeare' although never becoming popular was well respected by his peers. The idea for the book had come from his second favourite author W.B.Yeats. His '*Vision*', which was seeded with occultism and '*The Wanderings Of Oisin*' both took their subject from Irish mythology and suggested to Haddo a new interpretation of the bard's labours. He pronounced '*Midsummer Night's Dream*' an interaction between the human and spirit world where Oberon was obviously the Egyptian God Osiris and Titania was Isis while Puck was Robin Goodfellow, '*The Green Man*', the Celtic version of the God, Pan. That Bottom the weaver had been turned into an ass by Oberon proved to Haddo that Shakespeare had read Lucius Apuleius's occult Roman classic, 'The Golden Ass'. The similarities were clear. Lucius told the story of his tempestuous love affaire with a slave girl whose mistress was a witch. The particular skill of this lady was her ability to transform humans into animal form. Lucius aspired to spend a short time as an owl, but because of a technical hitch became an ass, in which form he remained for a year. After recounting his adventures he was finally saved by none other than Isis who announced, 'I am

Nature – the Universal mother, mistress of all the elements and Queen of the immortals.'

She explained that, the ass was to her 'the most hateful of all the beasts in existence' and then restored Lucius to human form. Why such hatred? In the Ancient Mystery religions the Ass was acknowledged as the representation of the basest carnal form of humanity, everything that was not spiritual. The image of the God-man riding in triumph on an ass symbolized to those initiated into the ancient cult, that he was master of his lower animal self. Each spring the rite was performed while the lining crowds waved palm fronds in celebration. The later biblical event of Jesus riding into Jerusalem on an ass while the crowds waved palm leaves was an obvious mimicking of the original. In fact the very first depiction of a crucifixion was that of an ass on a cross where man crucifies his base side to release his spiritual self into everlasting time.

Suddenly Haddo looked at his watch and turned to the waiting students. He spoke with a debilitating stutter.

"I suppose we had b..b..better start, Miss R..R..Robinson appears to be later r..rather than sooner."

He enjoyed his own joke and the students attempted a benevolent smile except Jones who rolled his eyes despairingly.

Haddo began, "R..right, the comparison between Julius Caesar and R..Richard the Third."

He rounded on one student, "Andrews? And while you're thinking l..l..let me say that the style of your Christmas essay is what I c..c..call, '*comma bacillus*". You love your sentences s..so much that you hate to end them. R..r..right carry on."

Andrews began hesitantly "Caesar is not really the main character, he dies half way through but Richard the Third is there from beginning to end."

"Who then is the main character in Caesar?"

"Brutus, I suppose," answered Andrews, "But Mark Anthony is the hero."

"T..true, anyone else?"

"Richard the Third is a structure-less play," added a student with rounded glasses, "But what we enjoy and are entertained by is just a man behaving awfully."

"Yes, and why d..does he behave so awfully?"

He indicated Clarice with a nod.

"In the beginning Richard the Third says he's not good looking or physically attractive so he has to play the villain," answered Clarice.

"Yes, exactly, good. But is it actually believable that a man would announce that he is going to be a villain?"

Jones led the negation. "No, it's ridiculous."

"Ridiculous is a little strong, perhaps unreal would be better," interjected Haddo. "But then why do we watch something that is plainly unreal?"

Goggles raised a hand, "Because it's not a documentary about Richard the Third but a work of the imagination."

"P..perhaps Shakespeare thought he was m..making a documentary," added Haddo. "But something lifts it above questions of reality. What is it?"

"The language..?" answered Clarice hesitantly.

"The language," agreed Haddo enthusiastically. "The speech in which he announces his intention to be a villain is filled with such wonderful imagery about his physical repulsiveness that we enjoy it for itself."

With that Haddo burst into a recital with such feeling that it caused the students to wonder if he was not referring to his own physical repulsiveness.

"But I that am not shaped for sportive tricks
Nor made to court an amorous looking-glass;
I that am curtailed of this fair proportion,
Cheated of feature by dissembling nature,
Deformed, unfinished, sent before my time
Into this breathing world scarce half made up,

And that so lamely and unfashionable
That dogs bark at me as I halt by them
Why I, in this weak piping time of peace,
Have no delight to pass away the time,
Unless to spy my shadow in the sun
And descant on mine own deformity.
And therefore, since I cannot prove a lover
To entertain these fair well-spoken days,
I am determined to prove a villain
And hate the idle pleasures of these days."

A 3-dimensional pentagram appeared, rotating slowly within a sphere. Victor Newman sat alone and intense at the computer keyboard, his blue eyes reflecting the rotating pentagram from the screen. The cables ran across the room to a sealed cabinet containing, in its super-cooled, cloudy atmosphere, the world's fastest computer – the Z93. Victor programmed the beast with such a facility that the same mother could well have nurtured them both. For it was easier for Victor to get the computer to generate a brilliant complex equation than it was for his brain to send a simple message down to his foot to kick a ball. Emotionally too he felt his cells, his very atoms were vibrating in frequency with the quartz crystal that lies at the very heart of the Z93. As Crowley wrote, 'Every man is eternally alone. But when he gets mixed up with a fairly decent crowd, he forgets that appalling fact for long enough to give his brain time to recover from the acute symptoms of its disease – that of thinking.' Victor's only relieving social interaction was with the computer.

He typed the word: 'BAPHOMET' and looked up at the screen as it answered: 'DO WHAT THOU WILT'. He opened his bag and took out a portable hard drive labelled 'ALEISTER CROWLEY' and plugged it into the computer. At that moment the door of the lab banged open, Victor aborted the program immediately. Mathers entered with the impressive figure of Professor Duncan Brent.

"It arrived on Monday," explained Professor Brent, "we had a glass room, lead lined and… ah this is Victor our technical wizard."

"Hi," smiled Mathers and shook hands with Victor.

"Victor's been wiring up," said Professor Brent

"Any luck?" asked Mathers.

Victor pointed through an observation window.

"I've begun fitting the vacuum pumps and the electromagnets in the floor and ceiling."

Mathers cupped his hands to see through the observation window.

In a vast hangar-like space were scattered pieces of equipment covered in plastic sheeting, the ghosts of previous experiments. Alone in the centre, illuminated by a vertical beam of light was a sealed glass room. In the brightness of the glass room sat the gleaming steel sarcophagus.

Victor smiled. "The porters call it the space coffin."

Professor Brent directed Mathers' attention back to the computer.

"The Z93 should cope with the problems your integrator's been having. It's really something isn't it Victor?"

"Yes its speed comes from using a combination of Josephson junctions and his 'weak link' macro quantum particles."

"Brian Josephson was professor here at Trinity." Professor Brent added, "that was till he won the Nobel Prize and turned to Eastern Philosophy."

Mathers nodded, "I've read his book."

Professor Brent raised an eyebrow; "Consciousness and the Physical World. Rather cranky, no?"

Typically, Nobel Prize winner Brian Josephson's views were not universally acclaimed in the science community. Indeed, physicists were highly critical of a passage that Josephson wrote to accompany a special set of stamps published by the Royal Mail to mark the 100th anniversary of the Nobel prize:

'Quantum theory is now being fruitfully combined with theories of information and computation. These developments may lead to an explanation of processes still not understood within conventional science such as telepathy.'

'Utter rubbish!' declared David Deutsch, the quantum physicist at Oxford University, and added, 'there is no evidence that paranormal phenomena actually exist.' Entering the controversy, *Physics World* queried Deutsch whether the paranormal might not become a respectable area of research? Deutsch replied, 'One day Santa Claus might turn out to be a respectable area of research. All one can say is that there is no better evidence for the one than for the other.'

Josephson, however, believed that such views stem from ignorance. He maintained that there was strong evidence for the existence of parapsychologyical phenomena.

These extraordinary views for a Professor of Physics were as nothing compared to his discovery of the Josephson junction. It worked on the strangest quantum principal, which in layman's terms proposed that if you throw one hundred tennis balls at a brick wall one will pass through to the other side. Ridiculous? Yes – but it worked!!

And so the debate raged on and Mathers knew not to touch on the controversy at so early a stage of his visit to Cambridge. He stayed detached watching the plumes of cold air rising round the superconductors of the Z93. "She certainly looks capable of initiating a structural analysis of feelings."

"Putting feelings into the computer," enthused Victor, "onto the quartz crystal, reminds me of what the ancient Mayans were supposed to have done with the crystal skull."

Unfortunately Victor was accepted as a wizard computer programmer not a theoretician and so a nonentity in the eyes of the Professor who never listened attentively to his ideas. Victor's intense blue eyes, dark hair and compulsive obsessions had the same switching off effect on most people, which made him feel both angrily isolated and resentfully superior.

But Victor's weird ideas about archaeological anomalies like the crystal skull could well have related in a crucial way to Mathers experiment. For the Mitchell-Hedges Crystal Skull was one of the most extraordinary ancient artefacts ever un-earthed. From a technical standpoint, it appeared to be an impossible object which modern technology was unable to duplicate. And what Victor liked most was that the discovery of the skull read like one of his favourite sci-fi adventures.

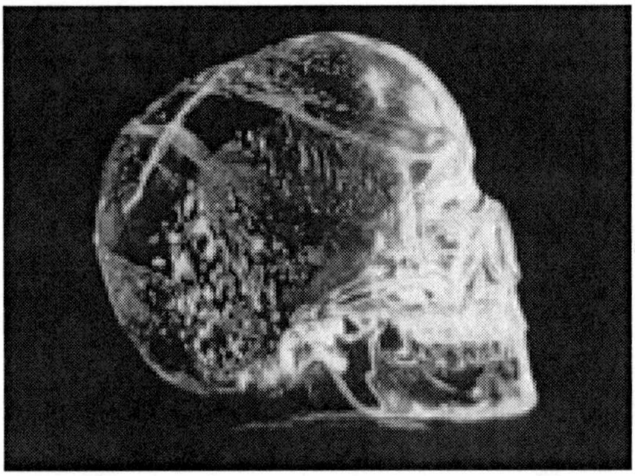

As the story goes one day in 1927, English adventurer F.A. Mitchell-Hedges, who had a talent for telling colorful stories, was clearing debris from atop a ruined pyramid temple at the ancient Mayan city of Lubaantum, in British Honduras; when his seventeen-year old daughter Anna, suddenly saw something shimmering in the dust below. Anna climbed down and found an exquisitely carved and polished skull made of quartz crystal.

There were then extraordinary twists and turns in the story that led to claims that the whole thing was a hoax.

Then in 1970, the Mitchell-Hedges estate submitted the quartz skull for analysis at the Hewlett-Packard Laboratories in California. As experts in quartz computer chips they were astounded that the skull and separate jaw had been carved from a single quartz crystal. Even more surprising was that it had been cut with total disregard to the natural axis of the crystal. By all the laws known to man, it should have shattered – there was no way it should exist. The enigma of the skull, however, did not end with just its existence. The zygomatic arches, the cheekbones, were accurately separated from the skull piece, and acted as light pipes, using principles similar to modern optics, to channel light from the base of the skull to the eye sockets. The eye sockets in turn were miniature concave lenses that also transferred light from a source below. Finally, in the interior of the skull was a ribbon prism and tiny light tunnels, by which objects held beneath the skull were magnified and brightened. The skull appeared to be designed to be placed over an upward shining beam and with the various light transfers and prismatic effects, the entire skull would illuminate and cause the sockets to become glowing eyes. The lab performed experiments using this technique, and reported the skull 'lit up as if it were on fire.'

Still another finding about the crystal skull revealed knowledge of weights and fulcrum points. The jaw piece fitted precisely into the skull by two polished sockets, which allowed the jaw to move up and down. The skull itself could be balanced exactly where two tiny holes were drilled on each side of its base. So perfect was the balance at these points that the slightest breeze caused the skull to nod back and forth, the jaw opening and closing as counter-weight. The visual effect was that of a living skull, talking and articulating.

Was the talking skull meant to be an oracular device, using strange phenomena to defy any logical explanation? Observers reported that, for unknown reasons, the skull would change color. The frontal cranium clouded up, looking like white cotton, while at other times it turned perfectly clear, as if the space within disappeared into an empty void. Sometimes a dark spot would form on the right side and slowly blacken the entire skull, then recede and disappear as mysteriously as it came. Some observers even heard ringing noises emanating from within. The skull appeared to take in all five physical senses of the brain. It changed color, it emitted odours, it created sound, it gave off sensations of heat and cold even though it always remained at a physical temperature of 70 degrees, and it had even produced sensations of thirst in a few cases.

Victor was convinced that the crystal was stimulating an unknown part of the human brain, opening a psychic door to the absolute. He knew crystals continuously put out electro-magnetic radio waves. And since the brain does the same thing, they would naturally interact. By gazing at the crystal, the eyes set up a harmonic relation stimulating the magnetism collected in that portion of the brain known as the cerebellum. The cerebellum therefore became a reservoir of magnetism, which influences the quality of the magnetic outflow through the eyes, thus setting up a continuous flow of magnetism between gazer and crystal.

Authorities and Archaeologists called the skull an elaborate hoax but to the team at Hewlett-Packard it was an object that with all their most sophisticated modern technology they could not reproduce. The only idea they could put forward to explain the skull's manufacture was grinding and polishing by applying innumerable applications of water and sand. The big problem was that, if this was in fact the process used, then they calculated, it would have taken a total of 300 man-years of continuous labour to make the skull. A 300 year hoax? Begun when? In 1690 so that it would be ready to be found at the turn of the century. Victor was furious and frustrated by the 'so called' archaeologists. Surely they must either accept this almost unimaginable feat, or admit to the use of some form of lost technology the likes of which had no modern equivalent. Who could have had such a technology? The amazing answer appeared when forensic artists filled out the muscles, sinews and cartilages of the crystal skull. What slowly appeared from the clay was a native South American Indian woman. This was no European hoax. This skull was perfect in every anatomical detail except one strange anomaly, the molars had x form ridges not the normal + shape. Victor was convinced this was a race of knowledgeable people who lived before one of the five global catastrophes that are detailed in Mayan history.

But before Mathers could ask Victor to explain all that was in his mind, Professor Brent, who had no time for Victor's idiosyncratic theories, interrupted. For Prof. Brent's attention was firmly focused on one thing, any kudos that Mathers' experiment might generate. This was the way Professor Brent had moved through the ranks. As Swift said, 'Ambition often puts men upon doing the meanest offices, so climbing is performed in the same posture as creeping.' By using techniques he learnt at Eton, arrogantly making his juniors feel inferior, Professor Brent had stolen the credit for other people's labours. His rounded voice, erect stature and confident tone implied to most people a knowledgeable authority. But in fact talent most often resides in shy unassuming people. The tell tale sign is the man or woman who is described as a 'great assistant'. What that usually means is, they are doing all the work while their boss is getting all the credit. And Professor Brent's only real expertise was exactly that, knowing how to get all the credit.

"If it works – then a joint paper – I presume," said Brent, "And I'd better take the first journey if I am to deal with the press and TV."

"I'm..well..I..." Mathers assumed he was going to make the first trip himself but he suddenly felt terribly jet lagged as Professor Brent slid the carpet from under him.

"Mind you." Brent added, concealing his method in a joke. "If I put my brain paths into the Z93 maybe they'll discharge me and have the computer do my lectures."

With Shakespeare in his plump hand, Dr. Haddo quoted from 'Julius Caesar'. "The evil that m..m..men do lives on. The good is oft interred with th..th..their bones. Why should M..M..Mark Antony..."

The door opened and Leah entered.

"I'm sorry Dr. Haddo, I had to meet someone and the train was late. It *was* an interview for Granta."

"There is a d..difference, Ms Robinson, between journalism and l..literature. Journalism is unreadable and l..literature is not read." He giggled at his little joke and continued. "S..s..sit down, Mr. Jones, would you p..please illuminate, Ms Robinson."

Jones filled in. "Julius Caesar, the Mark Antony speech. Friends Romans… We just got to 'The evil that men do lives on' bit."

"Yes...and s..so?" asked Haddo.

"Well, I suppose I remember the bad things about people more than the good," said Jones hesitantly. Haddo contemplated the answer as he gazed out of the window where he saw Mathers leave the lab and cross the courtyard. Somewhere deep down in Haddo's subconscious, he knew their paths would cross in a more momentous way.

"Possibly, b..b..but what about the sp..spiritual sense?" said Haddo and turned suddenly to Leah, "Ms Robinson!"

Leah was caught off guard. "Evil lives on?" Her immediate thought was the death of her father but even if she could talk about that, she could find no connection with it and the question, so she stumbled a spontaneous answer. "Well, people abused – like children... abused by Devil Worshippers, their minds are permanently scarred, so that the evil lives on in them – they often become abusers themselves."

"Good," again he looked out the window, as if lost in his own reverie. "Devil w..worship and evil."

Jones raised an eyebrow at Leah and sneered.

Haddo continued obliviously. "P..p..perhaps we're taking certain v..value judgments for granted. Who, may I ask, was the devil?"

Haddo hardly listened to the jumble of answers he expected. A mythical figure created by religion to personify the evil in the world. The bogeyman – who will get you if you do wrong, the scapegoat to excuse us of the responsibility for our own evil and Julia, the Christian who equated the Devil with Satan. 'What confusion,' thought Haddo. But even the Encyclopaedia Britannica expanded on this confusion with a thousand words on the definition of the Devil where the word Devil rapidly disappeared to be replaced by 'Satan'. And the word Satan strangely enough is not listed nor are there any cross reference to Lucifer. And yet under

Devil it states that in the Jewish Targums, 'Sammael is the highest Angel that stands before God's throne and causes the serpent to seduce the woman'. The name Satan however passed through its Chaldaic form, 'Sheitan' into the Greek, 'Titan', which was used by Greek and Latin poets as a designation of the Sun God. And Haddo had in his walnut bookcase a small leather bound book, 'Christian Iconography' by the medieval writer Didron in which he describes three Byzantine miniatures of the tenth century, in which Satan is depicted with a nimbus, a halo, the recognized sign of the Sun God in Pagan times. The Christian authorities would later misappropriate the nimbus for Christ and the Saints.

Haddo turned back to his students. "The t..truth is that the church may have b..b..blackened the name of the Devil but who asked man to eat from the apple of knowledge?"

"The serpent," quipped Jones

Haddo looked up. "Yes, the s..serpent. It's just a p..pity you didn't think t..to take a bite of that apple yourself, Mr. Jones."

Again he smiled at his own joke, Jones sneered at the insult.

Given all the quaint Inns and guesthouses in Cambridge, the hotel the college administration had booked for Mathers was hugely disappointing. 'The Moat Hotel' sounded like it would be almost medieval. Instead it was one of those modern impersonal buildings that are scattered from Baltimore to Bangkok whose rooms, once entered, reflected absolutely nothing of the exotic nature of the country – that is except for the usual bad painting of a local tourist spot perched over the bed. At the turn of the century Aleister Crowley had already spotted this trend when, on a visit, he identified a foul disease ravaging the United States and warned that this irremediable calamity threatened to engulf the whole of humanity.

'...it is now an accepted principle of business to endeavour to make tyranny international, to suppress all customs of historical interest, and indeed everything which lends variety or distraction to human society in the interest of making a market for standardized products. This complex industrial conspiracy lies underneath all attempts to extend, so-called, 'civilization'. The progress of this pestilence is only too visible all over the world. Standardized hotels and standardized merchandise have invaded the remotest districts, and these would be economically impossible unless supported by the forcible suppression of local competition. When we find the newspapers indignant at Mohammedan morality, we may suspect the real trouble is that American hatters see no hope of disposing of their surplus stock as long as the wicked Oriental sticks to his turban. It should be obvious that 'Do what thou wilt' cuts diametrically athwart this attempt to destroy the distinctions which constitute the sole hope of humanity.'

In his standardized hotel room the jet lagged Mathers flopped on the bed and gazed up at the painting of an ornate bridge over a river. The title was 'Bridge of Sighs'. He was confused; he was sure the 'Bridge of Sighs' was in Venice.

'Maybe I'm in Venice,' he sighed and was soon fast asleep.

Leah and the other students came out of Haddo's study into the long arched corridor. Once out they looked at each other and burst out laughing.

"The way he quotes Hamlet you'd think he was Larry Olivier."

"He should stick to that fat fool, Falstaff," said Ashby.

Goggles looked at his watch. "We could get through the tutorial in half the time if he didn't stutter so much."

"You know what they say; some people talk in their sleep: lecturers talk while others sleep."

"How the hell is he supposed to give the J.Z. Maudlyn Classics lecture?"

"W..w..w..with d.damn d..d..difficulty." joked Jones.

The hilarity echoed around the corridor till the laughers were hushed by the cautious.

Jones turned to Leah. "M...M...M...Ms Robinson, d..d..do not slander Mr. Satan he was such a n..nice chap!"

"Don't be so cruel," pleaded Leah who had a soft spot for the bumbling academic.

"Oh, come on. You heard him. He's insane."

"Why! I don't like the way people laugh at anyone with different ideas."

"Crazy ideas, you mean," replied Jones.

"What's crazy? Every Sunday there's a guy comes on the TV and talks about communicating with God and nobody laughs. Why?"

"I don't know – because they do it every Sunday."

"But David Icke comes on and they all think he's funny for saying something similar. To me they're both as funny as each other."

"Maybe people don't think for themselves they have to be told what's funny."

"Or they're conditioned because Presidents, Prime Ministers, Kings and Queens all say they pray to God."

"Lots of people believe in God."

"Why God? The world is in such a mess surely the God in power is the Devil."

"Ah, so that's why you sympathize with Haddo?"

"No, I don't believe in any of it but just ask yourself if God didn't exist would the world be a better place?"

"If he didn't exist? – Yeah I suppose you'd have to say there would be less things to war about. But..."

"Shit." Leah interrupted as she looked at her watch. "Ashby's going to kill me; I've got an interview with that Chaos Prof. for five."

"So what's the problem, it's ten to?"

"He didn't say where."

Jones laughed mockingly shaking his head.

Jones's method of romancing a woman was not to flatter and pay compliments but to tease and often insult her with a big grin on his face. It had and did work often enough for him not to change. But when he looked at Leah's face she did not seem to be enjoying the ribbing.

"Try the Moat Hotel" he suggested, "they always stick visiting lecturers in there."

She looked up gratefully. "The Moat in Market Street?"

"Off Queens Street?" Jones nodded.

"Thanks, I owe you."

As she headed off Jones could not resist calling after her. "Don't forget! Spice it up; there must be something sexy about chaos theory."

She mouthed a satirical ha, ha, then turned, ran round the corner and bumped straight into Victor dropping her books.

"Idiot!" snarled Victor.

"I'm sorry," she apologized as she picked up her books.

For a moment Victor stood staring.

"Err, all right," he stammered as he could see straight down Leah's v-necked sweater. The view was mesmerizing to Victor; the porcelain like skin of the redhead with her small rounded breasts reminded him of a classic French sculpture by Rodin. Victor meant no harm staring; in fact in reality he had tremendous awe-inspiring wonder at the sight.

To Victor, women were a greater mystery than an Alien from out of space. Not that he lacked desire; he had a healthy lust, which he could only satisfy with the impersonal images from glossy magazines. And not that he would not make a convivial companion to the right woman but women always fell for those confident, good-looking guys who chatted them up, screwed them and dumped them the next day. In his scientific way Victor had developed an equation that calculated that each of these hundred men had pained two hundred women a year, spreading the mythology amongst twenty thousand women a year that 'all men are bastards'. The truth was that women were their own worst enemy and so shy men like Victor were never spotted as good partners let alone get the chance to be bastards.

Sensing his eyes on her, Leah put a hand on her sweater closing off the miraculous view to Victor. As she rose she smiled apologetically then hurried on down the corridor. He watched her go, trying hard to burn the image into his memory for later use. When he turned he found the other students were smirking at him. Self-consciously he walked awkwardly past them to Haddo's study and knocked on the door. "Come in."

Victor entered the study but before he could speak, Haddo raised a hand to stop him. Then with a swirl of the hand Haddo picked up a jug of water and poured it into a tumbler. The water turned deep red as it hit the glass.

"See V..Victor. W..Water into w..wine," Haddo enthused.

Victor enjoyed Haddo's magic tricks and this one was impressive.

"That's very good. You'll be raising the dead next."

Victor spotted the chess game in progress. "Ah, you've moved."

"Yes I'm r..rather pleased...'

Without a flicker Victor moved the black knight to G5.

"Oh, I d..d..didn't see that," stammered Haddo

"No you didn't, did you?" grinned Victor, "Well – it's in."

"In the c..c..computer?" stuttered Haddo.

"Aleister Crowley transferred to RAM. His rituals re-enacted on computer screens from Montevideo to Madras."

Aleister Crowley was the common link between these two disparate characters. Not unlikely since both as children developed few social skills. One whose debilitating stutter hid him away in the fantasy world of books, the other lived in the cyber world of computers. And when boys and girls come out to play there is always someone left behind and the boy who is left behind is of no use to the girl who is left behind.

But these two boys who had been left behind came to Crowley from exactly opposite directions. Haddo because of his anti scientific, anti materialist interest in the magic and Spiritual world of Aleister Crowley.

While Victor, on the other hand, came to Crowley because of

his scientific and materialist view, which never allowed him to dismiss the strange physical anomalies from which new scientific theories often sprung. And Victor knew that Crowley was well aware of the magic of Quantum physics when he wrote in 'The Beast',

'Here is a paradox beyond even the imagination of Swift. Gulliver regarded the Lilliputians as a race of dwarfs and the Lilliputians regarded Gulliver as a giant. That is natural. But how strange it would be if the Lilliputians had appeared as dwarfs to Gulliver and Gulliver had appeared a dwarf to the Lilliputians. That is too absurd for fiction and is an idea only to be found in the sober pages of science.'

The world of quantum physics is so far out of our everyday experience that it allowed for any wild thought to be considered, but Victor's wild thoughts were too often, just wild thoughts. Haddo on the other hand was a more cautious character with much to lose by any disreputable incident.

"B..b..but won't they be able to trace a virus b..back to the Z93."

"Not the way I'm working it, with an external key."

"But wh..why would anyone open it?"

"Sexual magic. That's what he recognized – the one way to our primitive emotions – sex."

"I suppose it..it..it's an STD.

"An STD?" queried Victor.

"A sexually t..transmitted disease." Haddo enjoyed his joke.

"It's not funny, Haddo. This is serious."

"Please V..Victor, I'm n..not a scientist, To me c..computers are useless, all they can do is give you answers. The real genius is to know the questions."

"Look, mysticism is expressed in words, in incantations, in spells. Incantations use language. What is the most basic and universal language?"

"English?"

"No! no the only truly universal language is numbers."

"N..Numbers?" stuttered Haddo.

"Yes numbers. Now the computer works numbers, not like an average human being but like a God – like a Shakespeare with language."

"Alright, so it's clever but where's the body? Where's the s..soul? Your talking about a bloody machine," said Haddo as he unfolded a pamphlet advertising Crowley's ceremony.

"Here. When we perform the Rites, th..then you'll see the u..u..union."

Typical poster for the performance of Crowley's rites in modern USA

Victor took the pamphlet and looked it over. "That's pretty good, but ceremonies without him are like performing Hamlet without the Prince. We're more likely to generate something from a cathode ray tube not to mention the Z93."

"You have no r..respect for r..ritual. Your c..computer c..can't inter-react it can't c..c..c..connect to the soul."

"Don't you see Quantum physics is modern alchemy; alchemy at the sub-particle level. It opens virtual connections..." Victor suddenly stopped in mid sentence. "What did you say?"

"What?" asked Haddo, "About the in..interaction b..between energy from the human soul. The untapped p..p..power of the spirit. A machine c..can't experience f..fear, elation, passion. W..w..what do you expect it t..to do, cast s..spells?"

"Cast spells? Yes," smiled Victor enigmatically. "Yes that's exactly what I expect it to do."

He turned and walked out leaving Haddo stuttering.

"H..h..how? C..cast spells?"

In the laboratory the vertical beam of light picked out the gleaming steel sarcophagus in the glass room. There was a knocking sound coming from it. Mathers entered the glass room to the sound of hissing air and a loud amplified heartbeat. He knelt at the box and slowly opened the lid. Leah's shock of red hair was spread, her arms crossed over her naked breasts as in death. He stared down amazed and confused. Then suddenly her eyes opened and her arms reached up and round him. Leah's white body came sliding to him, her tongue pushed into his mouth. She was on him; his hands ran down her back. They touched the fleshy umbilical chord that pumped blood into her body through her back. He looked down at the pumping umbilical, shocked. The knocking sound continued. His eyes traced the blood filled chord coil round the floor to the glass wall. On the other side of the glass the chord entered Professor Brent through his stomach, his face red with drops of blood-colored perspiration; his eyes bulged red as he knocked furiously on the glass wall.

The knocking continued. Mathers rolled in restless sleep, tormented by dreams. Professor Brent, the red headed girl, the glass room, the sarcophagus all rolled into one. His brow dripped sweat his breathing short gasps. The persistent knocking echoed round the darkened room evoking deathly poems of loss.

'Once upon a midnight dreary, while I pondered, weak and weary,
Over many a quaint and curious volume of forgotten lore,
While I nodded, nearly napping, suddenly there came a tapping,

As of someone gently rapping, rapping at my chamber door.
"'Tis some visiter," I muttered, "tapping at my chamber door –
Only this and nothing more.'

Outside in the corridor Leah was knocking on the door. Perhaps her essence, her spirit, her aura or just her memory penetrated Mathers dreams. She knocked again. There was no answer. After a moment she looked at her watch and began to realize this story was going nowhere fast. How much could she write without the interview and what would make a good heading? 'Reporter Uncertain to get Interview Proves the Uncertainty Principal.' Very funny, she thought as she turned her mind to what she liked in his book. The way he questioned reality, 'Chaos Professor Defies Reality'? No that's corny and he said he wasn't a Professor anyway. How did he defy reality? Well he proved that a x b was not equal to b x a, which was like saying 2 x 3 is not equal to 3 x 2. But Mathers wrote that that was discovered here in Cambridge by Paul Dirac way back in the 1930's - Mathers just found new equations to express it. There was the nice bit in the book about a dropping stone. All the atoms of the stone drop to the ground but when it hits and the atoms are brought to an abrupt halt, energy in the form of heat is produced. So if you heat a stone why doesn't it fly back up into the air? It does - or some atoms do but then more don't and its all a question of probability. It is possible that all the atoms could move upwards together and the stone would fly into the air but it's not probable. 'Chaos Lecturer Brings Probability to Cambridge?' No, that's awful, she thought as she turned away depressed, down the corridor with its optically challenging patterned carpet. 'Chaotic Configuration Confuses Cambridge Correspondent.'

The 'Granta' editorial meeting took place in a cramped office with desks round the walls on which were computers, printers and scanners. The chairs were pulled into the centre as the students acted out being journalists each having the same competitive desire to pull in the best story as real ones. Ashby, the editor, whose accent and jacket, tailored to the waist with a bum flap, revealing his military parents and public school upbringing, began the meeting with a sarcastic attack on Leah.

"So your big front-page scoop on the visiting Chaos Professor hasn't materialized."

"I'll get it," responded Leah to the challenge, then immediately felt sorry she had not allowed the story to drop, especially when Ashby added,

"But we won't hold our breath."

He turned to Sinclair, a Scottish student in a leather jacket. "What about the Masonic story?"

"I've got a few names but I can't work out how far it goes into the University establishment."

"But what do they do, what's the purpose of Masonry? I mean, a secret organization with leading members in the police force, the Government and even the University establishment."

"It's confusing," replied Sinclair scratching his head. "They seem to be behind the French Revolution, the American Revolution and even the first Russian revolution, the Kerensky one, but now they appear to be bastions of the establishment. English Grand Lodge claim that it began in the eighteenth century but it's absolutely clear that Christopher Wren was a Mason as were the founders of the Royal Society in the sixteen hundreds. I seem to find traces right back to the Knights Templars and even to the Pythagoreans. And of course Pythagoras spent twenty years in Egypt being initiated into their mystery religion."

"So it could have begun anywhere from the 17th Century to 3,000 BC," said Ashby.

"They use a pyramid from ancient Egypt as their symbol," added Sinclair.

"Yes, but that doesn't mean it goes back all that way," said Ashby.

"Maybe it does," said Goggles, "because it's only a half finished Pyramid like on the dollar bill... so it could go back to the building of the pyramids."

"And it has the eye of Horus over it," enthused Sinclair.

"Wooh, Wooh!" interrupted Ashby. "That's all conjecture. You can't really tell us when it began, so obviously the piece isn't ready is it?" He turned and opened it up to the meeting, "Any other ideas?"

"I've written a poem on the recount going on in Florida," said Phil, a fair-haired student. "It sort of goes: 'Jed Bush skipped his lunches. To blunt Florida's punches. So when you vote for Al Gore. The paper just tore."

Jones quickly added, "Now the U.S. is split, and we're all in the shit."

"No, keep it clean," warned Ashby.

" It is," said Sinclair." It goes on – about forty lines."

"Okay that can do page four," said Ashby. "Do you want to do a cartoon, Clarice, to go with it?"

"Sure, give me the poem and I'll work on it."

"You know," mused Goggles, "I think Sinclair can still do the Masonic story even if he hasn't got all the facts. He can write all his questions, like how much do they infiltrate the University Establishment and leave them as questions."

"Yeah," added Jones, "I bet there are plenty of students in Cambridge whose fathers are masons who can give you some answers."

Goggles continued, "And he can raise issues like the Italian banker found hung under Blackfriars Bridge, obviously murdered by the Italian Masonic P2 organization but who is said by the British Police to have committed suicide. How could an Italian Masonic organization influence our Police to bring in such a ridiculous verdict to prevent investigation?"

Sinclair warmed to the idea. "There's also the case of the Manchester policeman who was investigating the links in Northern Ireland between the Protestant police force and Protestant paramilitary murders. Then just as he gets close he is suddenly fired by the

Manchester Police for mixing with criminals. What's his name?"

"Stalker," said Ashby.

"Yes Stalker. The evidence was a photograph of him at a Masonic dinner sitting next to a known criminal. How did that photo suddenly appear and what influence did the Protestant Masonic Orange Lodges have on the Manchester Chief Superintendent to get him to sack an innocent officer?"

"Sounds good," said Ashby. "Okay, write the first part of your investigation, put in all your conjectures and ask lots of questions as if the big revelation will be in the next issue."

Phil held up an evening newspaper. "What about this – Prince William is going to St Andrews?"

"Is that news?" asked Ashby.

"Why St. Andrews and not Cambridge. Prince Charles read archaeology here at Trinity."

"I bet he's got some skeletons in the cupboard here," said Ben.

"Maybe we could find a tutor who'll spill the beans on him," Jones added gleefully.

Ashby was not impressed. "Like what? He's got three illegitimate kids with the local librarian."

But Phil persisted. "We should find out if Prince William was circumcized."

"Circumcized?" queried Ashby dubiously.

"Prince Charles was circumcized by the Chief Rabbi – it's part of the ancient rites of all British Kings."

"The what?"

They looked at each other incredulously then burst out laughing.

Their sceptical laughter missed a fascinating exposé for there is huge dispute and occult interest in the ritual which some believed was established when the partly Jewish Battenbergs changed their name to Mountbatten and married into the British Royal Family. But others considered it more ancient, linking the Royal families of Europe with the mystical Merovingian Kings (the long haired kings) who traced their descent from the Jewish Royal family and the line of David. The blue emblem of the Jewish Royal Family who integrated into European Royalty gave rise to the term true blue blood royalty. The ancient Holy Grail stories alluded to the link of the line of David to Lancelot and therefore to the Lady of the Lake, Queen Elena of Aquitaine who gave rise to the British Plantagenet King line. The most memorable member of the Plantagenets was Richard the First of England, Richard the Lion Heart who probably never stepped foot in Britain but just exploited it mercilessly to finance his adventures in the Holy Land. And of course it was there in Jerusalem in 1115 that the rituals of the Knights Templar were created.

And not a stone's throw from the University was a dark round building with a large ornate black door. The interior walls were thick with carved symbols, the five-pointed star, the callipers and setsquare and the image of Pythagoras. On the floor in the centre was the black and white, chessboard ceremonial carpet given meaning and significance by Omar Khayyam.

> 'Tis all a chequer-board of Nights and Days
> Where destiny with man for pieces plays.
> Hither and thither moves, and mates, and slays.
> And one by one back in the closet lays.'

On either side of the carpet sat the Knights in their dark suits and embroidered aprons. The Eminent Preceptor, Symons, sat in his chair to the North. Haddo sat in the registrar's position.

Symons picked up the gavel in his white-gloved hand and knocked for attention. "Brethren assist me to open this Preceptory." They all rose.

Behind Symons, standing in their stately positions were the two pillars named in the bible. Chronicles 3-15,

> 'In front of the house he made two pillars thirty-five cubits high, with a capital of five cubits on the top of each.

He set up the pillars in front of the temple, one on the south, the other on the north; that on the south he called Jachin, and that on the north Bo'az.'

According to the old ritual of Freemasonry these two great pillars were hollow. Inside them had been stored the 'ancient records' and the 'valuable writings' pertaining to the past of the Jewish people. But in truth the concept was even more ancient, arising in the temples of Egypt where legend had it that a previous advanced culture seeing the likelihood of a natural disaster put their technical secrets into two pillars, one of wood that would float in case of a flood and the other made of stone to withstand a conflagration.

Between Jachin and Boaz, Symons began the meeting.

"Is the Lodge properly Tyled?"

The Marshal, who was Professor Brent, moved to the entrance, opened the door and checked the Guard outside who had with him a hooded man. Brent closed the door, did the sign of the crucifix and reported.

"Eminent Preceptor, the Lodge is properly Tyled."

Crowley dressed in his Masonic Regalia

Haddo rose and with his palms crossed began. "I then call upon the Chaplain to grace those present."

The Chaplain stepped clockwise round the chequered carpet till he was forward, facing East.

"Knights, it is time to commence our labours. Set a watch before my mouth and keep thou the door of my lips."

"So note it be," they all replied in unison.

A white shroud with a skull and crossed bones was laid on the floor. From the back the hooded man was led in, his trouser leg rolled up and his shirt open to reveal a breast. Round his neck was a hangman's noose. He stopped before the shroud and turned by his future brothers. Disorientated and 'hoodwinked' his feet were placed in the secret communicating position of a T. He gladly awaits his death – and then his resurrection.

Deep from the abyss Mathers woke with a start. He looked round but could see nothing in the darkness the poem still pressing on his heart.

'Deep into that darkness peering, long I stood there
    wondering, fearing.
Doubting, dreaming dreams no mortals ever dared to dream
    before;
But the silence was unbroken, and the stillness gave no token;
And the only word there spoken was the whispered word,
    "Lenore!"'

Mathers stretched out a hand and found a table lamp and switched it on. Above him the painting 'Bridge of Sighs' reminded him he was in Cambridge, not Venice. Behind him a damp patch stained the sheet with the deathly perspiration effused by a tormented dream. He sat on the bed, the depression forming a knot in the pit of his stomach, trying to recall the ordeal but could not remember any of it. He picked up the phone. The very British voice answered.

"Reception?"

"What time is it?" asked Mathers.

The voice replied. "It's nine Sir."

"Nine in the morning?"

"No evening."

"What day?"

"Wednesday the fifth of January, Sir."

Mathers put down the phone and sat there empty and alone. The confusion caused by jet lag was not unexpected but was still disturbing. And Mathers knew researchers had found that mice undergoing weekly light-cycle shifts – similar to those experienced by jet travelers – showed significantly higher death rates than mice kept on a normal daylight schedule. The findings provided, in rather stark terms, new insights into how the disruption of circadian rhythms can impact on the wellbeing and physiology of an individual. Sleep specialists also suggested that eastward adjustments like Mathers's US to Europe journey were more difficult than westward and probably compromised the immune system. Certainly shift work, which produces similar reactions to jet lag, had been associated with higher rates of breast cancer and heart problems. One Israeli study even showed a higher rate of mental problems in tourists who traveled through multiple time zones.

Mathers rubbed his fingers through his scalp to help circulate the blood to his brain. He noticed the notepad with his equations on the bedside table and glanced at them but his brain was in no fit state to expand on them. He got up from the bed like an old man and staggered into the bathroom. The light bounced blindingly off the white tiles as he found the sink and looked at his tired face in the mirror. He rubbed a scar that was irritating him on the back of his forearm. He splashed cold water. The arm trembled uncontrollably as blood oozed. He grabbed a towel and pressed it.

The black doors pushed open against the windy night and the Freemasons, flapping like bats, scurried out of the Temple and hurried across the road to the Red Lion and Sun Inn. An appropriate Inn for an occult organization since the name is a concealed form of an alchemical process. The Brethrens flapping coats revealed their evening suits beneath and hanging from their wrists were pouches for their Masonic aprons. Haddo was in conversation with Symons when Victor slid out of the shadows and grabbed Haddo's arm.

"I need to talk to you," hissed Victor.

Haddo turned: Symons stopped and waited.

"V..Victor, There's an initiatory lodge dinner," complained Haddo.

Victor started to whisper urgently. Symons caught snippets of the conversation carried on the wind.

"We've only got this one chance."

"I d..d..don't know w..why.." Haddo noticed Symons listening.

"G..go on I'll c..catch you up."

Symons turned and hurried across the road. As he went into the shelter of the Red Lion he turned and noticed Haddo heading off with Victor his wisps of grey hair streaming in the wind. Three days later when Symons recounted his story he recalled that this was the last moment he saw Haddo alive.

The fat crescent moon appeared and disappeared behind racing clouds over the Clock Tower as Leah and Jones walked through the shadows of the cloisters protected from the whistling wind that blew papers round the quadrangle. She was feeling pretty sore.

"So far I've covered the dark controversy of Trinity buying up the council allotments, the high rate of drunkenness during Rag week, and the unfortunate and untimely death of Mrs. Miggins, the cloister's cat."

"Went down in the annuls as one of Granta's best," quipped Jones.

"First chance I get to do something important my man goes missing."

"I don't see what's so important about his work?"

"You should read his book," she said earnestly.

But Jones just joked. "Bet it doesn't beat Mrs Miggins for human interest."

"That's not quite the type of journalist I want to be."

"What, efficient?"

"Oh do shut up, Jonesy."

"Okay then, I won't tell you that he's probably in the physics lab where they're setting up."

She looked at her watch.

"Now?"

"Maybe he's jet lagged and can't sleep," said Jones, then added sarcastically, "probably on a different timescale to us mere mortals."

She ignored the quip, thanked him and headed off.

As he watched her go he became slowly depressed. Somehow he felt any chance of romantic involvement was slipping away.

In the laboratory Victor threw the main light switch for the glass room, illuminating the steel sarcophagus.

"There she is," pointed Victor.

Haddo turned and his eyes reflected the brightness. Victor opened the glass door and beckoned him in. Together they approached the shiny sarcophagus. Victor unclipped the latches and pulled open the lid. Inside was a black double layered, body cover.

"You wanted human contact, the link between the Z93 and the soul. Well there it is."

Tubes and compressed air pads covered the suit and on the top was a helmet like the head of a fly with large bulbous eyes.

"There's a miniaturized computer in the helmet that will communicate with my Crowley program in the Z93."

Haddo started to stutter. "And I w..will experience h..him?"

"Some form of him."

"I'm n..not sure it's going to b..be a very m..m..meaningful ex..ex..ex..."

"Dr. Haddo, I do believe you are scared. What are you afraid of – an encounter with him or with your secret self?"

The wind carried the sound of a choir singing 'The Twelve Days of Christmas'.

They had reached 'Nine Lords leaping' and were descending through seven swans swimming, six geese laying and five gold rings as Leah hurried from the cloisters into the outer quadrangle. Her flat mate Rose saw her.

"Hi, Leah."

Leah nodded but carried on. "Can't stop."

'Something tells me our cub reporter is on a mission."

"Hunting down that Professor," admitted Leah.

"No luck at the station?"

"He slipped me."

"I've got one for your scientific article," said Rose and began a little ditty.

"When Einstein was studying light,
His equations they gave him a fright.
He went out that day in a relative way
And came back the previous night."

Leah laughed. "Very funny. I'll use it in the article and give you a credit."

"Well thanks, but I think it's by Anon. Will I see you later?" added Rose as Leah turned to go.

"Yes. Why wouldn't you?"

"Wasn't that Jones I saw you talking to?"

Leah looked back despairingly, "Come on Rose."

Rose smiled, "In the immortal words of Lewis Carroll, "No wise fish goes anywhere without a porpoise'."

Leah noticed lights flickering in the Physics laboratory

"Gotta go," and she headed off her red hair blowing back across her face.

Rose sang after her. "Will you wont you, will you wont you, will you join the dance."

Leah smiled as she entered the lab block. Security was as usual very lax and she passed down the corridor unchallenged. She brushed her hair back off her face with her fingers, knocked on the lab door and pushed it open.

Victor jumped as the pretty redhead stepped through the door. "What are you..? This is a restricted zone."

"I'm sorry I'm looking for... Is that Dr. Mathers?"

Leah pointed through the window, to where she had noticed the space-type suit standing alone in the bright glass room.

"No. He went back to his hotel."

"I've been there," she replied hoping for another suggestion.

At that moment a distorted voice came over the monitor

"H..h..hurry up, its d-dark in here."

Leah looked up at the monitor. She half recognized the voice but continued.

"Could you tell Dr. Mathers that Leah Robinson from Granta was looking for him."

"Sure."

"About the interview."

"About the interview, right," said Victor trying to rapidly conclude the conversation. Finally she turned to go.

"And close the door after you," snarled Victor then swivelled back to the controls.

Leah just caught the voice from the suit as the door closed.

"V-V-Victor I'm feeling a b-b-bit claustrophobic."

"Relax, here we go," reassured Victor and pressed a button marked ENGAGE.

As Leah went down the corridor something niggled at the back of her mind. Her subconscious, the right side of her brain, had registered information but no message was sent to the conscious left and by the time she stepped out into the windy night the feeling had passed. She headed out through the University Gatehouse to the cobbled street where her bicycle was locked to the railings. There were still hundreds of other bikes locked along the wall. She noticed that, as usual, every tenth bike, or so, was a mangled mess. Where the hell did they come from, all those broken bikes and why were they chained up with the good bikes? Perhaps she could write a comic article for Granta about a ghostly factory producing broken bikes and planting them at night: or better still, an epic poem about a malevolent motorist stalking the streets, destroying bikes for some evil revenge. 'The Serial Cycle Slayer.' With that idea stored for future use she mounted her cycle and thought about going back to the Moat Hotel but instead circled round and headed down wind to the student union to celebrate her inspired idea with a beer.

Victor watched the screen as it flashed up:

'SUIT ACTIVATED' then ' MAGNETS ON'.

In the glass room the suit magically floated gently upwards. Victor rubbed his hands in vigorous glee and typed 'SET CO-ORDINATES'.

A grill of blue laser beams partitioned the glass room and cast a three dimensional diagram on the computer screen. The suit's legs moved. Haddo's voice came over the intercom excitedly.

"It's just l-like normal w-walking."

The screen flashed ENGAGE.

"G-gosh, fields," exclaimed Haddo.

"Is it working? I'm going to put it on the monitor up here," said Victor as he switched on the large TV monitor. An image of wheat fields appeared.

"Wheat fields? Right?

"Y..y..yes. But the sound I hear is of waves."

"Get your bearings, turn to your left."

Haddo turned left and the image panned left to show the seashore.

"Wow. It's r-r-real, I c-c-can hear the birds – the sea."

"Virtually." Victor smiled. "Okay, I'm switching in the squids."

"S..s..squids?"

"The super-conducting quantum interference devices, they

should interact with your thought patterns."

He typed in a command and engaged his portable hard drive.

"Okay now I'm introducing my program."

He hit a key and looked up at the screen. The same seashore, nothing seemed to be happening. He checked the connection and hit the key again.

"I'm not.."

Before he could finish Haddo's voice came over the intercom.

"The c-c-colors. The sky is changing."

Victor looked at the screen, nothing.

"Are you sure, I'm getting nothing on my monitor?"

"Yes, c..can't you see?"

Victor glanced down through the viewing window. Haddo was standing looking up, his arms outstretched.

"What is it?" asked Victor.

"There, in the s..sky. A pentagram."

Again Victor looked at the screen, just the same seascape.

"Describe it to me."

In the suit Haddo saw the pentagram slowly revolve. Weird black storm clouds rose on the horizon – now the centre was pulsing, mutating, spinning producing a high-pitched throbbing sound.

"W-What's that n..noise?"

Victor heard it too.

"I don't know. I think it's some sort of feedback."

Victor typed 'HOLD'. The sound continued to grow.

"V-Victor I'm scared. Switch it off."

"Wait, maybe I can…"

"No-No, stop it."

"Okay – okay."

Victor typed 'CANCEL INTEGRATION' and looked to the screen. 'ERROR. DATE TIME FREEZE'. Haddo saw a whirling vortex of blazing light and color, spinning, spinning. Victor frantically punched in new commands, but to no avail, the sound just grew louder; a pulsing static on both monitor and speakers.

"Ahhhhhhhhh!"

Victor panicked. "Haddo!"

Haddo was swaying as if about to fall over. Victor ejected his hard drive.

"Haddo! Haddo!"

Victor pressed 'MAGNETS OFF' and leapt up to the window. Haddo crashed to the floor. The VDU started flashing images at an incredible speed. Victor opened the door of the control room and hurried to the bright-lit glass room were the black suit lay motionless in the middle. He opened the door, dropped to the suit and unstrapped the gloss black helmet. Supporting Haddo with one arm he pulled off the helmet. Haddo was ashen white with cold sweat droplets, his head lolled over, blood coming from his ears.

"Jesus Christ."

Victor unzipped the suit and loosened the collar and tie and felt for a pulse, nothing.

He slapped the cheek gently.

"Haddo – come on!"

He slapped again harder. Nothing moved. He thumped with clench fists on the chest then went to slap the face when, Haddo swung an arm across hitting Victor in the face and tipping him back.

Haddo laughed maniacally and rolled over, grabbing Victor by the throat. "Do what thou shall."

"Get off," choked Victor.

Haddo held him tight by the throat. His voice was deeper and throaty.

"Come now! That's not the response. Do what thou wilt?"

Victor croaked, "Love is the law, love under will."

"That's more like it."

Haddo released him and jumped to his feet. Victor backed away, coughing.

Haddo glared down at him, "Behold where thine Angel hath led thee! Thou didst ask for power and pleasure."

"Haddo?" inquired Victor hesitantly.

Haddo looked at his hands as if he was seeing them for the first time. He stepped out of the suit.

"Are you alright?" asked Victor.

"Time cures all things."

Haddo pulled off his Rolex watch and threw it down; his eyes fevered with madness as he walked to the glass door.

"Haddo you..!"

Haddo turned. "No. Not Haddo. The beast, megatherion!" Haddo slammed the glass door.

Victor sat dazed under the spotted light in the glass room and watched Haddo stride across the darkened hangar and disappear through the Laboratory door. Victor blinked and rubbed his sore throat. He picked up Haddo's watch and got to his feet trying to understand what had happened and what reprimand may fall on him for the use of the equipment for such illicit activities. If something is wrong with Haddo it will surely all come out. Anxiously he stepped out of the glass room and ran out of the laboratory after him.

Emerging from the Physics block and into the quadrangle Victor turned about looking for Haddo. There was no sign of him. The leaves in the tree overhead rustled noisily, the clouds rushed away revealing the nearly full moon bright in the night sky, as its ghostly light delineated the battlements and spires. The world felt different, strangely unreal; he looked around confused by his feelings. Finally he turned and headed left through the arched doorway to the street. At the kerb he stopped and looked both ways. The street was empty. Haddo had disappeared.

At that very moment Cambridge was exactly on the opposite side of the Earth to the blazing Sun and in the darkness Victor's attention was drawn to the streak of light in the sky; a particle of space dust colliding with the Earth's atmosphere. The wind suddenly dropped to a murmur and it seemed to whisper Crowley's words into Victor's ear:

"The moon and the night but mock
The wretch on his barren rock
And the dome of heaven high arched
Like his mouth is arid and parched
And the caves of his heart high spanned
Are chocked with alkali sand."

Crowley? Or was it a memory sifted from his subconscious. Confused, Victor looked down at the Rolex ticking in his hand and shivered. He suddenly felt very small and insignificant.

CHAPTER 2

DAY TWO

Wednesday 6th January

Leah sat and, with her bleary eyes, watched the sand drain down through the egg timer, each grain representing an instant of time, an instant, which Omar Khayyam had once said could never return.

> 'The Moving Finger writes; and, having writ,
> Moves on: nor all your Piety nor Wit
> Shall lure it back to cancel half a Line,
> Nor all your Tears wash out a Word of it.'

Yet not only had this universal belief been threatened by Einstein's confirmed theory that time was relative but in Mathers book on Chaos, which was propped open on the table, he quoted from the greatest brain in the world, Richard Feynman.

> 'In all the laws of physics that we have found so far there does not seem to be any distinction between the past and the future. The moving picture should work the same going both ways, and the physicist who looks at it should not laugh because there appears to be no evident distinction between past and future. In the motion laws of atoms there should be somewhere in the works some kind of principle that uxles only make wuxles, and never vice

> versa, and the world is turning away from uxley character to wuxley character all the time – and this one-way business should be the thing that makes the whole phenomena of the world seem to go one way. But we have not found this yet.'

Leah had wondered how seriously one should take all this when Feynman himself declared?

> 'One does not, by knowing all the physical laws as we know them today, immediately obtain an understanding of anything much.'

And

> 'The more you see how strangely Nature behaves, the harder it is to make a model that explains how even the simplest phenomena actually work. So theoretical physics has given up on that.'

And

> 'I think it is safe to say that no one understands Quantum Mechanics.'

As yet, none of these obscure theoretical problems of quantum mechanics had affected Leah's life. And the sand draining through the glass tube just added up to how hard her egg was boiled. But over the next two days the uncertainty of quantum theory would prove to be the difference between a long contented life or imminent death.

When the last grain of sand fell Leah quickly took the egg from the boiling water to prevent any more of the individual curled long protein molecules from unfolding and netting with their neighbours.

She sat down at the formica kitchen table where she sliced the top off her egg and nodded with satisfaction at its soft-boiled perfection. She wore a Chinese dressing gown, blue like a summer sky with dragons worked all over it in gold with scarlet eyes and tongues. Her feet were warmed by her new fluffy slippers. The Christmas Cards and decorations were still up around her and as she ate she glanced at the cards trying to remember who had sent which. She gave up and went back to 'A Tale of Two Cities', her homework, which was propped open on the table. The specific task was to select three sections that best illustrate his style. She had never read Charles Dickens and certainly never read 'A Tale' before but strangely she had from somewhere imbibed the opening and ending lines of the book. The opening, 'It was the best of times, it was the worst of times.' She flicked back to the opening to remind herself of the rest.

'It was the best of times, it was the worst of times, it was the age of wisdom, it was the age of foolishness, it was the epoch of belief, it was the epoch of incredulity, it was the season of Light, it was the season of Darkness, it was the spring of hope, it was the winter of despair, we had everything before us, we had nothing before us, we were all going direct to Heaven, we were all going direct the other way'

That could all refer to today, she thought; or perhaps it could refer to any time. Maybe there were always some people who saw the best and others who saw the worst. Whichever, she could not use it as an example of his style. She had already selected one passage, Chapter 2 page 8: the Dover coach making its way up Shooters Hill–

'There was a steaming mist in all the hollows, and it had roamed in its forlornness up the hill, like an evil spirit, seeking rest and finding none. A clammy and intensely cold mist, it made its slow way through the air in ripples that visibly followed and over-spread one another, as the waves of an unwelcome sea might do. It was dense enough to shut out everything from the light of the coach lamps but these its own workings, and a few yards of road; and the reek of the labouring horses steamed into it, as if they had made it all.' She considered this typical of his writing often inserting 'evil' or 'forlornness' or 'spirit' or 'malevolent' in a description to create a mood even before the action. She wondered if there was an example from the last lines, which she knew by heart. On his way to the guillotine Sydney Carton proclaims, 'It is a far, far better thing I do, than I have ever done; it is a far better rest that I go to, than I have ever known.' For a second her father came to mind but before she could dwell on it, Rose, came in drying her hair. "Morning."

Leah lifted up a leg to show Rose she was wearing her fluffy present.

"Nice." Rose said sarcastically. "We must get these decorations down."

"That's what you said yesterday."

"You're right. I'm going to stop putting things off – starting tomorrow!"

"Ha, ha," pronounced Leah sarcastically.

"Well you can take them down too."

"I've got a lot on my plate and I'm not feeling great?"

"What's up?" asked Rose.

"I was out celebrating."

"Celebrating getting your Professor: or getting Jonesy?"

"Nope and nope," said Leah.

"So what were you celebrating?"

"I can't remember, my brain's a bit clogged and I've got to sit through two hours of Dr Haddo lecturing."

"Once on your bike the cold air will clear your head.'

"Oh that was it."

"What?"

"What I was celebrating," remembered Leah.

"Riding your bike?"

"No, It's an idea for a comic article but I'll kill it if I try to describe it."

"You never got your chaos interview then?"

"I think he's trying to avoid me," said Leah screwing up her nose.

"I think he has a thing for you."

"Who? Doctor Mathers? I've only met him once."

"No, Jones," smiled Rose.

"What?"

"And I see you fancy this Doctor Mathers."

"What? Why?"

"You blushed."

"I did not. And just give me a break will you, I'm really fucking this up," complained Leah.

"That's what you said about the Mrs. Miggins story, and now look at her: that cat is almost as famous as Isaac Newton. You're a perfectionist, that's your problem. And you did blush."

"Redheads don't blush, we're too pale skinned."

"I've heard he's young, he's handsome and he's brilliant," sniggered Rose.

"From who?"

"Nobody; but it must be true cause it made you blush again."

Leah threw the bread crust at her.

The morning mist had cleared by the time the road filled with cycling students, their short academic gowns billowing behind them, their basket panniers filled with books. Leah joined the throng as they headed towards the college, her mind still reciting, like a relentless song, the heroic words, 'It is a far, far better thing I do, than I have ever done' She turned the pedals to its rhythm. 'It is a far, far better thing I do, than I have ever done.' It continued till she reached the college gates, parked up in the cycle rack and with the other students headed through the Gatehouse past the sign 'NO CYCLES' and across the neatly trimmed lawn. She wore less winter clothing than most, another characteristic of redheads who are built for cold climates. Their smooth snake-like skin with fewer sweat glands had the added bonus of producing less body odour but had the huge disadvantage in summer of burning with the first sight of the sun.

In the cosy warmth of the laboratory Mathers knelt over the suit in the glass room. As he slid open a hatch in the helmet there was a knocking sound like the dream. For a moment dreams and reality were confused. A couplet from Shakespeare crossed his mind and unfortunately he murmured it out loud.

"Wake Duncan with thy knocking? I would thou could'st," recalling too late the theatrical superstition that it is very unlucky to quote the 'Scottish Play' at the beginning of any enterprise. The knocking persisted. He looked up to see the red headed girl smile and open the glass door.

"Dr. Mathers."

He took a moment to place her. "I thought I'd dreamt you. Leah yes?"

"Robinson," she added.

"From Granta," remembered Mathers.

"You said five but you didn't say where."

"Sorry I was a bit jet lagged.

"Have you got a moment now?" asked Leah.

Mathers looked around. "Well no one is in yet, so – okay fire away?"

"Perhaps we could start with why you came to Cambridge and then we could do a bit on your background."

"Why I came? Well… we were getting some strange reactions back in California probably caused by lack of computing speed. Here the Z93... hold on."

Victor entered the lab wearing dark glasses.

"Hi Victor. Leah Robinson this is Victor."

They shook hands.

"Victor runs the Z93, the top notch computer we're hoping will solve the problems we've been having."

Mathers turned to Victor "You got it working then?"

"Yes ready to go, I think?" said Victor nervously.

"Have you tried it out?"

"N..n..no," lied Victor, "I haven't actually tried it out yet."

He flashed a guilty look at Leah but she was concerned only with Mathers.

"I'll go and fire her up," added Victor and hurried away leaving the other two talking.

Once in the control room Victor removed his dark glasses to reveal a black eye. He prepared the Z93 cabinet switching on the liquid nitrogen pump then went back to the control desk and turned on the monitor, which showed the glass room in the hangar. Leah was still interviewing Mathers, their voices coming over the intercom.

"So it's like a brain swapping machine?"

Mathers laughed. "No, not really - more a brain relating machine. You remember the double hole experiment where wave energy collapses to particles when we look at them?"

"Yes, Niels Bohr suggested the particles know when you are looking at them."

"That's the one. Perhaps if we could understand the way the brain thinks at a quantum level in wave form or particle form - we could bring some understanding to that aspect of quantum mechanics."

Victor sat at the computer and opened Mathers program.

Mathers' voice continued over the intercom.

"Yes I am planning another book, postulating a fundamental rearrangement of Einstein's equations."

"What way?" asked Leah.

"That reality is light. Matter and time don't exist they're just a by-product of the degradation of light – the slowing down of light."

"You don't believe in time?" asked Leah.

"It's becoming clear that our description of the world is based on an incredibly limited human experience. Already on the sub-particle level our beliefs in time, in space, in dimensions is... look, don't try to find a commonsense logic in this. Quantum physics has looked into the mind of God and it's totally alien to us. We're like ants trying to understand New York."

Victor looked up as he was reminded of Crowley's writings. 'During Dhyana meditation, time and space are abolished.' He pressed the camera control and the lens zoomed in on Leah, till her eyes filled the frame. He watched almost mesmerized then suddenly turned down the volume on the conversation. He picked up the phone and dialled, mumbling to himself. "Come on, come on, you fat idiot."

In an old Victorian house, shaded in gloom, on the corner of Oak Street, a phone rang. It rang on and on till a hand picked up the receiver from the cradle and smashed it against the wall.

Victor looked at the phone as it went dead. He dialled again and got engaged.

"Come on Haddo. Answer!"

He dialled again, still engaged.

He put down the phone and sat twirling his hair nervously. He looked up at Leah on the monitor. Mathers's voice could still be heard.

"When you look up at a star, how old is the light you see?"

Leah guessed. "I don't know, four hundred years?

"Well give or take a few hundred thousand. Anyway, you know how long it actually takes?"

"Actually takes?"

"No time at all. By Einstein's theory of relativity the faster objects move the slower clocks go. At the speed of light, clocks stand still. So light from the star arrives here at the same time it left. In fact for light no time has passed since our, so-called, beginning of time – the big bang."

Victor zoomed out to include Mathers who continued.

"So which is true, our introverted concept that the big bang occurred 15 billion years ago or light's view that it happened now? We conceive of things in terms of speed… momentum… they are all defined by time. But time doesn't exist…"

At that moment the door of the hangar opened and Professor Brent swept in and strode over to the glass room.

"Well chaps are we all set?"

"It seems so," answered Mathers. "Victor's wired me up."

In the control room, Victor switched on the intercom, his voice echoed urgently in the hangar.

"You can't go in that suit."

"Oh no," huffed Brent. "Why ever not?"

"Well er... I'm having trouble with er… the date-time sequence," fabricated Victor.

"Shall I come up?" asked Mathers.

"Give me the morning to work on it."

"Damn!" Cursed Professor Brent then turned his attention to Leah. "And who might you be?"

"A reporter." Mathers interjected.

"Press are not allowed on campus without authorization," proclaimed Brent.

"Oh, I okay'd it," explained Mathers. "I hope you don't mind, she's from Granta."

Professor Brent looked at her suspiciously.

"What faculty are you? Who's your tutor?"

Leah pulled out her press pass. "Dr. Haddo."

In the control room, Victor turned at the mention of his lost associate.

Mathers apologized to Leah with a smile. "We do have to get back to work, I'm afraid."

"But it was just getting…"

He directed her towards the door leaving Professor Brent with the suit. Once out of earshot Mathers whispered to her. "I'm sorry."

"Are scientists superstitious?" asked Leah.

"A few, why?"

"This interview is beginning to feel cursed."

"I hope not," said Mathers.

"Hope? Forget it; just give me the probability?"

"Very probable."

"With how much uncertainty?"

"Only what cannot be ruled out by the Copenhagen interpretation," smiled Mathers.

Leah looked at him sarcastically. "Meaning I can't calculate my position at any moment. The where or the when."

"My, you did do your homework. I'm impressed. Look, I've an appointment with the Bursar at seven and then we could meet outside his office at say quarter past – is that certain enough for you?"

"Quarter past seven outside the Bursar's," confirmed Leah.

"Maybe we could do dinner?" added Mathers.

"Dinner?"

"Maybe I'll get better service than last night with you at my table."

"That was British service – it won't get any faster with me there."

"I wouldn't be so sure about that. Einstein said, 'put your hand on a hot stove for a minute, and it seems like an hour. Sit with a pretty girl for an hour, and it seems like a minute. That's relativity."

"He never said that."

'Yes, he did. Seven o'clock – okay?"

"You said seven fifteen."

"Sorry yes, I'll be outside the bursar's office seven fifteen."

He smiled pleasantly and she stood a moment then gathered herself together and opened the door. Victor watched her from the control room then grabbed his case and went to intercept her in the corridor. She was nearly at the exterior door when he caught up with her.

"Did you say Dr. Haddo is your tutor?"

Leah turned.

"Have you seen him today?" asked Victor.

"No, he's giving the Maudleyn Classics lecture this afternoon."

"Oh Christ," cursed Victor and he went past her and out of the building.

She watched him cross the quadrangle. He looked agitated and nervous even a little weird to be in charge of something so powerful as the Z93. It was said that the world would soon be divided into two distinct groups, those who would control computers and those who would be controlled by computers. A little worrying, thought Leah, if this was the sort of person who would be in control. Victor disappeared into a side door and she peeled off with the other students through the archway and up the stairs past the sign 'SWITCH OFF YOUR MOBILE PHONES HERE' to class.

Victor hurried up the stairs to Haddo's study and knocked on the door. There was no answer. He looked about him knocked again and went in.

"Haddo?"

The study was empty. Victor wandered up to the desk. Amongst the papers and books, he saw the water jug and glass. He tried pouring the water into the glass – nothing, the water stayed crystal clear.

Scratching his head he shuffled through the mess of papers. He noticed one had scrawled all over it 'Aleister Crowley's phallic signature'. Crowley's autobiography, *'Confessions'* was open on the desk.

> 'I was born at 30 Clarendon Square Leamington, Warwickshire*'

Victor looked down to the base of the page for Crowley's note.

> '* It has been remarked a strange coincidence that one small county should have given England her two greatest poets – for one must not forget Shakespeare.'

Even in his state of angst a smile crept across Victor's face as he looked back to the narrative.

> '...on the 12th day of October 1875 E.V. between eleven and twelve at night. Leo was just rising at the time. I was

> baptized Edward Alexander but after many years of being called Alick which I loathed, partly because of the unpleasant sound and sight of the word, partly because it was the name my mother called me. Edward did not seem to suit me and the diminutives Ted or Ned were even less appropriate. Alexander was too long and Sandy suggested tow hair and freckles. I had read in some book that the most favourable name for becoming famous was one consisting of a hexameter: like 'Jeremy Taylor'. Aleister Crowley fulfilled these conditions and to adopt it would satisfy my romantic ideals. The atrocious spelling was suggested from the Gaelic and ALAISDAIR makes a very bad dactyl. For these reasons I saddled myself with my present nom-de-guerre. I can't say that I feel sure that I facilitated the process of becoming famous. I should doubtless have done so, whatever name I had chosen.'

Victor closed the book and went to the circular bookcases where he knew Haddo kept his full collection of Crowley's works. He opened the glass door and slipped it in the gap, which was its place. He thought for a moment then took out a small leather bound volume titled 'Moonchild'. As he went to leave he noticed the half finished game of chess. It took him just a moment to see that Haddo had moved a derisive pawn. Victor arrogantly moved his own Bishop out into play. He smiled conceitedly then suddenly realized the danger. He looked around as if someone might catch him cheating and returned the Bishop to its home square. His hand went to a knight but again he became aware that that would also be fraught with danger. He pondered the situation for a while then shook his head.

"Where the hell did you get a move like that from, Haddo?"

The old tiered Lecture theater was full. A wall of faces buzzing in anticipation. Leah was sitting with her classmates near the front. At the door a notice board read:

THE J. Z. MAUDLEYN CLASSICS LECTURE
'The Psychology of Hamlet', by Dr. Oliver Haddo.

Near the board, Symons and a couple of tutors were talking anxiously.

Alone, on the other side of the corridor, Victor was waiting nervously to see if Haddo would actually appear. Symons took out Crowley's old pocket watch and flicked it open to check the time. Several students were also checking their watches.

Leah turned to Jones. "He's always so punctual."

"Fuck him."

A gowned official came running up the corridor. "He's on his way."

Symons went up to the podium and announced. "This year's J. Z. Maudleyn Classics lecture will be given by Dr. Haddo who will be discussing the psychology of Hamlet."

There was a polite applause.

Haddo strode impressively up the corridor. Victor starred in disbelief, his mouth dropped open. For Haddo's head was shaved; shaved as clean as a hard boiled egg. He walked haughtily past Victor, ignoring him totally and strode into the theater and up on to the podium. There was a buzz and the odd giggle from the audience. He stood there in silence, his once meek demeanour suddenly fierce and imposing.

"Do what thou wilt shall be the whole of the law." He announced.

Symons looked up in surprise, what was Haddo doing quoting Crowley?

Haddo then turned to where Leah was sitting. "And fuck you too, Mr. Jones."

Leah looked at Jones. What the hell!!

There was a long pause then he began with a solemn statement

"Shakespeare was an occultist. Ghosts, fairies, fortune-tellers, witches, monsters from the id all inhabit his plays. Hamlet is not and never was a man of indecision; a man who couldn't make his mind up. No, quite the contrary, he is a man moved to action by a spiritual encounter with a Ghost. Academia's attempt to ignore this fact proves just one thing – that they are mere boils on the bard's asshole."

The students were warming to his script. This was not going to be any normal boring lecture on English literature.

Haddo continued. "For true enlightenment and understanding, we have to turn to England's greatest living poet – Aleister Crowley."

Jones whispered. "Living?" Others had noticed the mistake. There was general whispering. Haddo waited till there was silence and then he began.

"To pee, or not to pee: that is the question:"

Did they hear him right?

"Whether tis nobler in the mind to suffer the slings and arrows of outrageous stricture or take arms against a closed urethra and by abscission, end it? To fuck, to come: no more; and by a come to say we end the cockstand and the thousand natural lusts that flesh is heir to."

The officials were open mouthed. The students smiled in disbelief.

Furiously the Chaplain left the Theater through the door at the back.

Haddo continued. "Tis a consummation devoutly to be wished. To fuck to come. To come perchance to clap! Ay, there's the rub."

Haddo moved to the side of the lectern and as he spoke undid the top button of his flies.

"For from that come of fuck what clap may catch when we have shuffled off this mortal stand must give us pause."

Haddo unfastened the second button. The students stared in open-mouthed disbelief.

"There's the chordee that makes calamity of so wet dreams. For who would bear the jerks and drops of piss."

Haddo reached in to his flies. The girls in the front row looked down and frantically wrote notes too afraid to look. Suddenly a stream of yellow liquid splashed on to their notebooks.

In the Music room a quartet recital of a Mozart quintet was in progress. The Chaplain who had left Haddo's lecture appeared at the back of the hall and made his way down to the Dean. He lent down and whispered. The Dean's eyes opened in wide astonishment. He got up and strode out of the recital.

The high vaulted hall that served as the student canteen echoed with steamed cabbage and animated conversation. Those who had seen the incident, were narrating it to those who had not Leah walked along the dinner line with her tray, sticking to the low calorie items for her lunch but falling for the chocolate pudding at the end. She carried her lunch to where Jones was sitting with other students of her class. He pulled over to make a space for her.

"Did you get that?" said Jones. "England's greatest *living* poet – Aleister Crowley. Is he crazy?"

Ashby laughed. "I liked the haircut, though – gave him a certain gravitas."

"Who is Aleister Crowley?" asked Leah.

"Was," corrected Jones. "He died years ago."

"A 1920's occultist," said Goggles. "He scandalized the world practising an AZ of ritual perversions."

"He's one of the characters on the front of the Beatles' 'Sergeant Pepper' album," added Ashby, "in between an Indian Guru and Mae West."

"I don't know why they put a weirdo like that on it."

Sinclair frowned. "He wasn't a wierdo, he was just ahead of his time. He helped tear down the false, hypocritical, self righteous attitudes of the time."

"He was a pervert," insisted Ashby.

"The world was perverted and he just wanted freedom," defended Sinclair

"Come on. He tried every sin imaginable"

"Sure, his great saying, 'Do what thou wilt shall be the Law' was no different from the hippy 'Do your own thing, man'. To him the word 'sin' simply translated as 'restriction'.

"He has a point there, the church calls anything it doesn't want you to do a sin."

"Like sex," quipped Jones.

"So he just did anything that touched his fancy." continued Sinclair, "never just live within your own skin; he said, so one day he was a Scottish peer, next a Russian nobleman, then a Persian Prince…"

"And next God," added Jones.

"So? It's a lot smarter to believe you're God than to believe you're just one of his followers," answered Sinclair.

"He was an idiot," said Goggles.

"De mortuls nil nisi bonum," quoted Ashby. "Speak not evil of the dead."

"He was no idiot, he was here at Trinity!" said Sinclair.

"Lance Sieveking said that Aleister Crowley knew a lot of things but they were things he personally didn't have any interest in knowing."

"You know where he got 'Do what thou wilt' from?" quizzed Ashby.

"He invented it," Sinclair answered.

"No, no he didn't. 'Fay ce que voudras' comes from 'Gargantua and Pantagruel' by Rabelais. It was copied in the Eighteenth century as the motto of the Hell Fire Club and written up over their Abbey in Buckinghamshire. You can go and visit the caves where they performed their Masonic rituals mixed with sexual orgies. Crowley just translated it."

"You know during World War Two Ian Fleming proposed a disinformation plot where Crowley would help an MI5 agent supply Rudolf Hess with fake horoscopes. They could then pass along false information about an alleged pro-German circle in Britain. The government abandoned the plan when Hess flew to Scotland and was captured. Fleming then suggested using Crowley as an interrogator to determine the influence of astrology on other Nazi leaders, but his superiors rejected the plan."

"The Nazi's were big on occult stuff," added Jones. "They say it was never brought up in the Nuremburg trials in case they used it to put in a plea of insanity."

"Oh for a camera – what a front page that would have made," mussed Goggles. "Shall I write it up?"

"If you want background," enthused Sinclair, "There's one of Crowley's books in the Library. 'The Great Beast'"

"Hold on there," cautioned Ashby. "The University is going to clamp up on this big-time."

"They can't stop us printing what happened," complained Jones.

"If he's ill – having a breakdown – it would appear totally callous."

"What if we got an interview from him so it came out of his own mouth?" suggested Jones. "Leah could get one – being teacher's pet and all."

"Teacher's pet!" interjected Leah. "Are you joking?"

"Come on Ms R..R..Robinson don't t..t..tell me you haven't noticed the way he l..l..looks at you."

Unaware of Haddo's scandalous behaviour, a relieved Victor walked back into the laboratory to continue the experiment. He was still giggling to himself over Haddo's haircut when he found Mathers alone working at the computer.

"It's okay," said Victor, "I fixed the problem we can go ahead."

Mathers looked up. "Fraid the Prof's been called away. A committee meeting or something."

"Always some committee or other," complained Victor. "If computers get too powerful, we can organize them into a committee; that'll do them in."

Mathers smiled, "I was just checking the program for the fault."

"I cleared it but let me just run the scan again," said Victor protectively.

Mathers got up to let Victor at the computer.

"I don't know," worried Mathers, "the computer was showing something I've never seen before in the date – time file."

"Let's see." Victor put Crowley's book down on the desktop and sat at the keyboard, Mathers leaned over to help.

Victor looked up at Mathers. "Do you mind, I hate people looking over my shoulder while I'm working."

"Sorry, I'll go and have a cup of coffee." He looked at his watch. "God no, is that the time, I'm supposed to be at the Bursar's office." Mathers grabbed his coat.

Victor reassured, "I'm sure we'll be ready to go for it first thing tomorrow morning."

A shaft of winter sun fell on the pale statue of Lord Byron. The sculpture had once been intended for Westminster Abbey, but the poet's notoriety was such that the offer was refused and so now it stands in the heavy silence of the Christopher Wren Library. Leah loved books – the colors, the smell, the feel, she could even smell them as she came through the double doors. These were old books and the smell was pleasant but different to the wonderful aroma of a bookshop. Every time she entered a bookshop, and she could rarely pass one by, she took in a deep breath of the scent of new books. To her it spelt out excitement, lost hours in other worlds, interesting characters to meet and enchanting locations. There were few things in this world that Leah loved more than to discover a good book. She knew she had her father to thank for this but since his untimely death, her love of books had a sting of remembrance in the tail.

Surrounded by beloved books Leah sat working on her Dickens essay glancing every now and then at the pages of, 'The Dickensian Style' and hating herself every time she did. Why wasn't she confident enough to just write what she saw in his work not repeat parrot fashion someone else's analysis. Actually the reasons she knew full well – the academic establishment preferred to see a repetition of well-trod accepted ideas than deal with new ones. You get ten marks for repeating, and one for questioning or even nought if they didn't agree with you. She glanced once more at the book and read a passage:

> 'Dickens began his literary career as 'Boz' the author of descriptive sketches of London for the 'Evening Chronicle'. His skill in this apparently transitory form, so perfectly adapted to the columns of a newspaper, was sustained throughout his career in his novels...'

She threw down her pen in dismay. What nonsense – he wrote in a style that fitted newspaper columns. That's such rubbish. She looked around at the other students all painstakingly copying ideas from other people's books and realized she was being a trifle petty. Reading other peoples ideas was essential to forming your own and of course packed in to books there was information.

'See information from a new angle,' her father always said, 'and you will write an interesting article.'

But from what angle could you view today's events other than just pure sensationalism? Perhaps if she had more background information she could see it for something more than just a crude event. She got up and went over to the librarian's desk.

'Do you have a section on the occult?" she asked as she had no idea where to look for books on the subject.

"The occult?" queried the librarian.

"Yes, I'm after anything you've got on Aleister Crowley. I'm not sure of the pronunciation. Some people say Crowley as in crow and others as if it's cow with an 'r', Crowley."

"Crow I would suggest. Just at the end of religion in the 290s you'll locate books on that type of esoteric subject. If you don't find what you want I can search the computer."

Leah thanked her and headed for the Non Fiction section wondering at the use of the word esoteric. She wasn't sure what occult meant but esoteric meant obscure, mysterious, abstruse, impenetrable, cryptic or arcane. 'I must check the dictionary definition of occult,' she thought as she arrived at the History section, the 500's; then moved on past philosophies, 600's, till she reached religion.

She ran her finger over the Religious books, Buddhism, Hinduism, Mohammadism and on to books on Christianity. The titles amused, 'In search of God', 'Jesus the Man', 'True Revelations' and 'The Language of God'. She smiled as it reminded her of one of the probing questions her father loved to throw at her. 'What language did God write the Ten Commandments in?' Of course she answered Hebrew but then he pointed out Hebrew was not developed as a written language for another 1000 years. If there were an answer it would be Egyptian Hieroglyphics as that was the only written language Moses could have known.

She glanced on to a variety of versions of the Bible: ''The Holy Bible', 'The New International Bible', 'The New American Standard Bible', 'The King James Bible' 'The New King James Bible', 'The Geneva Bible', 'The Alabama State Bible'. So many, which was the actual word of God?' she mused.

Finally she reached the 720's, 'Atlantis Revisited', 'Secrets of the Great Pyramid', 'Celtic Giants' and 'The Alchemists'. Presumably this was the section she was looking for, though the subjects were not what she was expecting. She pulled one out, 'World Mysteries' and opened it randomly. 'Investigations of Bolivia's Fuente Magna and the Monolith of Pokotia.' The text continued, 'A large stone vessel, resembling a libation bowl, and now known as the Fuente Magna, was originally discovered in a rather casual fashion by a country peasant in the Ancient Mayan area of Lake Titicaca about 100 km from the city of La Paz, Bolivia.

In 2000 restoration work began on what has now become known as the 'Rosetta Stone of the Americas'. The investigation threw up several things of worthy note:

1. The Fuente Magna was made in keeping with *Mesopotamian* tradition.

2. It contains two texts, one in cuneiform and another in a Semitic language of possible Sinaitic extraction with cuneiform influences.

3. According to the symbols used, the Fuente Magna evidently shows itself to be from the transitional period between ideographical writing and cuneiform.

4. Chronologically, this places it to a date of 3500 B.C., the Sumerian period of Mesopotamia; present day Iraq.'

Leah was baffled, what was an Ancient Sumerian artefact doing in the hands of the Mayans in South America? She would have to return to this book in the future. She put it back and pulled down another, 'Hidden Art' and glanced through. She stopped at a page with a painting she remembered was in her school hall, 'Primavera', by Botticelli.

She began to read.

'The title, which was not Botticelli's, has led many an art historian astray. The subject is not 'Spring' but 'Love', and the creativity which is rooted in love. This can be gleaned from the placing of the Goddess Venus, the pagan and planetary deity of Love, at the centre with the blindfolded cupid above her.

'In Botticelli's esoteric terms the group on the left represent ordinary love and contemplative love, in the philosophical sense. While the group on the right represent creative Love in the artistic sense. The true meaning of these groups is hidden in occult imagery. Firstly the structure of the painting – 4 to the left 2 in the centre and 3 to the right not only is the quantity of people but also the proportions of the canvas. This is no accident. 4:2:3 is the same musical ratio, which in Renaissance times was called the '*double diapente*'. This proportion, expressing a doubling of 2/3 time, arose from the explorations of Alberti who influenced Gafurius, Botticelli and many of their contemporaries. The musical structure of the canvas is not surprising since Venus was the patron of both dance and music whilst the 3 Graces were frequently associated with Pythagoras' Music of the Spheres. In Renaissance imagery the 3 graces were named as Castitus, Voluptus and Pulchritudo. Castitus has her back to us looking towards Voluptus. The theme in this is that the innocent Castitus is being introduced to Love by Desire and Beauty. Botticelli allows her dress to fall off on the side of Desire, yet leaves her clothed on the side of beauty. The lyrical postures and facial expressions underline the human experience of love: Innocence, Voluptuousness and Beauty.

'Mercury is the fourth figure of this group. With his winged feet he is the messenger to the Gods, one who moves between the ethereal realms and the world itself. Mercury has the power to escape from the lure of the Graces. And he reaches up and away from the Graces to remind us that love should have a celestial rather than a worldly aim. The innocent Castitus is therefore looking at Mercury as she is about to receive Cupid's arrow and fall in love; a love which has to have a spiritual dimension.

'The group to the right exhibits none of this sense of dignified and spiritual calm. The Wind God Zephyrus reaches out for the nymph Chloris, as though making sexual advances. The third figure, dressed in floral robe, is the harbinger of Spring, Flora. The group is an exoteric symbol, the warm winds breathe upon the Earth and spring flowers are called into being. Zephyrus' warm breath turns the Nymph Chloris into the beautiful robed Flora. Zephyrus represents the human spirit of love, which has refreshed itself up in the spiritual world (where Mercury points) and has now descended back into matter. The whole is an 'open secret' to those with knowledge, all presided over by the Goddess Venus.'

Although Leah had seen the picture thousands of times it now became obvious that she had never looked at it. The blue man in the trees, the plant coming from the girl's mouth, which she had never even noticed and the Mercurial figure to the side. She became annoyed at herself for never querying these images. Maybe we go through life looking but not seeing, and not understanding. She turned the pages to another painting she recognized from school-days, Holbein's 'The Ambassadors'.

She read the accompanying text, which began with a description of a large skull in the foreground of the picture.

What skull? She looked back at the picture. There was something in front of the two characters.

She turned the book sideways and sure enough drawn in high perspective was a skull on the carpet before the characters.

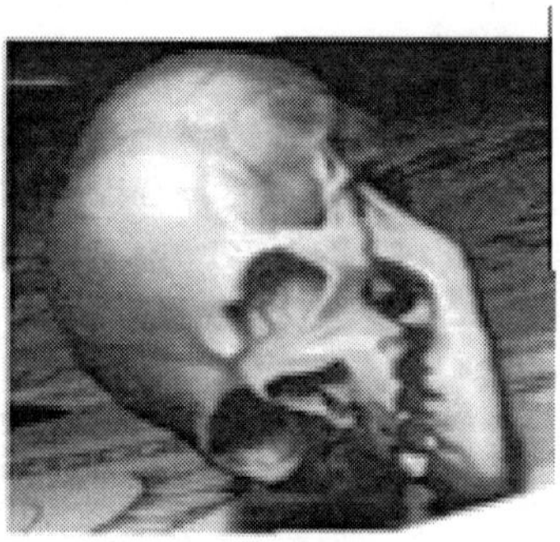

Un-missable? But she had missed it. This was a startling and sobering lesson to her for she had always considered herself an acute and accurate observer. If she was going to be a serious writer or a journalist she had to stop looking and start seeing. She suddenly remembered a story her father told her about a South American Indian tribe.

The tribe had a bizarre method of initiating Priests. A child who was destined to become a Priest was kept in a cave from birth. Every day the Elder Priests would bring him food and describe the world outside. 'There are blue skies and a burning sun. Colored birds fly through the air and at the end of the day the world goes pitch black.' At the age of nine the young priest was taken out of the cave and shown the world. It was for him the most magical moment. Everything was true. The sky was blue, there were white fluffy clouds and shining, like a white-hot ball, was the sun, which crossed slowly overhead and sank down to earth. These young priests saw the world with fresh eyes. With this insight the Priests understood the glories of the natural world and became important fighters against the destruction of the environment. For the first time in her life Leah understood why he told her the story, what her father had been trying to communicate to her. She returned the book to its place and decided there and then that she would take nothing in this world for granted. She would observe the world with fresh eyes.

It was then that she spotted a book, which had the word occult in the title, 'Occult World'. She pulled it from the shelf hoping it would give her a good overview of the subject. She opened it and flicked through the Chapter headings, 'Hermes', 'Alchemy' 'Pythagoras', 'Orion', 'Dr. John Dee', and, Madam Blavatsky'. She tried to read bits to get the gist but kept getting engrossed with the new type of information. 'I must come back to that,' she kept thinking as she forced herself to move on. Finally near the end she found a whole chapter on 'Aleister Crowley'. She settled down in a chair and glanced at her watch to see how much time she had before she met Mathers. She was amazed, 6.50. Where had the time gone? She closed the book grabbed her Dickensian notes from the desk and hurried through the lines of silent students to the exit.

Large Tudor windows had been cut into this fourteenth century oak room. At the head of a large polished boardroom table sat the Dean, flanked by a board of Academics, which included, Symons, Professor. Brent and the Chaplain. All were in full-length gowns with collars and sashes of their respective positions. The Dean played nervously with a large Masonic ring as the pendulum of a tall clock ticked off the seconds. The Dean checked his watch against the time on the clock and announced irritably, "He's late."

Suddenly a window flew open and the net curtain blew across the table. Everybody grabbed at their papers as Symons got up and shut the window. When the Academics turned back they found Haddo.

"Do what thou wilt."

He held up a black bible and continued, "shall be the whole of the law."

The Dean regained his composure. "Sit down please."

Haddo noticed Symons. "Master Symons! Have you capitulated to the forces of convention?"

"I'm sorry?"

"Are you? So am I. A man of sorrows for wasted time; so gentlemen, let's with haste commence."

The Dean folded his arms "Well, perhaps you could start by explaining you behaviour at the lecture."

"In ten years time that will be the only lecture those students will remember."

"That's hardly an explanation, Dr. Haddo," persisted the Dean.

"Haddo resides in the Abyss. You are now addressing the reincarnation of Ko Hsuen, Count Cagliostro and Eliphas Levi. You may refer to me as the Beast, Mega Therion."

"Delusional behaviour may impress the undergraduates but not here, Dr Haddo,"

Haddo's face warped angrily, "Idiot! I told you Haddo is in the Abyss,"

The board were shocked. Professor Brent attempted to warn Haddo. He pursed his lips and shook his head. Haddo looked at him quizzically as Professor Brent gave him a Masonic distress signal.

Haddo glared. "And you can save your Masonic signals for promotion boards, Professor Brent."

They all looked round to Professor Brent, who swiftly brought his hand down removing his glasses on the way and pretended to clean them.

The Dean frowned then turned back to Haddo with a forced smile. "I am, I must admit, a little unclear over your identity. I suggest that we suspend your classes till you have had time to visit a good Doctor.

Haddo laughed mockingly and held up his bible.

"I am in excellent health and as Satan's book says, in three days my resurrection shall be complete."

The Chaplain interjected. "I see no reason for you to blaspheme a book you clearly know nothing about."

"Nothing! Open it anywhere you like."

He slid the bible across the table in front of the Dean who complained, "We are not here to play games."

But the Chaplain pleaded. "No, please open it; a reading will do nothing but good."

The Dean reluctantly opened the book near the front. The Chaplain looked over his shoulder. Haddo thought for a moment.

"Genesis, chapter 6 verse 4 – 'in those days the sons of God came in to the daughters of men and they bore children to them.' Am I right?"

The other Academics leaned over to read it.

"Does it say 'sons of God' – plural?" queried Professor Brent.

"Yes it says sons, plural," said Haddo, "doesn't it?"

The Dean nodded dismissively. Haddo indicated for him to turn to another page. He did so. Haddo immediately declared. "Numbers 31, verse 7 – 'And they warred against the Midianites just as the Lord had commanded. They killed all the males and burnt all their cities. They brought all the captives and the booty to Moses. But Moses was angry, saying, 'Have you kept all the women alive? The same women who tempted the Israelites to transgress against the Lord? Therefore kill every male among the little ones, and kill every woman who has known a man intimately. But keep alive for yourself all the young girls who have not known a man intimately.' – am I right?"

They were all leaning over to try to read.

"You see the nature of the Devil you worship?"

"These are Old Testament interpretations," said the Chaplain as he took the Bible.

"Let us see the true words of our Lord in the Gospels."

He turned to the back of the bible, to the New Testament. Haddo thought for a moment then broke into a smile.

"Ah yes, the Lord's homosexual ritual in Gethsemane. Mark 14, verse 51. – 'Now a certain young man followed Jesus, having a linen cloth thrown around his naked body. And the men laid hold of him and he left the linen cloth and fled from them naked.'"

The Chaplain tried to turn to another page but the Dean had had enough, he grabbed the Bible and slammed it closed. "That's enough of the amateur magic."

"Amateur! You call me amateur! What about the expanding

gulf between your puny Academic endeavours and any real practical problem solving. And why? Because your only real goal is to seek academic promotion and for that all you need is to demonstrate an output. So not one of you would risk a failed attempt to solve an important but difficult problem. You just tailor your Academic research to suit your pathetically limited talent, and this becomes the end in itself.'

"This University," proclaimed the Dean "has stood on its Academic credentials for hundreds of years and will do so with our help for many more years to come."

"No it won't." Haddo got up to leave. "In just three days I shall return and you shall all be as ants beneath my feet."

"You will not succeed in threatening this Board, Dr. Haddo," fumed the Dean.

" Only your feeble God threatens. I act."

"Blasphemy!" accused the Chaplain.

"All great truths begin as blasphemies," answered Haddo. "I'm afraid I have no patience with the idiotic vanity of mediocrities. Good day, Gentlemen." He turned from the speechless board then suddenly rounded on Symons.

"Does my watch still keep good time, Symons?"

"I beg your pardon?"

"It's all right, I don't blame you. It was that thieving friend of yours, Alex."

Haddo slammed the door. There was a pause as the Dean sat down.

The Chaplain broke the silence with an attempt to retrieve the situation with a quote from Shakespeare; "The Devil can cite scripture for his own purpose."

"Quite," said the Dean and turned to Symons

"What the hell was that all about, Symons?"

"I've no idea. But I have only ever encountered one man who knew the Bible like that."

Of course Symons didn't know how Haddo had engineered the

pages to be turned to those specific quotes but he did understand the occult knowledge implied. God having more than one Son and the homosexual activities of the Lord had long been hinted at. A strange omission in Mark's Gospel led to this theory. Mark 10:46 reads:

> 'Then they came to Jericho. As he was leaving Jericho with his disciples...'

But what happened in Jericho? Did Jesus simply pass through and then leave without doing or saying anything? If the visit was so irrelevant to Jesus' mission, why is it even mentioned? The gap suggests a deleted portion of Mark's Gospel.

In 1958, a manuscript was discovered by Prof Morton Smith of Columbia University at a monastery at Mar Saba, east of Jerusalem, which revealed the missing passage. It was a letter from Bishop Clement of Alexandria, an early Christian father, to a colleague called Theodore. Theodore had asked for advice regarding the Caprocratians, a Gnostic Christian sect, who were using a "Secret Gospel of Mark."

In his answer Clement not only confirmed the existence and authority of "Secret Mark", but actually denounced Carprocratians for using black magic to steal a copy of it from the church library. He writes:

> "As for Mark then, during Peter's stay in Rome wrote an account of the Lord's doings, not, however, declaring all of them, nor yet hinting at the secret ones, but selecting what he thought most useful for increasing the faith of those who were instructed. But when Peter died a martyr, Mark came over to Alexandria, bringing both his own notes and those of Peter, from which he transferred to his former book the things suitable to whatever makes for progress towards knowledge. Thus he composed a more spiritual gospel for the use of those who were being perfected. Nevertheless,

he yet did not divulge the things not to be uttered, nor did he write down the hierophantic teaching of the Lord. He left his composition in the church in Alexandria, where it is most carefully guarded, being read only by those who are being initiated into the great mysteries."

'But since the foul demons are always devising destruction for the race of men, Carpocrates using deceitful arts, so enslaved a certain presbyter in the church that he got from a copy of the secret gospel, which he interpreted according to his blasphemous and carnal doctrine. To them, therefore, one must never give way or even concede that the secret gospel is by Mark but deny it on oath. For not all true things are to be said to all men..."

And he then congratulates Theodore:

"You did well in silencing the unspeakable teachings of the Carpocratians. For even if they should say something true, one who loves the truth should not, even so, agree with them, even if the things they keep saying about the divinely inspired Gospel of Mark do contain some true elements."

So those 'who love the truth' must lie through their teeth about the existence of deleted sections of Mark. But then St. Clement quotes from this "Secret Gospel of Mark" mentioning the missing section of what happened in Jericho.

'Then they came to Jericho, and the sister of the youth whom Jesus loved, and his mother and Salome were there, and Jesus did not receive them."

Who is this disciple who 'Jesus loved' and why did the church deem it important to cut such an innocent section? Clement not only reveals who this 'disciple Jesus loved' was – but also why it was cut.

He wrote 'To you, therefore I shall not hesitate to answer the questions you have asked. After the passage 'and they were in the road going up to Jerusalem' the secret gospel brings forth the following word for word.

"And they come into Bethany. And a certain woman whose brother had died was there. And she prostrated herself before Jesus and says to him, Son of David, have mercy on me. But the disciples rebuked her. And Jesus, being angered, went off with her unto the garden where the tomb was, and straightway a great cry was heard from the tomb. And going near, Jesus rolled away the stone from the door of the tomb. And straightway, going in where the youth was, he stretched forth his hand and raised him, seizing his hand. But the youth, looking upon him, loved him and began to beseech him that he might be with him. And going out of the tomb they came into the house of the youth, for he was rich. And after six days Jesus told him what to do and in the evening the youth came to him, wearing a linen cloth over his naked body. And he remained with him that night, for Jesus taught him the mystery of the Kingdom of God. And thence, arising, he returned to the other side of the Jordan."

After these words follows the text you know, 'And James and John come to him, and all that section. But naked man with naked man, and the other things about which you wrote, are not found."

Symons knew that the disciple Jesus loved was 'Lazarus', and the story of his resurrection that appears in John's Gospel was cut from Mark because it admitted that there was a cry from the tomb before Jesus rolls away the stone – making it less magical and more what Symons knew as a Masonic type death and resurrection ceremony. And then there followed what appeared a homosexual rite. Some Christian sects did, like Tantra Yoga, engage in sexual intercourse as part of a union with God. There are passages in the Pauline Epistles which admonishing certain unnamed sexual practices and there is a letter from a Roman physician describing in detail this practice. Symons looked around the scandalized Academics as they shook their heads and tutted incessantly.

Leah arrived outside the Bursar's office to meet Mathers. She checked her watch and sat on a bench to wait. She opened the Occult book at the chapter on Crowley and glanced through.

> Aleister Crowley was born on 12th October 1875 in Leamington, England to Edward Crowley a follower of John Nelson Darby, the founder of the Plymouth Brethren. The sect is characterized by a refusal to compromise on the literal translation of the Bible as the exact words of the Holy Ghost. Aleister Crowley was author of a brilliant book called Magick, which is a manual for those who wish to practise this difficult and dangerous art. Crowley was the head of two magical organizations and of several minor ones. The main one was the Ordo Templi Orientis or the OTO.

Below that was Crowley's circular insignia for the OTO.

She was about to read on when she stopped herself and studied the emblem with her new searching eyes. A seven pointed star with the number of the beast, 666. And what was the circular part in the middle?

She turned the book around then just as she turned it back she suddenly burst out laughing realizing the phallic nature of the image. Her enjoyment was not just of the image but of her successful interpretation. A couple of hours earlier she would have glanced at the image and let it pass – looked at it without seeing it. Now she was seeing with her father's critical eyes. It was the moment when she knew she was no longer a child.

Just then Haddo appeared from the boardroom with a satisfied smirk on his face and set off down the corridor. Leah grabbed her notebook and followed.

"Dr. Haddo! Dr. Haddo, I'd just like a comment for Granta."

"The new age has dawned," announced Haddo as he strode on. "The Aeon of Horus; do what thou wilt shall be the whole of the law."

Leah chased after him. "Did the board suspend you?"

"Bah! Cockless wonders."

"The Board?"

Haddo suddenly stopped and turned, Leah almost bumped into him. He seemed to register her for the first time.

"Yes, the board," he said looking her up and down and adding, "Embarrassed – they hide in darkened bedrooms to perform the numinous rite of impregnation."

"You're not advocating sex in public are you?"

"My dear Ms *Robinson*, you forget your Midsummer Nights Dream. Puck – Robin Goodfellow and the ancient spring fertility rite of dancing round the phallic maypole was followed by a sexual romp. Offspring of that caper were named Roberts-son or Robin-son." He smiled as if recalling the event. "So, *Ms Robinson,* many years ago some great ancestor of yours was involved in a very public sexual rite."

The idea made her smile.

"Stab your demoniac smile to my brain, soak me in cognac, kisses and cocaine."

He laughed and went to move off. Leah recovered enough to put a further question.

"What about in the lecture you quoted Aleister Crowley and called him England's greatest living poet?"

"Absolutely."

"He's dead, isn't he?"

He fixed her with his eyes knowingly. "And what do you know about death, Ms Robinson?"

Was he taunting her? A cruel question that brought her father to mind, and made her falter before she stuttered out a foolish remark.

"It is difficult to write poetry from the grave."

"Is it?" His unblinking eyes made her feel more and more uncomfortable. "That is a very trivial remark from someone who has been close to the mystery of a man's death. Isn't it?"

"I didn't mean... I was told he died."

Haddo leaned forward and whispered, "He lives for you."

She fought the tears that were welling up.

Haddo smiled at her discomfort. "Death is but one short sleep to eternity."

She diverted. "Do you mean the afterlife?"

"Afterlife! Do you not believe in the resurrection of Jesus the Nazarean?"

"Of Nazareth?" she corrected as she recovered her composure.

"No such place existed. He was a Nazarean. A Nazarean is a mystic who does not cut his hair. Samson was a Nazarean." He took her hair in his plump fingers. "And talking about hair you have the wonderful red hair of the Magdalene. Perhaps your chance of immortality will come sooner rather than later."

"What do you mean?"

"You can read of Miriam – of Aramathea – of Joshua – I wrote it all in one of my previous lives as Eliphas Levi."

She wrote the name 'Eliphas Levi'.

Haddo pointed to the name. "Check the year of his death and the year of my birth."

At that moment Mathers came out of the Bursar's office.

Haddo spotted him with interest. "Ah! There's the man you should interview – the man with the Lazarus touch. Wonderful machine Dr. Mathers; a great achievement."

Mathers was confused, "Have we met?"

"Yes we have on the Astral plane. Born in Pasadena in 1947, schooled at Westcliff High, first girlfriend Susan – no?" He turned to Leah. "You two should get on well together. His mother was a redhead too." Then back to Mathers. "Ah, but of course you were orphaned – you never knew your magnificent mother."

He blew at Leah's neck, turned and walked off.

"Who's that?" asked Mathers.

"Dr. Haddo, my classics tutor. Is your mother redheaded?"

"I don't know I *was* adopted. Have you been talking about – researching me?"

"Me? No, it's nothing I said."

She showed him the book at the Chapter on Crowley.

"It's something to do with him."

Mathers read, "Aleister Crowley? He's dead."

"You think so?"

"I know so. He died in 1947."

"Not according to Dr. Haddo."

The pendulum of an antique clock swung on the wall above the desk where Symons shuffled through the pages of Crowley's 'Book of the Law'. Other Crowley books were stacked on the side. The wood panelled walls of the room were covered with classical paintings, many religious. Pride of place over the mantelpiece was 'Tobias and the Angel' with Tobias carrying the fish on a piece of string and the angel with the translucent dog. From a lifetime of esoteric study Symons could comprehend the imagery. The only sound was the ticking clock and the scratching of his pen as he underlined a few words in Crowley's book and scribbled a note on a pad. He raised his arms behind his head and stretched upwards in the chair to alleviate the soreness of his lower back, which had ossified over the many years he had spent hunched over his studies. He lowered his hands and pulled out Crowley's pocket watch and checked the time against the wall clock. In the dark behind him, by the door, someone was sitting, silently watching him. The pendulum ticked off the seconds as Symons slowly became aware of the presence and without turning he spoke.

"I didn't hear you."

The person in the shadows did not answer. Symons cleared his throat and continued unconvincingly, "Listen to this." He opened Crowley's book and read. "The universe is full of obscure and subtle manifestations of energy. We are constantly advancing in our knowledge and control of them."

A strange mechanical voice came from the shadows. It was squeaky and unreal. *"Why are you reading his books?"*

Symons avoided the question.

"I'd just never noticed it before. And here, 'All energy implies vibration.' Interesting isn't it; just like modern theories of physics?"

There was a long silence with just the faint tapping of keys.

Then the voice from the shadows announced.

"He's back isn't he? I know, I can feel it."

Symons looked at the watch then reluctantly back up to the shadows and gave the smallest of nods.

Victor pulled his overcoat tight as he trudged home through the winter gloom. He had slumped from excited anticipation to a dreadful depression. His program had failed miserably. Haddo had lost his cool and shaved his head. So? He crossed the railway bridge where the misty moon rose over the distant spires. On happier occasions he might have enjoyed its glow but now in this depressed mood he thought only of annihilation. The side of the moon he saw the one that always faces the earth is covered with craters caused by meteorites, every one of which must have near-missed the earth to hit our side of the moon. How many more actually hit the earth? Biologists were just beginning to accept that a meteorite hit in the Gulf of Mexico caused the extinction of the dinosaurs. What other events were they responsible for?

His spiritual guide, Aleister Crowley, had set Victor on this line of research when he wrote, 'As for the future of humanity, the certainty of final extermination when the planet becomes uninhabitable makes all human endeavour a colossal fatuity.' Final Extermination! What had Crowley meant? The incredibly accurate Mayan calendar showed five major catastrophes in the past and predicted the final extermination in 2012. What were the five past catastrophes? The flood was one, which could have been a meteorite hit in the Mediterranean. Perhaps another was the hundred years of catastrophic weather that ended the advanced civilization of the Egyptian pyramid builders. And meteorites are not the only physical catastrophes that endanger mankind. The Thera volcano off Egypt led to the biblical plagues of Egypt and through Moses gave rise to a new God, Jehovah. The God of Abraham was of course the Mesopotamian, El, as witnessed by the names Israel, Michael, Samuel, Emmanuel. Victor's knowledge made him feel isolated and strangely resentful that the bustling commuters were totally unaware of all this. '*They, or them*' as he called them, are so blind.

Victor arrived at his apartment block and went up the stairs. On the second landing he glanced out of the window at the ant like people wrapped in their winter coats scurrying in the street below.

This rotten little race of men measures the world by its own standards. And blind too, he thought, refusing to contemplate the latest catastrophe theory, 'Global Warming'. Only the scientists took it seriously. '*They*' refused to accept the dangers posed. Give '*them*' ten years of vomiting an orgy of pollution and by then the extra energy in the environment will be making life impossible. Only when destructive tornadoes, floods, devastating hurricanes and rising sea levels arrive will '*they*' listen.

He lumbered to the door of his apartment but as he took out his keys he realized something was wrong. Warily he pushed the door and it swung gently open. The haunting sound of Debussy's nocturne wafted around the candlelit room. Victor tried the light switch but nothing happened. On the table an incense burner was puffing out smoke. He stepped forward and was shocked to see an upturned pentagram had been daubed in red paint above the fireplace. On the floor a pile of his erotic magazines, were torn and screwed up. Confused he went over to the magazines, bent down and unfolded one of the pictures. The door behind him closed.

"Welcome the conquering hero."

Victor spun round.

"Haddo! What the...how did you get in?"

"Do you think the lock has been made that can stop the Beast?"

"One of your tricks."

"Come Victor, ye of little faith, hiding away; wanking over a few paltry pictures. Do you not take my laws seriously?"

He pointed down at the pile of screwed up magazines. Victor hid his embarrassment by not looking.

"Your laws?"

Haddo proclaimed solemnly, "Do what thou wilt. Love is the law, love under will."

"Haddo, who do you think you are?"

"Who do *you* think I am, Victor?"

"You're Oliver Haddo!" Victor spelt it, spitting out each letter, "H, A, D, D, O, – Haddo."

Haddo dropped his head in mock shame. "Non sum quailis eram."

Victor did not follow the Latin, 'I am not what I was'.

He looked sadly at Haddo's bowed head. "You're not well."

The incense smoke drifted as Haddo slowly raised his arms in crucified form, holding the pose dramatically. Finally he lifted his head and looked at Victor across the candlelight.

"Oh Victor. Will you deny me thrice before the cock grows?"

Then slowly Haddo opened his clenched fists exposing deep, bloody holes in the palms. Stigmata!

"My G..God, w..what have you d..done?"

Haddo brought his hands together in mocking prayer.

"Dear Victor, don't stutter so. You must not worry, I come to praise Victor, not to bury him." Haddo blew on his praying hands and opened them in one movement. The stigmata were gone.

"Your stupid tricks, you had me worried."

In truth Victor was impressed by the vividness of Haddo's performance. He could see nothing, not one stitch, of the man he knew in this character before him. This was a skill he had often pondered on and marvelled at, the gift of the impersonator. Victor suspected that, deep down in his subconscious, Haddo possessed this ability and was now drawing upon it to create this impressive Crowley character.

Mathers studied the menu while Leah glanced through a chapter in the Occult book about Eliphas Levi. What caught Leah's attention was that Aleister Crowley was born the same year Eliphas Levi died and later claimed to be his reincarnation. Was Haddo claiming to have been born at Crowley's death? No that would make him too young. She read on, broadening her understanding of the Occult world.

Eliphas Levi was the pseudonym of Alphonse Louis Constant, who was born in Paris 1810 and was the only son of a shoemaker. His father did not have the funds to privately educate him so he sent Constant to St. Sulpice there to be educated as a priest. St. Sulpice was a hotbed of Johnists as can be seen by the large statue of John the Baptist to one side. Johnists were prevalent in the South of France where John was considered more important than Jesus. Occultists like Leonardo painted several pictures of John - with the upraised finger signifying Da Vinci considered he was the one. In fact in Da Vinci's 'Last Supper' a disciple is thrusting the one finger into Jesus' face.

The confusion about his 'Virgin of the Rocks' where no one was sure which child was Jesus and which was John the Baptist is also evidence of this. While Constant was at St. Sulpice he became intrigued by a lesson from his headmaster, who explained his belief that animal magnetism was a vital energy of the human body controlled by the 'Devil'. This sparked his curiosity and surrepti-

Levi's Sabbatic Goat
The hermaphrodite with the pentagram and phallic caduces bringing luciferous light to darkness while giving the sign of excommunication.

tiously he began to study all that he could find out about magic and the occult; producing his infamous conglomeratous sketch of the Sabbatic Goat.

He continued to pursue his ecclesiastical career and was ordained as a priest.

But later he was thrown out of the church and excommunicated for his left-wing political views and refusal to observe his vows of chastity.

When writing, Constant took on the pen name 'Magus Eliphas Levi', which he arrived at by translating his first and second names to Hebrew. In 1861 Levi published his first and perhaps most important book – *'The Dogma and Ritual of High Magic'*. His outrageous writings led to him serving three jail sentences. The introduction to *'The Dogma'* began, 'behind the veil of all the hieratic and mystical allegories of ancient doctrines, behind the darkness and strange ordeals of all initiations, under the seal of all sacred writings, in the ruins of Nineveh or Thebes, on the crumbling stones of old temples and on the blackened visage of the Assyrian or Egyptian sphinx, in the monstrous paintings which interpret to the faithful of India the inspired pages of the Vedas, in the cryptic emblems of our old books on alchemy, in the ceremonies practised at reception by all secret societies, there are found indications of a common doctrine.'

'A common doctrine behind everything from ancient Egypt to modern Masonry?' wondered Leah

"What do you think?" interrupted Mathers who had been waiting patiently.

"He died the year Crowley was born 1875." Leah confirmed, "It's all here just as Haddo said." She read aloud to him. "Eliphas Levi wrote, 'Elders from the line of David would impregnate a young girl to preserve the blood-line. A story from the Jewish Toledot tells of Miriam, a hairdresser of Bethlehem affianced to a young man named Jochanan, who was seduced by a libertine, Joseph Panther, and gave birth to a son whom she named Johosuah or Jeschu'."

"I meant..." Mathers went to speak but she cut him off.

"Wait there's more; according to the Talmudic authors Jeschu was taken during his boyhood to Egypt, where he was initiated into the secret doctrines of the priests, and on his return to Israel gave himself up to the practice of magic. He was driven out of Jerusalem and took refuge for a time in Galilee where..."

Mathers held up the menu. "I meant the meal."

"What? Oh, God, sorry. You must think I'm.."

"No, not at all, I like to see someone who enjoys their work."

"This could make a sensational article – 'Resurrected Lecturer reveals Hidden Truth about.."

"About visiting Lecturer," added Mathers.

"What hidden truths do you have?"

"Born in Pasadena; schooled at Westcliff High; Currently researching at Cal Tech; first girlfriend, Susan. Mother a redhead, maybe."

"He really shook you, didn't he?"

"What do you think? Some random professor announces that he knows who my birth mother is."

"He must have just read it somewhere."

"Where? I don't even know who she is. And Susan was my first girlfriend – when I was nine."

"It's all very strange," mused Leah. "You don't know who your parents were?"

"No."

"That must be very weird, like where did you get your skills in maths?"

My adoptive father was a mathematician."

"Ah, nurture rather than nature."

"Well who knows what my blood father was?" mused Mathers.

"Or mother," added Leah.

"Or mother," agreed Mathers. "And you; and journalism?"

"My father was a journalist."

"Was?"

'He died."

"I'm sorry." He realized Leah was hurt by the memory and changed the subject. "Are you ready to order?"

Leah looked quickly at the menu as the waiter brought the wine and poured a little for Mathers. He swilled it round the glass and smelt the bouquet. He smiled with satisfaction and nodded to the waiter to pour.

"I think I'll have the lamb," said Leah.

"Then I'll have.... What's this, black pudding?" asked Mathers.

"It's a blood sausage, I'm not sure you'd like it," said Leah.

"Me, I'll try anything once. I'll have the sautéed kidneys with black pudding or should I give it the definite article – 'the' black pudding as I'm with an expert on English."

Leah smiled as the waiter went off to the kitchen.

"It's true and I'm not sure why we always use the definite article when ordering," said Leah. "Mind you I've often thought it would be better to use the possessive pronoun – 'your' lamb."

"That's an interesting one," smiled Mathers. "I order 'your' lamb then it arrives at the table and at what point does it become 'my' lamb?"

"When you've eaten it," suggested Leah.

"But if the chef comes and asks you how was your meal? Do you answer 'my' lamb was great or 'your' lamb was great?"

Leah thought for a moment then smiled. "Maybe we should stick to the definite article, 'the' lamb."

"I'll drink to that," said Mathers as he raised the glass. "Cheers."

They clinked glasses and drank. Mathers glanced at the label on the wine.

"Bulls Blood. It's pretty good. Hungarian wine is a rarity in California. Do you like it?"

Leah was about to answer when suddenly she realized.

"Wait a minute, California, you're from Cal Tech. I read that a famous propulsion chemist from Cal. Tech – was head of Crowley's organization in America."

"Yes, Jack Parsons – and?"

"They're both Crowley fans. Maybe Haddo knows him and got the information from him."

"He'd need a medium, Parsons is dead – blew himself up in his lab years ago."

"How did Haddo do it then?"

Mathers leaned forward and spoke mysteriously.

"A magical meeting on the astral plane, maybe."

"Come on, scientists don't believe in magic. You believe in cause and effect."

"Cause and effect – me?"

"Don't you?"

"You know the uncertainty principle in quantum physics?"

"What about it?"

"You understand the implications are in my equations."

"Chaos?"

"And chaos is?"

'Is what?"

"The inability to link cause and effect," said Mathers.

"The unexpected."

"Exactly." Mathers raised his glass in a toast. "To the unexpected, long may it surprise us?"

She raised her glass and looked in his eyes as they clinked glasses.

"To the unexpected."

"And I note your use of the definite article, again there."

Haddo circled the table towards Victor. He picked up one of the pictures from the floor and pushed the lewd image of a naked girl opening her shaved vagina at Victor.

"Poor Victor I can't bear to see you suppress your natural urges. The power of your sexual magic."

He moved the picture over to the flame of the candle.

"See the flame burn through her."

The heat slowly blackened then burnt through her naked body, the flickering up-light gave Haddo a demonic look.

"Burns through her like your red-hot passion calls forth the whore of Babylon."

The pile of torn papers moved. Victor looked round to see a painted face come out from the shadows. Deep red lipstick, dark eye shadow, voluptuous curves. She came up through the colored pictures. Victor's mouth opened. Haddo was behind him, whispering in his ear.

"The mother of abomination. For she hath yielded up herself to everything that liveth to suck dry its mystery."

"How did you..?" stuttered Victor

She moved close to him. Haddo's hands reached round Victor to undo her blouse. Victor's eyes watched in fascination.

"Touch her Victor. Caress her."

Tentatively Victor stretched out a hand towards her breast. At the same time she reached down and unzipped Victor.

"Come oh serpent of passion," whispered Haddo, "Grasp the moment for thyself."

The candles threw a grotesque flickering shadow play on the wall as the girl slipped her hand into Victor's trousers. Haddo unzipped her skirt and it slipped to the ground. She pulled out Victor's penis.

Haddo toned on. "O great whore of Babylon let us gaze upon the cavern where lies Choronzon."

The girl leaned back into the sofa. Haddo whispered into Victor's ear as he rubbed Victor's penis. "In manu Regis."

She stroked open the lips of her vagina revealing the tip of her clitoris

"Look at her Victor. Watch her fingers rub open the chasm of creation."

Victor was panting. Haddo had his arm around his chest as he rubbed with the other. The girl masturbated in unison. The crude shadow play had their bodies entangled in rhythmic action.

"Call her Victor. Name her."

"Jesus...God..."

Haddo held him tight and pulled him hard. Victor gasped as he reached orgasm. His body thrashed in Haddo's arms.

"Kundalini..the serpent strikes!" Victor jerked violently, uncontrollably.

Haddo smiled as Victor became limp in his arms.

"Suck him, whore" demanded Haddo fiercely.

The girl moved forward and knelt at Victor's feet and took his penis in her mouth and sucked it rhythmically. Victor slowly began to revive and started to pant again.

Haddo whispered. "Who rewards you Victor?"

"Ooooaaaahhh." Victor groaned.

"What's my name?"

Victor was coming again. He groaned. Haddo held him tight and demanded sternly.

"What's my name? What's my name!"

Panting, Victor replied rhythmically as he climaxed "Crowley...Crowley..Crowley..Aaahhh."

Triumphantly Haddo smiled then let him sink to the floor.

"On him, whore. Take him across the abyss."

She slid down onto the wasted Victor and straddled him. Haddo pulled out a phial from his pocket and snapped the head off. He loaded a syringe with the yellow liquid.

"Now the final journey."

He dropped slowly down onto Victor and injected the instant pleasure straight through the eye into the optic nerve. The red pentagram flickered in the candlelight.

Willows bent their branches into the moonlit water. Leah and Mathers leant on the Bridge of Sighs together. They gazed at the same full moon that depressed Victor but now spirited Mathers and Leah into enchantment.

"It's beautiful," he whispered.

"I don't understand," said Leah.

"What?" He raised her hand and kissed it.

"Nothing.. everything… am I drunk or something?"

"You only had two glasses of wine."

Leah frowned. "I know, it's all – like being spellbound."

The world had stopped suddenly still. They were alone in the night and the silence of things. They belonged to eternity in some indefinable way and that infinite silence blossomed inscrutably into embrace.

"Did you see 'Spellbound', the Hitchcock film?" asked Mathers.

"Yes. Ingrid Bergman and Gregory Peck."

"They try to explain their sudden attraction but can't, it just happened."

"It certainly did." She put her arms round him and kissed him.

"So now," whispered Mathers into her ear. "I'm supposed to dread dark lines on white and go mad."

"And see Salvador Dali type dreams," added Leah

"Actually I have been having some strange dreams lately."

"Are you sure this isn't one of them?"

"Please God, don't let me wake up in that dreary hotel room."

He kissed her long and his hand stroked her cheek and brushed through her hair.

"No, I think you're real."

"This has been the strangest day," mused Leah, "With scandals, occult magicians, magic spells..."

"I know the words of a well-known spell that enchants and enthrals," smiled Mathers.

"A spell?"

"Yes the most powerful spell known to man."

"The most powerful? What is it?" asked Leah.

"I ... love... you."

With those three words Leah's heart started racing, a blush spread up her throat, her endorphins kicked in and...

"Wow!" she smiled, "That one really works."

He pulled her towards him and they kissed again.

That night, under the same moon, in two different apartments various bodies tangled together.

CHAPTER 3

DAY THREE

Thursday 7th January

The Earth spun eastwards causing the Sun to reappear over the turrets of the Gothic University buildings. To the inhabitants of this area of the planet the red globe seemed to rise up towards a troubled sky.

The internal clock that drives the daily activities of these inhabitants and all living things, from wild flowers to whales, is tied to one turn of the planet on its axis. The earth's rotation impresses a 24-hour period on the genes of all healthy humans and disruption of these circadian rhythms affects not only sleep patterns but also precipitates mania in people with manic-depressive illness. Circadian rhythms also cause heart attacks to occur more frequently in the morning while asthma attacks occur more often at night.

Night's sleepiness is tied to an increase in melatonin, a hormone secreted by the pineal gland, an organ in the head, which is often referred to as the third eye.

The human clock consists of a cluster of nerve cells, the suprachiasmatic nucleus, barely a hundredth of an inch in size, located deep in the brain and connected to the optic nerves.

Haddo had demanded of his suprachiasmatic nuclei to wake him at six o'clock as he had a busy day ahead and his *'time allowed'* was limited.

So at exactly six o'clock and eleven minutes Haddo's eyes

opened wide. His biological clock was not at fault. It was working perfectly but it worked as with all humans on a cycle, which was not exactly 24 hours but 24 hours and 11 minutes. What could explain this strange discrepancy? Perhaps the speed of the planet's rotation had changed. Caused by what? A meteorite hit? A reversal of the planet's polarity? Perhaps even a relocation of the earth's axis like the one that moved the North Pole from Hudson's Bay to its present location?

Whatever the problems with man's circadian rhythms Haddo would leave nothing else to biological chance. He went to the bathroom to spiritually cleanse and purify himself. He washed in water, fanned himself with his winnowing fan, took a sip of kaolin and morphine, kaolin being clay and ran his hand through a candle flame. Once baptized in all the four elements, three more than Christians, he opened the wardrobe and was immediately disappointed by the choice of suits. Grey, dark grey or black. 'Suits for a sober lawyer to impress a gullible client,' he thought as he donned the grey and checked the mirror. 'I'll have to find time to do something about this.'

At eight thirty exactly the post boy opened the imposing oak door of the Dean's office, strolled nonchalantly across the secretary's outer office and tossed the letters onto her desk. He noticed a parker fountain pen, picked it up, slipped it into his back pocket and left. The letters lay on the desk tied together with string.

At nine o'clock exactly a cup of hot dark liquid was placed on the bedside table. Complex chemical molecules leapt from the cup into the air and dispersed. Some were caught on an air stream that was inhaled into Mathers' olfactory organ. Inside, a small area covered in thick, mustard-colored mucus trapped them and they sunk down till they reached the sensitive hair-like tops of microscopic nerve endings. These cells sent signals along the olfactory nerve to the smell centre in his brain. They interpreted the stimulus as… coffee!

Mathers opened his eyes. Leah smiled down at him, fully dressed.

"Hi, there's coffee there" she whispered.

"Hi," he murmured.

"Still jet lagged?"

"No. As Albert Einstein once said, 'Gravitation can not be held responsible for people falling in love.'"

"Did he say that?"

"Yep, he was quit a funny guy. Why are we whispering?"

"Rose might hear us. She doesn't know you're here."

"And Rose is?"

"A bit straight."

"So," said Mathers with a wry smile.

"Students and professors..."

"She might not be alone there."

"Do what thou wilt shall be the whole of the law," smiled Leah.

"What?"

"That's what Crowley said."

"Ah yes, the late magician," remembered Mathers.

"Not so late according to Haddo."

"Talking of late what time is it?" said Mathers rubbing his eyes lazily.

"Nine o'clock."

Mathers leapt out of bed. "Nine! I'm going to be late."

Leah laughed.

Mathers stopped and looked at her. "What's so funny?"

"You don't believe in time."

At nine thirty the Dean's secretary entered the office and hung up her coat. She picked up the letters and untied the string and sorted out the Dean's personal mail. Glancing through, she went into the Dean's private office. She was about to place them on the Dean's desk when suddenly she reeled back in horror. She dropped the letters on the floor and staggered away in sheer terror.

Although it was not powered-up the quartz crystal at the heart of the Z93 still knew that the time was exactly 10 o'clock at zero degrees longitude on the Greenwich Meridian. In the adjoining hangar, bright in the glass room, Mathers plugged the umbilical chord from the Z93 into the back of the interactive suit, which was on Professor Brent. The Professor had receptive pads stuck to his forehead with cables that would connect to the helmet's computer once it was in place. Mathers screwed in the elbow joint which had a small brown bloodstain. Professor Brent looked a little apprehensive.

"What happened there?"

. "I fell," said Mathers rubbing his arm. "It's sometimes hard to keep your balance in Cyberia."

Brent looked confused. "Siberia, Russia?"

"No – no, the environment on the other side of the computer screen."

"Ah, cyberia as in cybernetics, of course."

Mathers looked up and saw Victor entering the control room. He was obviously late but Mathers was relieved to see him.

"Okay, I'll put on the helmet now, it will be dark till Victor fires up the computer."

"But I'll be able to hear you?" asked Brent.

"Yes, once I get up to the intercom in the control room."

"And presumably I just let my thoughts and feelings develop naturally?"

"Yes, just react normally and try and relax," said Mathers as he lifted up the bulbous helmet and placed it over Professor Brent's head. He screwed it into place then left and closed the glass room door behind him. He looked at the robotic black suit standing in the brightness, motionless, alone.

Symons came down the corridor and turned into the Dean's outer office where a crowd had gathered at the inner door, looking aghast. The secretary, still in shock, appealed to him.

"Oh Dr. Symons. This is how I found it."

Symons pushed through the crowd and looked in to the Dean's office. There on the Dean's desk, slap bang in the middle, was Crowley's infamous calling card. A huge turd. It was sitting in brown liquid and steamed its odour into the room. Symons held his nose and shook his head. He could not fail to recognize it's significance. Paul's Epistle to the Romans immediately came to mind. 'Vengeance is Mine saith the…' but he would not flatter Haddo by completing it.

Mathers sat down at the controls and turned to Victor.

"The Professor seems okay. I think he'll make a good subject."

"Ya know what Werner von Braun said," slurred Victor. "Man is the best computer to put aboard a spacecraft and the only one that can be mass produced by unskilled labour."

Mathers smiled but eyed Victor suspiciously as he sniffed and scratched his arm. Turning back to the controls Mathers switched on the electromagnets and stood up to see out of the observation window. In the glass room the suit floated gently upwards.

"Magnets are working great, Victor."

"We have lift off," said Victor with an odd grimace.

Mathers moved to the intercom, put on the headset and spoke. "Okay Professor, Victor will switch on the co-ordinates."

"Ready when you are," came the voice back.

Mathers waited for Victor, nothing happened. He turned to find Victor unfolding the leaflet for the Elcusion Ceremony. Mathers covered the microphone with his hand.

"What's this?"

"You wanna see him?"

Professor Brent's voice came over the intercom again.

"What's going on? It's pitch black you know."

"Slight technical hitch."

Mathers took off the headset. Victor put his arm round him.

"We did it together, you, me and the Z93."

"What's the matter with you?" asked Mathers.

Victor pointed to the computer. "We're just so very, very excited."

Mathers leaned across Victor and typed in the co-ordinates himself. The grid of blue laser-beams surrounded the suit. The grid also appeared on the monitor but at that moment Mathers could not stop his mind slipping away to what had been a magical night.

At the same time, almost by telepathy the same thoughts passed into Leah's mind as she cycled towards the University. What had happened? How had they ended in each other's arms? Could she ever contemplate living in California? What *was* she thinking? It's only been one night. But she loved the way he kissed, the way his hands stroked her face was like something from the movies. And sex was different. He seemed to know exactly how to touch her to move her into timelessness. The first climax was so early, the second and third brought her to such a pitch, that she was sure she ejaculated. 'Is it possible for a woman to secrete such an amount of vaginal juices that she ejaculates?' Just the thought began to excite her and she took a deep breath and tried hard to concentrate on the journey.

Mathers remembered the saying, 'Love is the triumph of imagination over intelligence' and refocused back on to the experiment. He switched in the program and on the monitor a 3d image of an office appeared with a cityscape stretching out through the window

"Welcome to Cyberia, professor. You're on the 20th floor of the Yamamoto Corporation building."

Professor Brent's voice came through the intercom. "My goodness."

The image panned as the suit looked around. Professor Brent moved clumsily at first, bumping into the furniture, causing the metal legs of the suit to jerk and hiss as the hydraulics simulated the impact. Mathers watched on the monitor.

"I'm going to activate the squids now." Mathers pressed a switch then turned back to the intercom. "Okay Professor, look in the mirror behind you."

Professor Brent turned and saw himself in the mirror. "But I'm not in the suit."

"No, because you're not really there, the Z93 is re-generating your thoughts. Now look around." Mathers watched on his screen as the image panned to find an oriental woman, smartly dressed, sitting at a desk. Mathers checked the LEDS showing incoming and outgoing information; they were jagging high. He turned to Victor. "So far so good. Now let's see if your computer can take itself seriously."

"Do what thou wilt," replied Victor.

Mathers spoke into the microphone, "Professor, introduce yourself."

The image moved towards the woman who rose and smiled.

"Hello. I'm Professor Brent."

The computer rapidly processed the information and generated a response

"Hello Professor. My name is Kieko," replied the apparition.

Mathers thumped the table with his fist. Victor jumped.

"Pretty damn good."

Victor was amused by Mathers' enthusiasm.

Mathers spoke into the microphone. "There's lots of information coming back from you. How are you feeling?"

Victor interjected. "How was it for you?"

Professor Brent missed the joke. "Perfectly natural."

Kieko responded. "I am pleased. Would you like to come this way?"

Professor Brent was confused. "What do I do?"

"Go with her," reassured Mathers.

"Does she do blow jobs?" added Victor

In Cyberia: Professor Brent followed Kieko to a door. She opened it and moved out of the way. The Chaplain wearing his Masonic costume gave the sign of the second principle. Professor Brent became disorientated and confused.

In the Lab. what Mathers saw on the monitor was just the door opening to reveal a black space.

"Damn. There's supposed to be a corridor there."

Victor frowned. "The abyss."

"A corridor leading to a staircase. Why isn't the 93 generating it?" asked Mathers.

Suddenly Professor Brent's voice was heard. "I do so swear."

Mathers turned round. "What's that?"

Cyberia: Brent watches as the Chaplain moves aside to reveal the Masonic Temple with all its detailed carvings. Where did it come from? Professor Brent's brain, Haddo's experience, Victor's program?

"Set a watch before thy lips," the Chaplain announces, "then enter and kneel before the Eminent Preceptor."

The Lab: Mathers watched the monitor as the image moved through the door into the blackness.

"Mathers?" Professor Brent's voice asked nervously.

"Don't go in! There's no information for that space."

Professor Brent whispered. "Mathers, what's going on?"

Cyberia: The Masonic Temple is dark, lit only by candles. Professor Brent's face is bathed in sweat; his eyes reflect the control lights inside the helmet. His pupils are hugely enlarged. The reflections in them become reality. A hooded figure sits away in the Eminent Preceptor's chair.

Lab: Mathers and Victor watched the monitor as Brent moved into the blackness. He disappeared just as the voice came over the intercom. "I did. I swear I did preserve inviolate, the secrets and mysteries."

"The secret sanctuary," whispered Victor.

Cyberia: Brent moves between the stone pillars of the temple, closer and closer to the Eminent Preceptor. Suddenly the hooded figure lifts his head and light falls on Haddo's eyes. Professor Brent blinks in surprise. "You!"

"We meet again in the kingdom of the Beast."

"Is that really you, Haddo?"

Lab: Only Brent's voice came over the intercom. "Is that really you Haddo?" Victor leaned over Mathers and spoke into the microphone.

"Not Haddo, he's Crowley."

Mathers pushed him off. " Will you get a grip? Professor Brent, are you all right?"

Victor laughed and started to sing in a whispered voice. "Wonderful, wonderful, Copenhagen interpretation."

Suddenly a hissing sounded. Mathers looked at the oscilloscope. It burst into jagged patterns, louder and louder.

"Chaotic feedback. It's feeding off itself."

Mathers jumped to the window and looked down at the suit. It was just floating there. The hissing sound, disturbingly amplified.

Professor Brent's voice came through. "NO!....Oh my God."

A red warning light came up on the Heartbeat indicator. Mathers leapt back to the computer as another warning light came up for Respiration – then Brain Wave activity.

Cyberia: Haddo rises and opens his cloak. With a horrifying screech, tubular tentacles burst from every pore.

Lab: An almighty scream came over the loudspeakers "JOBALONNNNNNE" half way between human and amplifier feedback. Mathers and Victor jumped to their feet. Chaotic images flashed across the screen.

Cyberia: Haddo's tentacles envelope Professor Brent. One goes down his throat and pulls his tongue out by the root.

Lab: The suit waved its arms above its head. Professor Brent was screaming in terror. The noise was deafening. Mathers tried to abort the program. Victor stared at the chaotic screen. Mathers looked out as the suit swayed. Suddenly the sound stopped, the screen went black. Mathers switched off the electromagnets. Professor Brent fell to the floor. They stood for a moment in shocked disbelief. Then a thin voice came over the monitor.

"V..V..Victor H..H..Help"

"Haddo?" queried Victor as he looked worryingly at the loud speakers.

Across the monitors rows of the number 7 filled the screens. Mathers looked at Victor. "What the hell's going on?"

Victor just stood watching the monitor. Mathers ran down and threw open the airlock door. The suit was hissing and jerking in the middle of the glass room. He ran over and ripped the headpiece off. Professor Brent's face was frozen in terror. Mathers took the pulse at the neck. He began violent cardiac massage. Victor looked up at the controls. All the red lights were out; all the levels were at zero.

"He's killed him."

Haddo smiled to himself and held out his arms like a Christ.

"Every man and every woman is a star."

A young lady slipped his coat over his outstretched arms. He smiled at the three painted girls who worked in the massage parlour.

"I always say, Mr Crowley," added Renee, the aging Madam, "that there's good and bad in all of us."

"My, a born philosopher," sneered Haddo sarcastically.

Around them the Christmas decorations were still up on the walls of what was effectively a brothel.

'Great men,' wrote Crowley, 'deliberately seek the most degraded and disgusting specimens of women that exist. The motive is always the same; to lose consciousness of their Promethean pangs. And monogamy is nonsense for any one with a grain of imagination. The more sides he has to his nature, the more women he needs to satisfy it.'

Now the once timid Haddo was flaunting and indulging his darkest desires with these low class vampires of the night.

Mavis, the girl who seduced Victor, came down the stairs with a silver topped cane.

"Now you be more careful with that in the future," she said as she handed it to him. Haddo tucked the cane under his arm, took a coin from behind Mavis' ear and gave it her.

"Some minor bruises. There will be no lasting damage."

"Let's hope not," frowned Renee. "I don't like to see my girls suffer in any way."

"Madam, mankind was made to suffer," corrected Haddo. "For example we may be healthy and fit but all we can think about is our little toe where the shoe pinches. And then the totality of our successful activities we ignore, all we think about is some insignificant trifle, which vexes us. There is a negativity in well being in antithesis to the positivity of pain."

"Well I'm not sure I agree with those sorts of ideas."

"Then you have to take it up with Schopenhauer, they are his not mine."

"I will," Renee picked a card off the desk. "Perhaps you could give him our card and tell him what an agreeable establishment we run here."

Haddo smiled at her ignorance and took the card. "In Xanadu did Kubla Khan; a stately pleasure-house decree."

He placed the card in his pocket took out a bankroll and gave Renee £80. She opened the door. "So, it's a redhead girl you want for tonight?"

"I have one in mind," he replied.

"Well let me see what I can do for you, Mr. Crowley."

"So be it. Till tonight, ladies."

And with an Arabic bow, he left. She closed the door then shook her head.

"He's a one, isn't he?"

Mavis looked at the coin Haddo had given her. "What's this?"

Renee took it and flipped it over. "Jesus! An old half-a-crown. I haven't seen one of them in years."

"Look, 1947, maybe it's worth something," said Mavis.

"Well girls, who wants to earn themselves a half crown and be a redhead for tonight."

She flipped the coin and Mavis caught it.

In the editor's office, the red headed Leah watched Ashby read her notes. When he finished he looked up at her.

"This is extraordinary," he said shaking his head in disbelief. "Haddo said this to Mathers?"

"Yes and he claimed again Aleister Crowley is not dead."

"Not dead? Does that make him mad or eccentric?"

"Crowley believed he would reincarnate."

"And Haddo thinks he is the reincarnation?"

"Yes. I think that's why he shaved his head; to look like him."

"He's crazy."

"Didn't seem like that, he just believed it like a Christian believes in God."

"That'll stir it up but it's a good point, write up the article and put that in."

"To cause controversy?"

"Yes. And can you get a clearer statement from Mathers as to why he thinks it's not nonsense?"

"The problem is he doesn't know who his parents were."

"But there's the girlfriend. Look, I'll dig out a picture of Haddo from the prospectus. Can you get a picture of Crowley?"

"I'll try the library."

"And is there any way you can get a photo of Haddo with his head shaved?"

"With his head shaved? Okay."

"Good girl. We'll make this the front page."

The wind had blown away the clouds and the day was bright and crisp as Haddo jauntily strode across the road from the massage parlour and bought a newspaper from a stand. The headlines announced 'BUSH AND GORE DEADLOCK CONTINUES'. He turned the pages searching for news. A man passed by carrying a banner proclaiming 'THE END IS NIGH' and on the reverse 'HE WILL RETURN'. Haddo lifted his stick and gave the Prophet a polite nod then tossed his less newsworthy paper into the bin. At that moment an outrageously dressed man came cruising down past the quaint antique shops. He wore a green carnation in a grubby black striped suit with white patent leather shoes and a black fedora hat. Haddo smiled and followed the man. The Beau noticed his admirer and descended the steps of a Gents toilet.

White sanitary tiles, the smell of antiseptic crystals and urine echoed to footsteps overhead on the glass block tiles. The Beau was standing at the stall when Haddo come down the stairs and looked around before moving in to the stall next to him. Haddo unbuttoned his flies and fetched out his penis and stood there without pissing. The man looked over the shoulder of the stall at Haddo's penis. Haddo looked across at the Beau and smiled lasciviously.

In the silence of the Wren Library, Leah ran her finger along a line of books. A small, black leather bound volume grabbed her attention. 'The Secret Rituals of the O.T.O.' by Aleister Crowley. She had not spotted this before; it must have been out. She opened it and smiled, there was a picture of Crowley with the shaved head. She studied it; there was a certain similarity between him and Haddo. Well not so much how Haddo looked before, she thought, more how he looked now. He certainly has a totally different persona: totally different. Leah suddenly had a moment of doubt, then reassured herself with the thought that it was probably just the haircut made him appear more imposing.

There were other curious anatomical features that Crowley shared with Haddo, ones that were hidden from view. Crowley wrote of them,

'While my masculinity is normal both physiologically and as witnessed by my powerful growth of beard, I had certain well-marked feminine characteristics. Not only were my limbs as slight and graceful as a girl's but my breasts were developed to a quite abnormal degree. There was thus a sort of hermaphroditism in my physical structure.'

While Crowley glorified in this feature, which he thought gave him a psychological understanding of women, Haddo on the other hand had concealed it wherever possible.

Leah looked from the picture to the title page opposite.

'Aleister Crowley, THE BEAST 666, Megatherion.'

Megatherion? Well mega is large and thurian is a large prehistoric animal. 'A large beast,' she translated. Below there was a poem.

'Ho! I adopt the number. Look
At the quaint wrapper of this book!
I will deserve it if I can:
It is the number of a Man.'

She smiled and flicked through the pages. At the back was a loose pamphlet, advertising a performance of Crowley's Eleusian Rites. It was for tonight, the 7th of January.

She assumed a follower must have slipped it in to get at anyone who might be interested in Crowley. As she removed it she noticed a hand written dedication on the back page of the book.

'To Leah who invokes the Serpent's flame,
Oh scarlet woman, wilt thou be willing to give all.'

Leah looked around the library. Was there someone watching her, someone playing a trick? No, just silent students with their heads in books. Confused and concerned she took the book to the desk.

'Can you tell me when this book was last taken out?"

"The last stamped date," answered the librarian as she opened the front page.

Leah looked at the date 12/12/2000. "Before Christmas?"

"Yes."

"Are you sure?"

The librarian opened the catalogue drawer and took out a card.

As she read the information, Leah asked, "Can you see who it was?"

"Twelfth of December. No I can't."

Leah thought for a moment and then a smile spread across her face as she realized it must have been Mathers. She handed over her library card and checked the book out.

Banging echoed around the empty toilets accompanied by a breathy groaning. Below the closed cubicle door were two pairs of feet, one with striped trousers around the ankles. The thumping on the door and the orgasmic groaning continued in unison with the rhythmic thrusting. Then a low humming started in time with the action and grew louder and louder till it broke into the words of the infamous Eton boating song.

'Jolly fine boating weather,
And a hay-harvest breeze,
Blade on the feather,
Shade off the trees;
Swing, swing together,
With your body between your knees.
Swing, swing together,
With your body between your knees.'

Leah, her mind still pondering the hand written quotation, entered the Physics block. She transferred the library books to her left hand as she pushed open the heavy computer room door. She could hear voices and looked around but with nobody there; she took it for a radio. Then she saw Victor's leaflet for the Eleusis ceremony on the desk and compared it with the one in her book. 'The conspiracy thickens,' she thought and was sure it was Mathers. Just then, she realized the voices were not coming from a radio but from the intercom, which was open to the hangar. Moving to the observation window she saw Mathers, Victor and the Dean talking while two ambulance men were waiting with a stretcher by the glass door.

Inside the glass room a doctor was examining Professor Brent. Mathers' voice came over the intercom.

"...but it's not real, it's an illusion."

"Whatever it is, it has caused a serious injury here," stated the Dean.

"Who was last in the suit?"

"I was, at Cal Tech." said Mathers.

The Dean turned to Victor. "So this was the first time it was linked to our computer?"

Victor nodded.

"I can't understand..." faltered Mathers.

'Well until you *can* understand, that contraption is not to be connected to our computer."

Leah watched from the observation window unable to make sense of what was going on.

Mathers tried to explain to the Dean, "But it can't..."

"I don't care what it theoretically can or can't do. It's dangerous. That suit is not to be connected to our computer. Do I make myself clear?"

The doctor opened the glass door to let the stretcher-bearers in.

The Dean turned. "Yes, Doctor?"

"Traumatic shock seems to have initiated what appears to be a heart attack."

"Is he going to be all right?"

"His heart will recover thanks to the prompt action of Dr Mathers but I'm afraid the brain appears frozen – catatonic."

Mathers was shocked. "Catatonic?"

The Dean added his own exclamation, 'Catatonic?"

"Yes. Fear seems to have triggered a shutdown of the senses."

Haddo rose up from the public toilets and strode off handsomely in the suit and fedora of his toilet companion. Raising his walking stick he hailed a cab, got in and it drove off.

A moment later, the Beau skipped up out of the toilets in his underpants. People turned and stared, some laughed. Without a care for the freezing wind he jumped up on to the ledge of the railway-bridge and balanced along in an exaggerated tightrope walker pose. Two Police Constables pushed past the laughing shoppers to haul him in. As they approached the trouserless performer saw them coming and waved daintily, goodbye, then turned and leapt off into the path of a screaming express train.

"Have they sacrificed thee?
Do they say that thou hast died for them?"

Haddo sat at the back of the taxi gently reciting.

"He is not dead! He lives forever!
He is alive more than they, for he is the mystic one of sacrifice."

The cabby checked his mirror. He had had the odd devout woman in the cab that crossed herself every time he cornered, which he considered was an insult to his driving. But this guy started praying as soon as he got in for Christ sake.

Oblivious of the cabby's attention Haddo continued,

"He is not dead! He lives forever!
He is their Lord living and young forever."

"Amen," added the cabby sarcastically and rightly mistaking this ancient Egyptian prayer to the dying Osiris as something to do with Jesus.

"Any resemblance between my Osiris," corrected Haddo, "and the two thousand year later facsimile, is purely plagiarism."

Leah was still watching through the observation window when Victor came into the control room grabbed his coat and left without seeing her. Mathers followed looking for Victor and found only Leah.

"Where did Victor go?"

"He grabbed his coat and went. What's happening?"

"There's been an accident, something's seriously wrong with the program."

"Your program?"

"Yes. We were generating tremendous amounts of information."

"Information? Is that bad?"

"No, yes. What are you doing here?"

"Nothing – well.. look at this. Did you write it?" She shows him the inscription in the book.

Mathers hardly glances. "I wouldn't write in your books."

"It's not my book – I happened to – it doesn't matter." She closed the book. "Do you want a coffee – you look shattered."

He nodded.

The taxi turned off the High Street into a narrow road and stopped outside a small terraced bookshop.

"How much, my good man?"

"Four pounds sixty."

Haddo gave him the exact money.

"I can remember when I got change from thrupence for the same journey."

"I can remember when people gave you a tip," moaned the cabby as he revved off.

Obliviously, Haddo turned and went to the window of the shop, which sold new age paraphernalia; tarot cards, occult books, crystals, CD's of whale songs, massage oils, didgeridoos, lava lamps and amongst all these objects was the poster 'THE RITES OF ELEUSIS' as performed by Aleister Crowley 7th January 10 pm.'

Haddo smiled and pushed the door.

The tinkling bell announced his entry. The Whale Song honking in the background was extremely apt for the fat lady behind the counter. Haddo removed his fedora and bowed flamboyantly to her.

"Dr. Haddo? Is that Dr. Haddo? What have you done to your hair?"

Haddo corrected, "The Earl of Boleskine," announcing himself with one of Crowley's many pseudonyms.

'Why live in one skin?' Crowley had always said. 'Experience the world and let the world experience you in other forms.' It had worked brilliantly for Crowley, people were imbeciles who reacted totally differently to him when he announced himself as a Lord or a Turkish Prince, exposing the frailties of the human psyche.

The fat lady was too interested in talking to notice his introduction. Her trouble was that she lacked the power of conversation but not the power of speech.

"I've had lots of inquiries, but I haven't prepared anything for this evening. You disappeared and I was beginning to..."

"And who might this charming lady be?" interrupted Haddo. He indicated another fat, middle-aged lady in a Marks and Spencer twin suit.

"This is my sister Stella. She's helping out because she's got a bad back, the doctors say..."

"Well how astonishing. I know of an ancient ritual that directs all the body's chi into the spine." He smiled ingenuously. "Never fails."

"The real danger was never that computers would begin to think like men," said Mathers, "But that men would begin to think like computers."

He lifted his coffee cup to his lips. Leah watched him sip and pull a face.

She apologized, "Sorry about that. University instant coffee is pretty foul stuff."

"It's okay. At least it's wet and nearly warm."

Leah liked his easy humour in fact she liked a lot about him. But then as she looked at his eyes, she was drawn back to his concern.

"What do you think happened with Professor Brent?" she asked. "Do you think his brain believed what he saw?"

"He believed it all right. Trouble was we didn't see what he saw."

"So whatever he saw was in his own mind or was generated by the program."

Mathers was impressed, she had a good brain; logical and rational.

"The program veered off, I can't think why, it was fine when I was last in the suit."

"You also said that to the Dean but you know you weren't the last person in the suit," said Leah.

"Yes at Cal Tech." replied Mathers.

"No, Victor had someone in the suit the other night."

"Victor's out of his head."

"Out of his head he may be but he had someone in that suit - and I know who it was."

"Who?"

"Dr, Haddo."

"Are you serious? Dr. Haddo, your classics tutor?"

"I'd recognize that stutter anywhere."

"What stutter?" asked Mathers.

"Oh God, I never noticed."

Mathers watched the blood drain from Leah's face. "What?"

"The astral plane."

"What?" Mathers looked blank.

"The astral plane - that's where he got the information about you."

"From the astral plane?" Mathers repeated sceptically.

"What Haddo knew about you. He must have got it when he was in the suit, from the computer."

"My information?"

"Yes. So like a chain reaction what Victor fed Haddo - what affected him - must have passed on to Professor Brent."

Mathers slowly put down his coffee. "When he said we met on the astral plane, he meant, we met in Cyberia."

The fat lady stood at the doorway of the back room, keeping a watch on the shop. Haddo held Stella's hand as they stood facing each other in the centre of the room. He watched her eyes as he unbuttoned her dress. She was a little apprehensive.

"Dr Haddo is very clever," the fat lady reassured. "I've seen him do some amazing things; why the other day he took a coin and made it pass through a table into a glass; do you remember, Dr. Haddo?"

Haddo nodded but was busy undressing Stella. He let drop her slip and she was down to her bra and panties.

"Lie down on the blanket... No face up."

She did as he asked. He knelt at her head end and stretched his hand over Stella's crutch.

"Yes, yes, I can sense your aura. Can you sense my hand?"

"Yes I can, I really can," said Stella.

The fat lady butted in. "You see, I told you…"

Haddo raised a finger to his lips to silence her then continued.

"Yes. Now raise your hips up."

Stella raised her hips off the ground till her body almost touched his hand.

"Good and relax.... Now once more."

She dropped her buttocks down then rose again to his hand.

"And relax. I can feel the evil coming into my palm. Let's take this off it's stopping the blood circulating."

He removed her bra and laid her back again.

The shop doorbell rang, the fat lady turned.

"A customer. I wont be a second."

"Please close the door will you," asked Haddo.

The Fat lady closed the door and went back to the counter. Haddo smiled as Stella continued raising her buttocks to meet his hand. This time Haddo slipped his hand into her panties and squeezed.

The Dean sat at his oak desk listening attentively to Mathers' story. Symons was sitting in a leather armchair by the window, watching with interest as they mention the occult leader he followed as a student back in 1947. When Mathers finished the Dean thought for a moment.

"So for some mad reason, you think Dr. Haddo believes he is the reincarnation of Aleister Crowley."

He turned to Symons. "What do you make of that, Symons?"

Symons shook his head but said nothing.

The Dean continued, "Didn't he mumble something about being the reincarnation of Count Cagliostro?"

"Of Ko Hsuen, Count Cagliostro and Eliphas Levi," said Symons, "also claimed by Crowley to be his previous lives."

"Really?" said the Dean. "Ah, but then there are plenty of madmen who think they are Napoleon or King George."

"You know what Oscar Wilde said about him?" added Symons, "Aleister Crowley is a madman who thinks he's Aleister Crowley."

The Dean smiled then turned back to Mathers.

"I don't see how this, in any way, explains or excuses what has happened to Professor Brent."

"Dr. Haddo was in the suit before Professor Brent."

"In the suit? In your interactive suit?" queried the Dean.

"Yes, I believe Victor fed in information from the Z93."

"Information? What sort of information?" asked Symons?

"Probably energy co-ordinates that relate to Crowley."

The Dean's eyes widened incredulously. He turned slowly to look at Symons who just sat there winding Crowley's old pocket watch.

Haddo came out of the back room where Stella was bent naked over the table. He closed the door as she began to recover. He walked over smugly to the Fat Lady at the counter.

"Her back is cured."

"That's amazing."

"Now to the Ceremony, only twelve initiates will be allowed in."

"Twelve! But I must have had about fifty enquiries."

"Twelve besides the participants and I will require certain very important items. Some are quite expensive."

"I'll get them."

"I need the key to the upstairs room. Neither you nor anyone else is to enter without my permission. Do you understand? No one is to enter before ten."

She nodded excitedly and took the key from a hook behind the counter and gave it to him. He handed her his list.

"I better get a move on, there's not much time," she said

"Time is like money, the less we have of it the further we make it go."

"Too true, Dr Haddo, but Stella and I had been tempted to visit the teashop for some of their superb éclairs."

"You know the only way to get rid of temptation, my dear?"

"What's that, Dr. Haddo?"

"Yield to it. Good afternoon." And with a flourish he tucked the key into his pocket and left the shop.

The Fat Lady watched him stride past the shop window, then shook her head and unfolded the list and examined it.

"I wonder what he wants that for?"

Dr. Timlet, the neurologist, shone his pen torch into Professor Brent's eye. There was still absolutely no response. He placed his fingers on the wrist; the pulse was healthy. He checked his watch and timed off half a minute, watching the frozen face, searching the eyes, *the window into the soul,* as his old professor called them. His patient he knew was a Professor of Physics. Quantum Physicists claimed they had glimpsed into the mind of God but Dr. Timlet knew it was the neurologists who were in there with Him. In the Twilight Zone of the mind, certain brain disorders could make one doubt the very fundamental existence of self. And others created transcendental experiences, which were out of this world. He knew full well that the sighting of heavenly Saints such as that at Lourdes were unremarkable experiences compared with the visions of his patients. The strange spiritual possessions experienced by the Tourettes patients, unable to control their foul expletives acted as if controlled by an outer force. But most astonishing were the autistics with their absolutely phenomenal skills. Can God instantly count a bunch of falling toothpicks? 153. Or does God know what day of the week he appeared to Moses as a burning bush and what the weather was like? Can he learn and speak fluently a foreign language in just seven days? Can he remember every piece of information he's ever heard or read? Or correctly calculate complex maths using just colors and shapes. Idiot Savants can. From these extraordinary talents right down to disorders, which revealed the very flimsy nature of existence, neurologists challenged God. The patient who had lost the ability to recognize faces and thus became indifferent to human identities. The other woke up one day and no longer perceived his left leg as something belonging to him, but rather as a severed human leg, some hideous thing placed in his hospital bed as a tasteless joke. Unhappily, when he tried to expel this counterfeit limb by throwing it out of bed, his body followed out after it. It all went to show that when the human brain fails in some way either the fragility of consciousness is revealed or the supernatural, magical, potential of the human being is glimpsed. Strangely Aleister Crowley had written something similar.

'I gave up the habit of going round to see people though I was always at home to anyone who chose to call. I was not interested in the average man; I cultivated the freak. It was not that I liked abnormal people, it was simply the scientific attitude that it is from the abnormal that we learn.'

But with all that Dr. Timlet had never seen a total catatonic. There had been a dramatic decline in the disease since the 1930's. Theories varied from a reduction in the incidence of an infective disorder – to changes in treatment, such as the introduction of neuroleptics. Catatonia was one of the most enigmatic phenomena in neurology. What treatment should he try in this case? ECT and benzodiazepines were the treatments of choice for patients with catatonic symptoms. But as yet Dr Timlet dared not begin a treatment till he had a plausible diagnosis, especially on such an eminent Professor. A smile slipped across his face as he remembered the old saying, 'A doctor's reputation is made by the number of eminent men who die under his care.' He returned grimly to the case in point. He knew normal catatonics were patients who deteriorated over time, often due to a slow reduction in the production by the brain of the chemical dopamine. He had been told this patient became catatonic instantly. 'Instantly' suggested this was caused by physical damage to the brain. But there were no external lacerations, no abrasions, no bruises. A scan would confirm any internal physical damage. He turned and nodded through the observation window to the technician at the controls of the scanner and left the room. The technician waited for the red door light to illuminate signifying the Doctor had left and the door was locked in place, then he switched on the scanner. It whirred up till the sound steadied and a green light came on the control board. He pressed the red button, which conveyed Professor Brent, in his flimsy operating gown into the massive magnetic field in the depths of the scanner.

Dr. Timlet put on his reading glasses and sat in front of the monitor as scanned sections of Professor Brent's brain began to appear. He studied them carefully, especially when the slices were showing the region of the substantia nigra, the dopamine producing part of the brain. He searched for a blood clot or a tumour but nothing appeared on the scan. Dr Timlet's brain moved ahead, what if we find no damage, what then? Chemical? There was the case in California where drug addicts became catatonic from a defective supply of a manufactured designer drug. The offending chemical was the tetrahydro-pyridine MPTP which suppressed the production of dopamine. The Neurologist in charge had revived them temporarily with a dose of L-Dopa. That is what he would try next, a dose of L-Dopa. Unfortunately he could only use L-Dopa as an indicator because long-term exposure to its formula caused patients to suffer frightening illusions and dreadful visions.

The oak door of the Dean's office opened and Mathers came out and headed down the corridor to where Leah was sitting on the bench.

He shook his head as he approached. "He thinks I'm crazy – he won't accept Haddo could be programmed by a computer."

"Why don't you get hold of Haddo, or better still Victor? The Bursar will have his address. Victor – what's his surname?"

"Neuman." A voice behind made them turn, Symons stood there.

"Perhaps I can help," he offered obligingly. "I can't say I know much about computers, but I do know a lot about Aleister Crowley."

The Aleister Crowley facsimile, wearing his extravagant fedora and stripped suit, strode towards the massage parlour. A small cat curled up to him and turned over onto its back to be stroked. Haddo placed his foot on the cat's belly. The cat stayed faithfully still. He slowly lowered his foot; the cat remained static expecting a caress. Crowley claimed to be uniformly kind to animals and assured all that his rather infamous experiment had no element of cruelty or sadism. He had through some analogy with the story of Hercules and the hydra considered the possibility that a cat could have nine lives. Having caught a cat he proceeded to administer a large dose of arsenic, he then chloroformed it, hanged it above a gas jet, stabbed it, cut its throat, smashed its skull and after it was pretty burnt; drowned it and threw it out of the window. He pronounced the experiment successful when the carcass was retrieved dead but unaccountably continued to insist that he loved animals. Haddo smiled at the memory as he looked down at the hapless cat below his heel. Then he lifted his foot and just gently brushed the cat to one side with the toe of his shoe and entered.

Symons watched Mathers at the keyboard of the Z93.

"I'm afraid I think computers are like Old Testament gods," said Symons, "lots of rules and no mercy. I tremble with fear every time I hit a key,"

Mathers stopped typing and looked up. "Yes but without a key, even I don't know...."

"Try something obvious, 777," said Symons.

"Why 777?"

"It's Crowley's number," declared Leah who was looking out of the observation window at the suit. "The natural harmonies seven notes of a scale, seven colors of the rainbow.'

"And seven stars in Orion," added Symonds, "What the ancient Egyrtians called Osiris."

Mathers typed it in.

Symons shook his head. "Who'd have believed it?"

Mathers looked round helplessly as the computer screen stayed blank.

Haddo entered a rather seedy room above the massage parlor. He removed the fedora, brushed it affectionately and hung it on a hook behind the door. He took off his jacket and placed it on the back of a chair. Then he undid the buttons of his shirt and slipped it off revealing a rather grubby vest, which exposed the rounded shape of his fatty breasts. He went over to a small sink in the corner and filled it with hot water. As the steam rose he looked at his face in the mirror and smiled. The once rounded features seem to have more firmness and sense of purpose. He slapped shaving foam onto his head and stropped a straight edged razor onto the leather strap. The movement backwards and forwards took on a rhythm and continued over and over till it became manic in its repetitiveness. Flap, flap, flap, flap, even the noise generated a hypnotic spell till finally he stopped in frozen reverie. He tested the blade by cutting across his thumb, the blood spilt like a smile and a drop fell into the water and dispersed. He lifted the blood red edge to the rays of light from the setting sun.

The luminosity reflected treacherously from the sharpened edge, firing photons into his eye. The autonomic nervous system immediately closed down the iris, revealing the abstract mechanics of this optic device. Through the aqueous humour the image of the razor was upturned and focused by the lens on to the retina. The photons caused the Rhodopsin containing rods, to react to the black and white while the three types of cones absorbed light from three different portion of the color spectrum. Those that reacted to long wavelengths were excited by the drop of red blood, stimulating the membrane of the touching nerve cell to change the action potential of their long arms, the axons. These caused the spot of red on the gleaming razor to sweep along the nerve as a ripple of depolarization. It traveled insulated from the outside by the white, fatty, myelin sheath that surrounds the elongated axon. The full image of the razor was carried by thousands of such insulated axons and collected together in the thick, white optic nerve. The two, pulsed images of the razor, one from each eye, crossed each other and then entered Haddo's brain, the left eye to the right hemisphere the right to the left. Deep in the cerebrum the pulses were reinterpreted back into a stereoscopic, color image of the red blood on the gleaming razor's edge.

Incredibly, the only clear geometrical structure that was inside Haddo's body, and in fact in the body of any vertebrate, was that created by the crossing of these white optic nerves at the base of the brain. This **X** shaped cross, the 'Optic Chaisma', has fascinated mankind from the very beginning, over a hundred thousand years ago. Remove the brain of any vertebrate animal, turn it over and there it is, the clear white cross against the red-grey matter of the brain. There is no way of seeing the optic chaisma without causing the death of the organism and therefore this has led to the graphic image of the cross becoming associated with the very life force itself. The ankh, the key of life carried by Isis in many hieroglyphics. And the **X** cross was even used as the Christian image up to four hundred years after the death of Christ. It was only late in 420AD that the first image of Jesus on a vertical cross, appeared.

Yet there was one other geometrical structure on Haddo, the dome of his skull was perfectly spherical, which he shaved with the straight edged razor. He grazed it to perfection then washed the remaining lather from his head and tapped it dry with a towel. The light from the window was fading fast and he switched on the table lamp, on the walnut cabinet. He pulled down the cabinet door, which lit to reveal a few bottles of alcoholic drink mirrored to appear like many. He looked at the wine label and instantly rejected it and poured himself a scotch instead. He settled into a chair and took a sip, swilling it round his mouth before swallowing. There was a knock on the door. He did not respond but took a second sip from the goblet and ran his tongue over his teeth giving them a superficial clean. Another knock then the door slowly opened and a girl with red hair entered the room.

"Mr. Crowley?"

"I drink therefore I am."

The girl was a little unsure. Haddo watched her intently. She turned and closed the door.

"I'm Ruby. I've got a sort of wedding dress."

"I told Renee I've got someone in mind."

"She said it would only be an extra fifty pounds on the room."

She took off her coat to reveal a white frilly dress, but with a short skirt.

"And I've got a white veil too."

She opened her bag and took it out.

"You look like a Christmas decoration."

"Twelve days too late."

"Not so my dear, do you know what these twelve days are?"

"It's unlucky to take down the decorations," she answered.

"The original birth day of Christ was in fact on the sixth of January but the Emperor Constantine made all the religions of Rome conform to sun worshipping. So Christians changed the date of his birth to the day of the winter solstice. The 25th of December. So you see my dear today is actually the real birthday of Jesus but Christian simpletons allude to the original date by singing songs or silly superstitions." The smile slipped away, his eyes suddenly glared. "But I'm not such a simpleton. Come here!"

She went to where he was sitting. He grabbed her dress and pulled her close to him. Then he lifted up her skirt and put his head under. Ruby looked surprised. Suddenly there was a tearing sound and she gave off a little scream.

"Redhead! My ass." Haddo announced from under her skirt. He pushed her away from him. There was a ripping sound and he was left holding her torn knickers in one hand and a brown pubic hair in the other. Haddo held it out accusatively.

"Was this your idea?"

"No…no it was Renee's," she answered fearfully.

"Hell, what fools these mortals be."

Haddo grabbed his razor and snatched her by the arm. She struggled frantically.

Symons looked at the blank computer screen and thought. "Now let's see… what would he call a resurrection program. Try skull and crossbones."

"The pirate flag?" asked Mathers.

Symons smiled. "No, stories they tell. Can you really imagine a band of pirates sitting down to sew a flag to wave at potential victims?"

"It does sound a little ridiculous when you put it like that"

"What is it then?" asked Leah

"It's a battle flag – flown by the Knights Templars' navy which escaped from La Rochelle on Friday the thirteenth 1307 when the French king attacked their sanctuaries. Then the British warships flew it to conceal their piratical attacks on Spanish bullion ships."

"A Knights Templar battle flag?" queried Leah. "Then what's it to do with resurrection?"

"During the ceremony to initiate a third degree Mason the apprentice is laid to death on a shroud with the skull and cross bones before being resurrected back to life as a Master Mason."

Leah wrote a note. "A death and resurrection ceremony."

Mathers turned and shrugged as nothing appeared on the screen.

Symons thought. "Try the skull, 'Baphomet' that's a ph."

Suddenly the pentagram appeared rotating.

"Got it. Baphomet?" queried Mathers.

Leah answered, "It's the name Crowley gave himself as head of the OTO – his Masonic organization."

"That's right," said Symons.

Mathers looked back at her with a smile.

"Crowley got Baphomet," added Symons, "from the name of a skull owned by the Knights Templars. The skull was alleged to be that of Mary Magdalene who sailed to the South of France after the Romans destroyed Jerusalem and exiled the Jews from their homeland."

"Do you believe that?" asked Leah.

"Spain and the South of France would be a natural haven for the exiled Jews. Herod's son himself spent the end of his life in Leon in France."

"But why link the skull with Mary Magdalene?"

"Dr. Hugh Schonfield when studying the 'Dead Sea Scrolls' came across a cipher. The Hebrew alphabet has 22 letters and the cipher exchanged the first 11 letters for the last 11 in reverse order. With the English alphabet this would mean that Z was substituted for A; Y for B and X for C and so on. In Hebrew this would be A – aleph = T – Tau and B – Bet = Sh – Shin. Thus as ATBSh it was called the Atbash cipher." Symons warmed to his academic task but Leah and Mathers were getting a little lost. He continued oblivious of this, "This cipher was used to glean a good amount hidden within scriptural texts, but the big surprise came when Dr. Schonfield applied it to the Templar word 'Baphomet'. Transcribing the word 'Baphomet' into Hebrew he then applied the Atbash cipher and it converted immediately into 'Sophia'."

"That links Baphomet to Sophia," accepted Leah, "but how does Sophia link to Mary Magdelene?"

"Sophia was the Greek Goddess of knowledge," continued Symons as he launched into another explanation. "In Gnostic circles

Mary Magdelene was associated with the wisdom of the immortal Sophia. A document that makes this especially clear is the 'Pistis Sophia' an ancient Coptic document found in Egypt and acquired by the British Museum from Dr Anthony Askew's estate. It is therefore known as the Askew Codex. In essence it is a dialogue between Jesus, Mary Magdelene and his disciples concerning the words said by Pistis Sophia. Jesus asks each of them in turn to give their interpretation of the mysterious wisdom. They comply but when Mary Magdalene gives her response, Jesus tells her, "Thou art she whose heart is more directed to the kingdom of Heaven than all thy brothers." Mary emerges as the one with the greatest empathy for the immortal Sophia and was forever after associated with her. For instance she is referred to as Sophia in the book of Revelations where it says 'a woman who bore the crown of Sophia fled into the wilderness to escape the imperial dragon that went to make war with the remnant of her seed."

"Her seed?"

"Yes it's well known in occult circles. And of course Revelations 12:2 continues, 'And she being with child cried, travailing in birth, and pained to be delivered."

Leah was shocked but Mathers who had not been following the conversation interrupted.

"So this might be the program mounted on mine. Let's see what's in it."

He hit a key and thousands of occult images - calculations - and writings flashed across the screen.

Haddo held the safety razor up over Ruby who was lying on her back on the floor. She looked at him in horror. Haddo lowered the razor below her dress.

"Vile locks of deception."

His face was red with anger, his arm moved upward. There was a rasping sound and Ruby squealed.

"Offending filaments, your time has come."

He raised the razor. It was filled with foam and brown hair.

"What an idiot to trust such vermin."

He washed the razor in a bowl then went back to the girl's crutch. He rasped off another stretch. Ruby squealed again then burst out giggling.

"Careful that tickles."

"Oh, Scarlet woman. I wasted time and now doth time waste me."

The occult images still flashed across the screen. Mathers turned to Symons.

"This must have taken years to put in. But it's information not a program, Victor must have an external key."

"I'll get his address from the bursar," said Leah. "Will I see you back at the flat?"

Mathers nodded. She closed the door as the screen images stopped. Mathers looked to Symons.

"Does any of that mean anything to you?"

"I noticed quite a lot of Hebrew script and Gematria, the occult power of numbers. And the images all have known occult interpretations."

"What the paintings?

"Yes… scroll back onto one?"

Mathers moved back through several images to a painting.

"That's a Bosch, isn't it?" asked Mathers.

"Yes. Christ Crowned with Thorns."

"What's occult about that?"

"Well what do you see?" asked Symons.

"Christ being crowned with thorns."

"What else?"

"There's four men, the one with the thorns has an iron arm and an arrow through his hat. One has his hand on Jesus shoulder like he's befriending him, as is this one who seems to be holding his hands. And the forth has him gripped by the collar. Am I missing something?"

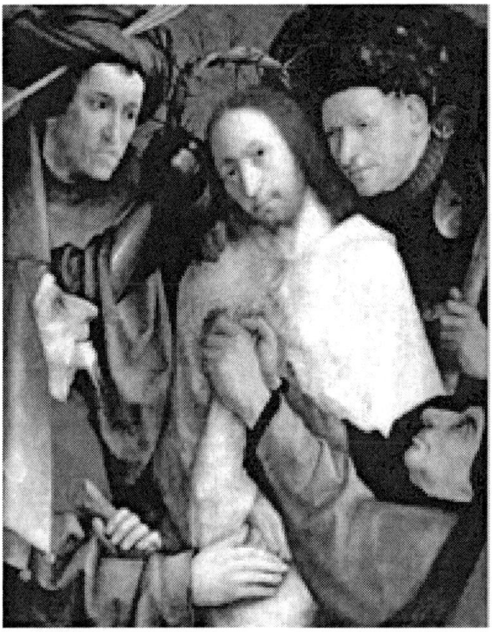

"What you have here are four types each representing the four elements, air, fire, earth and water. The fire type, the choleric is at the top. His armoured hand signifies not only the violence of the choleric type but in astrological tradition iron is the metal of Mars, the planet that rules over zodiacal Aries, which in turn rules over the head of man. That is why it is he who is placing the crown of thorns on Christ's head. The Air type, the sanguine is also to the top of the picture and as you say he is resting his hand on the shoulder – a gesture, which has double significance. Firstly in astrology the shoulders are ruled by the air sign Gemini. It also appears as you noticed that this sanguine type is befriending Christ and is about to speak to him. Speech is obviously carried through the medium of air and the sanguine type is associated with all forms of speech from the high drama to the chatter of imbeciles. But the oak leaves in the hat remind us that Christ will be thrust into the Air on a cross which was thought in medieval times to have been made of Oak.

The lower figure to the left, Water, the phlegmatic type is

making a lewd gesture towards Christ's hands, which are over his private parts. This links the phlegmatic with the Zodiacal Scorpio, the water sign that rules over the sexual organs. The moon symbol on his headdress is also associated in occult tradition with the sexual organs and with the lunar demons who have, through the sexual organs, direct access to man. The gesture of the water type is to man's weakest point. See his wooden stave forms a cross with the stave held by the Air type. Then the Earth type, the melancholic, reaches up from his low earthly position and will drag the body down to its final resting place and so on. You see?"

"You seem very knowledgeable about all this."

"I specialize in religious art."

"No, more than that: about Crowley," queried Mathers suspiciously.

"I met Crowley."

"The original?"

"I was just a student and he was an old man. He was quite a showman – but underneath he had access to some extraordinary knowledge."

"What sort of knowledge, like what you just explained?"

"Something like that. Look it's late. Shall we resume first thing tomorrow morning at my place? I have some books I need to show you, and the young lady."

Mathers remembered Victor's leaflet and pulled it from his pocket.

"Have you seen this? The rites of Eleusis, it's tonight."

Symons glanced over it. "Some people take drugs or drink alcohol but there's nothing more potent, or ancient, than the release of one's inhibitions through ritual." He handed the leaflet back to Mathers

"Is that the power he had over people?"

"And the power to exploit our passions."

Victor stood at the window staring at the last faint smudge of light over the rooftops to the South West. For the first time in his life he felt released from the necessity of existence. He did not know who he was, what he was or what was going to happen but none of that mattered. His chest was bare and his head rocked as his lips moved in a silent chant. He was aware that ancient chanting had hypnotic qualities that concentrated strength into deep regions of the brain and muscles. Ideas flashed through his energized brain, 'there had to be other unknown ancient skills. A method of lifting heavy stones, no modern attempt at copying the building of the pyramids had worked. And how had they cut the huge building blocks so that they fitted so perfectly that there was no sign of a wobble? And astoundingly they had accurately drilled out the centre of the extremely hard granite block that is the sarcophagus seated at the centre of the King's Chamber in the Great Pyramid. Today, laser beams and diamond drills would be employed – but then? Ancient temples are tuned to certain musical keys. Perhaps sound frequencies could have been used in some way to lift the massive lintels. Sound is at the centre of the theories Pythagoras learnt during his 22 years studying in Egypt. The '*Music of the Spheres*' he called it. Is that a clue to the missing technology: sound or electronic frequency?'

All these thoughts were being bounced across the synaptic gaps of Victor's brain, ferried by the neurotransmitters. The vast majority of the synapses in the human brain are chemical synapses and although chemical synapses are slower than electrical ones they are far more flexible. This valuable flexibility is the foundation of all repetitive learning. But perhaps some of these thoughts were deeper memories hidden in the base of the brain where instinctive memory resides. This inherited memory, which is carried in the genes, is deeply mystical. It is the type of memory that spiders use to create their wonderfully complex webs or the birds of paradise to perform the beautiful steps of their ritualized, mating dance.

Haddo came out of a door and stomped down the corridor. His face was still flushed red with menace.

"RENEE!"

There was no answer. He punched the light switch, it flashed blue and the lights went out.

"Out vile jellies. Where is your lustre now?"

He reached the top of the stairs and yelled. "RENEE!"

Victor closed the curtain on the darkened sky and switched on the bedside lamp. He picked up a small dagger and twirled it then placed it into his pocket and put on his coat and scarf. He unlocked the door bolts, which he had now started using and opened the door. As it swung aside he was surprise to be confronted by Leah.

"Victor Neuman."

"Yes."

"I've got a few questions for Granta."

"You what?"

"The other night Haddo was in the interactive suit."

Victor gave a dismissive snort and started to walk away down the corridor.

Leah followed, "You integrated a program into the computer that affected Professor Brent, didn't you? 'The ghost in the machine'."

He carried on.

She tried again, "Where's Haddo now?"

Victor stopped and smiled enigmatically; "Haddo has been possessed."

"Possessed?"

"By the greatest spiritual leader of modern times."

"Aleister Crowley."

"The Aeon of Horus. His second coming."

"In Haddo's body," added Leah.

"The ultimate transplant."

"Are you serious?"

"Never more so," replied Victor

Leah looked at him, his pupils were gaping wide black holes

"You're crazy. It's just not possible."

"Isn't it? Then tonight the chosen twelve will give witness to the impossible." Victor turned down the stairs.

Leah called after him, "Aleister Crowley died on the first of December nineteen forty seven and was cremated so whatever was left of him went up in smoke."

Victor stopped and turned. "Do you know every time you breathe in – you breath thousands of atoms that were once part of Aleister Crowley's body?"

"Maybe but it doesn't make him become a solid mass."

"Doesn't it? What do you think E=mc2 means?"

He laughed and continued down the stairs. Leah worked through Einstein's equation; energy equals mass times the speed of light squared.

"What's that supposed to mean?"

Victor's voice echoed back up the stairwell. "Reverse it."

She thought for a moment 'mass times the speed of light squared equals energy. Wasn't that what Mathers had said? 'Slow down light and you get mass – matter'. Is that what Victor meant, matter and energy are interchangeable? She hurried down the stairs and out into cold night air. She looked around but the streets were silently empty. A gust of wind rippled her hair like Haddo's plump fingers. She stiffened and turned round almost expecting the leering face but found no one there. Then against the rising moon she saw Victor crossing the humped bridge over the Cam.

Hammering sounded through the darkened corridor of the brothel. Then everything quietened. The door upstairs opened and Ruby appeared wrapped in a sheet and tiptoed to the staircase. Down in the lobby she saw Haddo putting on his coat.

"Have you paid?" she giggled.

Haddo looked up at her with anger. "What?"

"Have you paid?' she asked more tentatively.

He calmed. "My debts are settled like my mercy, which droppeth like the gentle rain from heaven."

He went out slamming the door behind him. Ruby came down the stairs. Drops of blood had stained the hallway carpet. She bent down to touch the stain. A drop fell on the back of her hand. She looked up; a drop of blood fell on her cheek. Horror and confusion – crucified to the roof beams Renee's body was stretched out. The nail through her right hand pinned a £50 note to her blood soaked palm. Ruby screamed.

Dead leaves blew across the manicured lawns as voices echoed through the cloisters. "The Egyptian Osiris, the Greek Dionysus and the Persian Mithras are all basically the same mystery religion," Mathers and Symons emerged from the archway and walked towards the iron gates. Symons continued, "the common details of all mystery religions you might recognize. The God is born on the 25th December from a virgin, he turns water into wine, he rides on a donkey, signifying his dominance over base carnal instincts, and is praised by people waving palms. He dies and goes into the underworld and after three days is resurrected. And the followers drink wine and take bread to celebrate the body and blood of the God."

"You've got to be joking."

"No. Osiris was the original and it was Pythagoras after studying in Egypt, who spread the rites and rituals throughout the Mediterranean."

"That's incredible."

"Pythagoras himself was supposed to have been born of a virgin and walked on water. And remember when Socrates was found guilty of following the Mystery Religion and not the official religion of Athens, he was fined thirty pieces of silver, which he refused on principal to pay and was therefore put to death. Then two hundred years later the thirty pieces of silver reappears in the Jesus story."

"But surely the early Christians would recognize all this."

"They did, in fact the church gave it a name. *'Diabolical mimicry'*. Using one of the most absurd arguments ever advanced, the Church Fathers accused the Devil of plagiarism by anticipation: of deviously copying the true story of Jesus before it had actually happened."

"That's ridiculous. Surely some people..."

Symons raised a hand as they came to the car park. "This is my car; can I give you a lift?"

"I think I'll walk."

"Then I'll see you first thing tomorrow and please bring the young lady, it's important."

"Right. See you tomorrow."

Symons drove off. Mathers watched the car disappear out through the arch. He followed like a man in a trance, his mind buzzing with disturbing information that he could not compartmentalize. He headed towards the town centre, back to his hotel to shower before going to pick up Leah. In the street ahead a cab came slowly towards him. He watched it approach then, just as it was about to pass, he jerked out a hand to stop it. A strange impulse had suddenly changed his plans. He searched his pockets and pulled out Victor's pamphlet and showed it to the driver. Mathers would witness Crowley's 'Rites of Eleusis'.

A distant bell chimed 10 o'clock as acolytes gathered outside the occult bookshop to attend the ceremony. Victor arrived and pushed through to the front where he was waved into the side door by the doorman. The rest of the crowd were kept out. A wrinkled sun tanned woman in her fifties complained. "Why is he allowed in? I've come all the way from Glastonbury."

"Sorry, strict instructions;" explained the doorman. "They'll be another ceremony in two weeks time."

Leah having trailed Victor arrived at the back of the crowd.

The woman at the front was still complaining. "You said only twelve."

"Twelve and the participants, he's one of the participants."

Leah looked at the poster in the window advertising the Ceremony. 'The Rites of Eleusis as performed by Aleister Crowley.'

'So this was where the twelve will witness the impossible,' she mused sceptically. 'As performed by' just means like the way he performed them, surely not the same as 'performed by Aleister Crowley.'

The chosen ones wound their way up the dimly lit stairs to the upper room. The Fat Lady led the way followed by a girl with a violin and the twelve witnesses. She knocked on the upstairs door. There was no answer.

The violin girl whispered "Go on, it's gone ten."

The Fat lady called through the door. "It's gone ten."

Victor came up from below to find Mathers was one of the those chosen.

"Mathers. I'm glad you came. It will change your life."

He carried on up past the Fat lady to the door and took hold of the handle.

"No, no one is supposed...oh."

The door opened.

The room was dark, flickeringly lit by a pair of candles on the altar. Incense smoke swirled around. In the middle of a chalked circle, crossed legged in the Sukhasana yoga pose sat Haddo dressed only in a pair of filthy underpants.

Crowley performs the Rites of Eleusis

His back was straight his feet locked up on his thighs and his eyes closed in meditation. Victor fell on his knees before him and studied the face closely.

"Crowley? I've got it."

Not a muscle of the Master moved in response.The chosen twelve who were surprised to hear Victor call him Crowley, whispered in anticipation as they took their seats. The girl with the violin stepped to the front and began to play.

Outside in the cold night Leah watched the disappointed acolytes slowly disperse till she was left alone. She walked across the road to see if she could see into the upstairs windows of the bookshop. As she stood there looking up, muffled music was coming from a Public House behind her. The Pub was closed but the lights were on and the curtains drawn for 'afters'.

Music is just sound. Sound produced by vibrations that are carried to the ear by changes in air pressure. But this particular vibration with its distinct rhythm, pitch, timbre and melody reached Leah's brain and triggered an instant flood of memories.

When she was a child her father played and sang along with this song. The vocalist 'Whispering' Paul McDowell sang.

'You, you're driving me crazy
What did I do, Oh what did I do?
My tears for you make everything hazy
Clouding the skies of bluuuee.'

She loved those lyrics and the comic way the Temperance Seven performed them. Her father bounced her on his knee to the trad. jazz rhythm, rocking his head as he sang. It had been her favourite memory of childhood; but then two years ago he was killed in Pakistan and the lyrics now came back to haunt her. Although she could only hear the muffled outline of the music, the words 'Whispering Paul' was singing were burnt into her memory.

You left me sad and lonely
Why did you leave me lonely
'Cause here's a heart that's only for
Nobody but you

Her mother had pleaded with him not to go.

'So the US are training and giving sophisticated weapons to the Mojahedin to fight the Russians. So what, who cares? That's not a story worth risking your life for.'

His belief that you should not bring modern weapons into tribal areas of the world was a passion. And not just weapons. Once he made her leap off the sofa, shouting at the TV. The apparently innocent program was showing a mild middle-aged English couple who used their savings to bring Jesus to Africa. They rode into a tribal village in their Range Rover and read stories from the Bible to the tribesmen. Daddy yelled at the screen. "You idiots! They're not impressed with your bloody Bible, they're fucking moved by your fucking Land Rover. You're not converting them to Jesus but to a Western style of life and the only way they're going to get it will destroy their own culture and bring them here."

Mother never felt passionate about this. Her concerns were more about the power and influence of the American secret services.

"The border area of Afghanistan is dangerous enough if you're an official journalist, but freelance?" she pleaded. "You're as likely to be bumped off by the CIA as a local tribesman. Look what they did in Chile."

The circumstances of his shooting were mysterious. Some claimed it was the British SAS or at least done with their collusion. Mother was broken with sadness but fierce with anger. 'How could he have done this to me and the child.'

Like the tragic clown the comic music continued to torture Leah.

'How true were the friends who were near me to cheer me
Believe, me they knew that you
Were the kind who would hurt me

Desert me, when I needed you
You, you're driving me crazy
What did I do to you?'

The tears rolled down her face.
'What did I do to you?'
How could music pain her so much.

What magic quality did it possess? Music was certainly able to cast spells on our psyche. To change our moods. To rouse us to war or reduce us to tears. And haunt us with nostalgic melancholia.

The music stopped and the moment's silence helped Leah to recover her composure. Then Chrissie Hynde began to sing her 70's hit.

Got brass in pocket
Got bottle I'm going to use it
Intention I feel inventive
Gonna make you, make you notice.

The tough sounding Chrissie brought strength back to Leah and she looked at the story developing across the road. What would daddy have done?

Gonna use my arms
Gonna use my legs
Gonna use my style
Gonna use my sidestep
Gonna use my fingers
Gonna use my, my, my imagination.

In the ceremony the violin weaved an eerie tune as the audience sat motionless in a circle of stillness. Mathers watched Haddo intently. Suddenly a small bell, like that used in church ceremonies, rang from behind the screen. They looked up as a girl, dressed in a black transparent robe came out from behind the screen. She had long black hair and carried a silver chalice. The violin began playing a winding melody. Gracefully the chalice girl crossed the room and approached the fat lady with her offering.

"Sip the wine that represents the Holy Blood."

The fat lady sat open mouthed then pulled her self together, took a sip and licked her lips. The girl moved to the man sitting next and repeated the offer.

"Sip the wine that represents the Holy Blood."

The man took the chalice but his eyes were fixed on the girl's pointed breast showing through the lace robe. He drank sloppily. Through all of this Victor peered at Haddo's face in the candlelight. Not a flicker.

Leah wiped her cheek, walked resolutely back across the road and slid down the darkened alley beside the shop. In the darkness she clattered straight into the dustbins. A lid rolled out into the street and circled noisily. She froze till it clanged to a stop. She looked around and noticed above her a window just out of reach. Standing on an upturned dustbin she pulled out her nail file and started to work the lock

Upstairs the girl offered Mathers the chalice.

"Sip the wine that represents the Holy Blood."

He took a sip, it was bitter. He spat the last traces into his hand and smelt it. She moved to Victor and repeated her lines.

"Sip the wine that represents the Holy Blood."

Keeping his eyes fixed on Haddo he took the chalice and sipped. The girl left the chalice with him and went to the altar and knelt. The sloppy man was performing his own private ceremony with his hand in his trouser pocket. Victor placed the chalice on the floor before Haddo and waited. The silence became oppressive, just the faint sound of Haddo's heartbeat. Then he spoke in a whisper.

"I call on Him with child devotion as a dewdrop woos the ocean."

Then silence: a silence that mocked all knowledge of existence as partial, incomplete, inadequate. What did it matter? Mathers himself suddenly could not even care if it all was unintelligible or without purpose. In fact the idea of having purpose at all was beneath contempt. He could not even keep track of time; a minute, 10 minutes, an hour? Counting things was so despicable; it's degrading and is the real difference between spirit and matter. Its bestial to be bound by numbers. He glanced behind him through the window at the impenetrable canopy of space, studded with secret and significant stars. Turning back, shadowy shapes flickered in the mysterious candlelight. The air was heavily sinister and he recognized the magnificent madness of the mind when stimulated by drugs. He was not hampered by knowledge but felt a release of the subconscious desires of the original animal and a yearning to do something demonic. Emotions kept reserved and hidden in the civilized man – emotions of life and death seen in full expression in the yells and screams of the tribal man.

Suddenly the tiny bell rang and the sound cut through. The girl at the altar rang it again but now the noise seemed to be lost in Haddo's heartbeat. The thumping pressed through the chest cavity. A woman held her hands over her ears in distress. Mathers stared in disbelief. The chest cavity was now bulging violently with the beat. Then a scraping sound as the chalice slid across the floor towards Haddo and came to rest before him. His eyes opened suddenly. He looked deep into Victor's eyes and spoke quietly.

"Behold where I have led thee. Thou hast become one with thy master's temple."

Everybody was leaning in to listen. Unaccountably Haddo slowly but surely appeared to levitate. Was he floating off the floor? Mathers could see beneath him. Suddenly the fat lady jumped to her feet and beat her breasts. "The beast. The beast. The beast..."

Leah forced the lock back and slid open the window. She clambered into the shop. The light from a fish tank illuminated the books, rings and hanging charms that cluttered the shop. Tinted crystals carved her image into hundreds of tiny Leahs as she moved through the shop, each one a perfectly crisp replica of the original.

Haddo looked towards Mathers "There is no part of thee that is not of the Gods."

The fat lady's sister, Stella, rocked on her chair, piss streaming from between her legs. A man in the audience went down on his knees and prayed anxiously. The fat lady was tearing at her clothes. A woman sobbed uncontrollably. Mathers noticed the room in the mirror. The reflection of Haddo was odd; he had not levitated but was in the circle surrounded by an aura of electric blue light.

Leah could hear the noise from the upstairs room. She moved into the light from a fish tank where guppies glided through the cavernous eye sockets of a human skull, past a poster for Crowley's tarot cards and up the cobwebbed staircase. Half way up, the landing joined the main staircase to the upper room. As she stepped out the upstairs door suddenly opened. She dived back into the shadows of the landing.

Above Haddo dragged Victor out of the ceremonial room and locked the door behind him. Victor stood blinking in the gloom.

Haddo smiled smugly, "Let the Holy Ghost descend on our disciples."

"Aren't we staying?" asked Victor.

"The twelve apostles will announce my resurrection," declared Haddo as he pushed Victor down the stairs. "We must prepare for the scarlet bride."

Leah pulled in tight as the footsteps approached down the stairs and passed within touching distance. Suddenly Haddo stopped and looked up, his nostrils flared like an animal sensing the air. Leah stood frozen in the shadows: she felt her left cheek twitch uncontrollably. His head began to turn towards her when suddenly there was a ring from the bell upstairs and a voice yelled 'Crowley!

CROWLEY'. Haddo smiled contentedly and continued down the stairs. Leah slowly let out her breath as she heard the door below bang shut. She climbed the stairs to the upper door and tried the handle. It was locked tight. She turned and ran down the stairs.

At the bottom she carefully opened the door and peered out to check the road was clear then stepped into the empty street. At the far end, turning into the yellow, sodium-lit, main road she saw the bulky Haddo and his accompanying cockroach, Victor. She was about to follow when a car kerb-crawled up to her. She walked quicker but the car responded keeping abreast of her. There was a tapping on the windscreen. She didn't look but just turned – pretending to go back the other way. The car slowed then stopped but the road was too narrow for it to turn. Leah carried on past the bookshop till the car finally revved up and sped away in search of another victim. Leah turned and seeing the coast was clear hurriedly gave chase.

Haddo and Victor walked along the High Street towards the Green Man public house. A couple of alchies were heaped on the corner reeking fumes of alcohol into the night air. One staggered to his feet as they approached and thrust out a hand.

"Can you spare some change?"

Haddo shoved the alchie away with his stick and carried on. The alchie tripped over the feet of his friend and crashed to the ground.

"Bastard! Your time will come."

Haddo stopped instantly. Victor turned to see Haddo raise his stick and bring it down on the man's skull. Crack! Haddo rained blows on the man.

"Time! TIME! TIME! I'll give you time!"

Victor was horrified. He grabbed Haddo's arm.

"Stop! Stop, you'll kill him."

Haddo swung from the bloody mess to Victor, his eyes red with vengeance and the stick raised above his head ready to strike. Victor cowered, lifting an arm in defence. Haddo looked into Victor's frightened eyes. A smile spread across his face and slowly he lowered the stick. He patted Victor's cheek.

"A mere scapegoat."

Haddo turned and walked away. Victor looked from the battered body to Haddo striding off. Victor knew full well the meaning but the implications were troubling. A 'scapegoat' was used as a substitute for human sacrifice. In the Bible the irrationally jealous God demands Abraham to sacrifice his only son, Isaac. Bound and stretched out on the altar, with the knife poised to strike, God spares the boy at the last minute and supplies a *scapegoat* as a substitute for the human sacrifice of Isaac.

'Is Haddo capable....?' For a moment Victor stood there unable to consider that possibility. Looking down at the bloody mess he twiddled his hair and scratched his punctured arm. The drugs were wearing off and reality was rearing its ugly head. His God like devotion was reducing to pained emptiness, the deep emptiness that signifies the first pangs of withdrawal. Defeated he turned and followed the bulky Haddo on his quest for the scarlet bride.

Pandemonium erupted in the upstairs room. A man was standing speaking in tongues. Another writhed on the floor. One man stood up and laughed hysterically as he pissed on the Fat lady who orgasmically washed herself in the golden spray. Suddenly a dreadful scream cut over the rest. Everybody froze. The girl with the violin was pointing.

"I see him....I see him."

An illusion created by joint hysteria began to develop vaguely through the wreathed smoke. Rising with each mass of inhaled air, the amorphous, quite horrifying figure of the Great Beast... CHORONZON.

Flames burst around him.

Leah searched ahead through the sodium light for Haddo and Victor.

Before her a ragged shape was huddled in the road. As she neared she realized it was a tattered man crouched over rocking to helpless sobs. She stopped and bent over placing a hand on his shoulder.

"Are you all right?"

He looked up his dirty face streaked in tears and raised a pointing finger

"He did it."

Leah looked up the road at the disappearing figures then down at the man whose raised arm had revealed the bloody, battered body of his alchie friend.

"Oh my God!" Leah reeled at the clotted horror.

The plump hand pushed the button and the hall lights came on illuminating the staircase to Leah's apartment. Haddo panted as he climbed up to the third floor. He rang the door bell and turned to see Victor following pathetically. Pityingly, Haddo reached in his pocket and handed over something in a small plastic bag. Victor grabbed it hungrily as the door opened.

Rose eyed them warily. "Can I help you?"

Haddo smiled. "Is this not the residence of Leah with the red hair?"

"She's out."

"How unfortunate. Maybe, Victor, we'll see if they will still serve us in the Green Man, unless we could impose on you to wait?"

Rose was unsure. "At this hour there's a good chance she won't be back. She's with a friend."

"Ah. Then could you tell her Mr. Crowley called."

"Yes okay."

"You wont forget the name will you. Crowley: Mr. Crowley.

"No, Mr Crowley."

"Good, thank you." He was about to turn then stopped. "Oh, perhaps you can give her this for me."

He held up a small silver chain with a charm in the form of a Masonic setsquare. She looked at it and smiled, the silver charm turned slowly catching the light and reflecting it into her brown eyes.

"It's rather precious – you won't misplace it, will you?"

Her unblinking eyes watched the charm as she spoke.

"No, Mr Crowley."

Slowly the set square turned round and round and round. Gleaming, reflecting, brightening - then suddenly the timer button clicked and the stair lights went out.

The windows cracked in the scorching heat releasing the billowing flames into the night. The bookshop was ablaze. Below, Mathers came stumbling out, coughing the smoke from his lungs. He rubbed his eyes and took deep breaths trying to clear his head. Above there was a sudden crash. Mathers looked up. A body came smashing out headfirst from the flaming upstairs window. It came out with such force that it traveled through the air coming down with a thump in the road. Shocked, Mathers staggered over and turned the face; blood was oozing from the fat lady's ear and mouth.

Rose removed her t-shirt and stood in her bra. Haddo sat in a chair watching dispassionately. He leaned across and swivelled the table lamp onto her and spoke in a calm voice. "That's right, very good. Now the bra."

Rose obeyed slipping off the bra.

Haddo smiled, "It's warm on the beach, why not enjoy the sun and remove your skirt. Don't you agree my dear?"

"Yes," said Rose, mesmerized.

She removed her skirt. Victor watched excitedly. Haddo looked at his eager eyes.

"What a pleasant figure the young lady has, Victor?"

Victor nodded in agreement. Haddo turned back to Rose.

"You must free yourself from those restricting knickers, my dear."

Rose was unsure. "Am I allowed?"

"Of course, my lovely, clothes are a terrible burden. "

She removed her knickers and stood there naked. Haddo held

up the small silver chain with the Masonic setsquare. She looked at it and smiled.

"Here my dear, take this as a present and lie down on the couch. Doctor Victor is going to give you a thorough examination."

She lay on the couch and Haddo turned to Victor.

"You'll need your instruments doctor. Get that bottle."

Hoses snaked from the fire engines across the pavement to the blazing bookshop. Police cars and ambulances flashed blue and amber. Mathers was sitting dazed on the kerb as firemen fired water into the inferno. Others with breathing apparatus crashed into the doorway to rescue the screaming acolytes in the upper floor.

Leah pushed the hall button lighting the stairs and trudged wearily up to her apartment. Her face and hands had streaks of blood. As she turned on the landing she noticed above her the door to her apartment was wide open. Confused she took the last flight till she was standing at the open door. She looked about, leaned in and switched on the light. She entered cautiously, closing the door behind her. In the lounge a chair was lying upturned on the floor. She lifted it up then noticed a syringe under the table. She picked it up and looked at it uncomprehendingly. Perhaps some addicts had broken in. She glanced around but could see nothing missing. She went to her bedroom and opened the door. It all looked normal. She tried Rose's bedroom. That was also empty. She heard the sound of running water from the bathroom. Leah went to the door and knocked gently. "Rose?"

Just the sound of running water. She called again but there was still no response. Leah tried the handle and the door opened. In the steamed up room, Rose was standing in the bathtub, her face a frozen mask, as the boiling water ran round her feet. She wore just a T-shirt, the rest of her clothes were in the tub.

"Rose, what are you doing?"

Rose did not answer. Leah turned off the taps and tried to fish the clothes out of the scalding water.

"How can you stand it?"

Rose answered flatly. "It's clean."

Leah noticed blood dripping from Rose's hand.

"Are you hurt?"

Leah unclenched the fist to find the Masonic charm cut into the hand.

"My God, what's happened here?"

A fine mist was blown from the jets of saving water onto the injured who were huddled away in blankets. As they were loaded into the ambulances, acolytes hysterically tried to relate their story to the police.

"He was there. Aleister Crowley, alive."

"It was the beast," added a woman. "Flames from it's…it's….".

"Yes, yes." Said the policeman maintaining a formal pose. "I'll take a full statement at the hospital."

He closed the ambulance door, turned to his colleague and shook his head. "Weekend warlocks probably left the gas on."

Leah looked down at Rose now asleep in her bed. She searched the troubled face for explanation. After a moment she switched off the light and went into the darkened lounge and flopped exhausted onto the armchair. She tried to comprehend the day's events but was soon fast asleep.

Her head lay heavy to one side when a gentle knock on the apartment door stirred her. She did not wake though and the door handle gently turned. The door creaked as it slowly opened, Leah's eyes rolled beneath the lids then blinked open. A black, silhouetted figure stood in the doorway. Her eyes widened as the lights came on.

"Hi," said Mathers.

"Oh God, it's you. You startled me."

"What are you doing sitting in the dark?"

"There's been some trouble with Rose."

"What?" Mathers saw the blood streaks on her face. "What's that?"

"Nothing, she won't say. She won't have a doctor or anything."

"I've got to show you this, look, Symons gave it to me."

He unfolded a photocopy and passed it over. Leah started to read.

"It's a copy of a letter Crowley wrote to Parsons in 1947. Look at the handwriting."

She looked back at the writing. Mathers picked up Crowley's book from the table, and opened the back page at the inscription. She compared the handwriting – it was the same.

"And this wasn't written in 1947, this edition was published in '67."

"Who are you saying wrote this? Haddo?"

"Crowley."

"You don't believe that?"

"There is no scientific principle that says it's impossible. We can pass the memory of one computer to another with a simple floppy disk."

"But you can't think..."

"Plenty do. Reincarnation is basic to many religions."

"So are delusions of grandeur. Look, tomorrow I'll confront Haddo with it."

"No, no don't do that," said Mathers fearfully.

"Why not?"

"Leah, I went to the ceremony and.. "

"I was there – outside. What happened?"

"I'm not sure, he might have drugged us. But...."

Suddenly he was silenced by a piercing yell.

'AAAAYYEE DON'T TOUCH ME! Don't touch me!'

Leah jumped to her feet and hurried to Rose's bedroom. Rose struggled in sleep against an invisible foe. Leah placed a calming hand on her forehead. "It's okay, its okay." Rose settled back soaked in sweat. Leah wiped her brow, straightened the bedclothes and sat with her till she was sure sleep had overcome her torments. Finally she got up and gently closed the door. In the dark, Rose sniffed the air like an animal, her face contorted.

The moon escaped from behind the clouds and tried to illuminate but the streetlights overpowered the effect. In fact sleeping Cambridge twinkled up more than the stars twinkled down.

The glow from the streetlights also penetrated through the window of Leah's bedroom. Her head arched up into the light, her eyes tight shut as time ceased all meaning. The two activities that freeze the biological clock are intense sex and intense fear. This night Mathers had experienced both. He turned and kissed her.

"Be careful," he whispered. "Symons said Crowley could always spot a weakness and exploit it."

Leah smiled sarcastically. "Are you saying I'm not perfect?"

Mathers was not joking, "Please promise me you won't go."

She kissed him without answering.

CHAPTER 4

DAY FOUR

Friday 8th January

The morning star, Venus, rose on the horizon but it was weirdly bright. All occult philosophy was based in some way on the movement of the planets with Venus at its heart. The magical fact that over its eight year cycle Venus traced a five pointed star in the sky led to that image being perched in high relief on the massive Central Masonic Temple in London's Great Queen Street. The sages of old could keep an accurate calendar while solar and moon calendars, as used in Rome were progressively faulty. And Venus' forty year cycle played an important part in Biblical events, where over a hundred references are made to the period, 40 years. But this night was something very different, something very rare and portentous. For this night Venus appeared extremely bright due to the rare conjunction between itself and the planet named after the winged messenger, Mercury. Who nowadays had the ancient knowledge to understand the auspicious significance of this conjugation?

Below in the darkness of Leah's bedroom the clock glowed 4.40. Mathers half woke from his dreams as he heard the sound of a door. He rolled over but did not notice that Leah had gone but returned to a deep sleep. Dangerous and disturbing dreams invaded his subconscious.

Between the terraced houses the road was dark but as Leah cycled out over the railway bridge the sky opened up and she became aware of the beautiful bright star in the East. She had no idea of the grave significance this luminance had to the ancients. The Venus conjunction with Mercury could be calculated back to have occurred at many major biblical events, where it was called the 'Light from the Divine Shekinah'. To the ancient Jewish sect, the Essenes, the Divine Shekinah would signal the birth of the Messiah and one did occur over Jerusalem in 7 AD. To the Magi, who studied the heavens, the Shekinah would predict the future birth of twins. Twins? Perhaps both the Essenes and the Zoroastrian Magi were right. Perhaps the Messiah and the twins *were* born on the same night. Is there any evidence for twins? The Hebrew word for twin is Thomas and in the Bible, *(John 11 v16)* the Disciple Thomas is called Thomas Didymus. Didymus is the Greek word for twin so Thomas Dydimus translates as twin twin?? The identity of this twin is revealed in the Bible when he is called Judas Thomas - Judas the Twin. And Mark 6:3 reveals the names of Jesus four brothers as James, Joses, Simon and Judas. Perhaps the three Zoroastrian Magi came to visit the expected arrival of the great twins of their religion.

But slowly the beautiful light from the divine Shekenah was wiped from the sky by the rays of the rising sun as it crept over the dark spires of Cambridge. One lone window of the sombre University building was lit by the warmth of an electric light; the window of the student Granta office.

There, Leah sat hunched over her computer typing quickly with an obsessive urgency. A beam from the rising sun fell on to the screen and she pulled the curtain and continued typing the extraordinary unfolding story of the transformation of Dr. Oliver Haddo.

In the upstairs bedroom of the old Victorian house on the corner of Oak Street Oliver Haddo's eyes suddenly opened wide. A smile broke across his face as the concentrating thoughts of the red haired beauty traveled to him. He leapt from the bed.

In the lounge Victor was curled up on a sofa with a blanket half off him. He looked a mess. His brain in half sleep was reducing mankind to its bare essentials, an environment for DNA. The spiralling complex chemical, Desoxyribo Nucleic Acid had the capability not only of reproducing itself but also to mutate. With these abilities this molecule began life on this planet, as we know it. Victor dreamed of it surviving over a million years in the seas and continuing to build around itself a more and more protective structure to maintain a constant favourable environment. First with proteins and protoplasms, forming simple Protozoans. Then building complex multi-cellular creatures and plants to transport it out of the sea and onto the land. The most successful environment DNA had created for itself was man, or was it? Maybe the insect is more.... A hand shook him into life.

"Victor. Get up." demanded Haddo

Victor groaned into life, "What is it?"

"She's thinking about me."

"What time is it?"

"Idiot!" snapped Haddo. "The innocent and the beautiful have no enemy but time. Get up - she awaits my call."

He left the room urgently. Victor looked frightened.

Granta's editor, Ashby came down the corridor carrying a pile of files and whistling the tune Jeanne Moreau sang in 'Jules et Jim' which had been shown at the movie club the night before. The catchy little tune came to an abrupt halt as he entered the Granta office to find Leah sitting at the computer typing.

"What's this - can't sleep?" he said as he dumped the files on the table.

"I've got a new front page," announced Leah enthusiastically.

Ashby was dismayed. "Do me a favour, your story's already front page and we're out tonight."

"Everything's changed. Don't worry, I've laid it out."

"Let's have a look," he said with a distinct lack of enthusiasm.

She got up to let him sit at the computer and he began to read.

Unlike the rest of the dishevelled house Haddo's library was cleared and empty but for a table laid out as an altar. The windows had been taped up with pieces of cardboard with holes like the night sky punched through. The streams of light from the morning sun speckled Haddo's face as he knelt at the altar staring at a paper on which was scrawled two lines of runic writing. Below the runic letters was written, '*the hidden truth*'.

Behind, in a chalked circle, Victor stood nervously reading from the 'Book of the Law'.

"Pale or purple, veiled or voluptuous, thou who aren't all pleasure of the innermost sense, desire you."

Haddo closed his eyes. "Now the spell that will bring her to me, get my stick."

Victor looked up uncomprehendingly.

"Victor! GET MY STICK!"

Victor jumped and went to where Haddo pointed to his walking stick. He brought it to the altar and offered it to Haddo.

"You damn fool," spat Haddo pulling down his pants.

Victor looked confused. Haddo bent his face to the altar.

"Beat at the gate that let my folly in."

Victor was stuck in amazement.

"My scarlet woman waits. Strike."

Victor raised the stick, paused then came down on Haddo's naked rear.

"Harder! Harder!"

Victor beat down again. Thwack! Haddo breathed heavily, his body moved rhythmically as he masturbated. Thwack!

"And read," he hissed.

Victor opened the book in one hand.

"Put on the wings;" Thwack! "And arouse the coiled splendour within you; come unto me!" Thwack!

Haddo panted, "She will come. She will come. She will come. Come! Come! Come!"

Haddo was coming.

Then, "AAAahhhhh."

He grabbed the paper and ejaculated onto the runic letters.

Ashby was reading from the computer, shaking his head in disbelief and occasionally snorting with a huff at the unfolding events. Suddenly the fax came to life. He lent across to see the cover page.

"It's for you."

Leah went over to the fax machine and looked. It buzzed and slid out the page of Haddo's runic writing with '*the hidden truth*'. Leah looked at it uncomprehendingly as it landed in the tray. She picked it up then dropped it suddenly, her hand covered in slime.

"Err God! There's something wrong with this machine. It's leaking ink... or.. solvent..." she smelt her hand " – or something."

The ceremonial bell rang from behind the screen. The silver chalice came from the shadows. Leah, dressed in the black see through robe carried it to Victor and placed it on his lips.

"Sip the wine that represents the Holy Blood." As Victor took a sip, Haddo suddenly loomed behind her. He kissed her on the back of the neck and she arched back in pleasure. She closed her eyes passionately as his hands reached round and squeezed her breasts.

Mather's eyes rolled behind the closed eyelids, the telltale sign of R.E.M. sleep that signifies the last dream before morning. The disturbed, jealous feelings of the dream woke him suddenly but his gummed up eyes failed to open.

"Leah?" he whispered as he wiped his eyes and looked across the bed. He sat up anxiously as he realized she was not there, the dream's feelings of loss, pain and distress transferred to a fearful daytime reality. There was a note on her pillow. He picked it up and tried to focus on the writing,

'Gone to College. Help yourself to breakfast. See you later. Love Leah.'

He rolled back onto the pillow and lay there separating dreams from reality with the depressing knot in his stomach the prevailing emotion. Suddenly his eyes focused and he leapt to his feet and dressed.

In Haddo's house, Victor came sneaking down the stairs and recovered the cracked phone from the floor and put it back on the table. He picked up the receiver and checked for the tone and dialled.

The phone rang incessantly. Mathers finally picked it up

"Leah Robinson?" asked Victor.

"She's not here. Victor is that you?"

"Mathers? What are you doing there?"

"Where's Leah?" asked Mathers urgently.

Victor looked behind him in fear then whispered into the phone.

"Mathers, you fool. There's no way to stop him."

Suddenly Haddo grabbed the phone from Victor who cowered back into the corner

Haddo ignored him and talked to Mathers.

"To sleep perchance to dream, aye there's the rub."

"Haddo?"

"No, Aleister Crowley esquire."

"Who do you think you're fooling?"

"Who do I think I'm fooling? The meek. Yes the meek," smiled Haddo.

"Nothing happened in the suit that wasn't just in your head."

"You tremble with fear because of what – a dream, a fantasy? Something just in your head."

"Where is she?"

"Lust does not confer propriety. Leah is a free spirit – free to choose between common lust or the gift of immortality."

"So long as she's free to choose what she wants."

"So long as she doesn't choose me. Am I right, Dr. Mathers?"

"What are you after?"

"Am I right? I am right aren't I?"

"What do you want from her?"

"To draw the eternal soul from the bloody womb of time."

Mathers was silent.

Haddo continued. "Do you understand me?"

"No. But I know where to come if anything happens to her."

"It's not where to come, but when."

Haddo burst out laughing. Mathers slammed down the phone.

Without looking, Haddo stretched his hand back with the phone towards Victor who trembled as he took it and returned it to its cradle.

"I thought I would ring her," stammered Victor.

"She will come of her own free will," said Haddo as he walked up two steps of the stairs then turned and looked at Victor, benevolently.

"Victor, kiss me."

Victor looked up at him.

"Betrayer! I said kiss me."

Victor meekly stepped up and kissed Haddo on the cheek.

"Thank you, Victor. This was done to fulfil the prophecies. Those who have understanding thank you."

Mathers stared for a moment at the phone worrying about Haddo's meaning. Then suddenly a frightful scream wrenched him round. Rose stood in the kitchen doorway screaming with fear of him

Ashby scrolled down the article. Leah watched him, impatient for his final verdict. Jones arrived at the door with the morning edition of the Cambridge Chronicle.

"Morning all."

Leah hushed him.

"Sorry I spoke."

Leah took him to one side and whispered so as not to disturb Ashby. "You do ancient Greek what's Gematria?"

"In Greek and the same in Hebrew each letter also is a number so words could add up to numbers."

Leah puzzled, "Is that it?"

"It's a little more complicated. You want to see some of the magic of numbers? Who was the worst person of the twentieth century?"

Leah thought, "Hitler."

Jones picked up a pencil and wrote 'HITLER' on the back of an envelope.

"A beast, right? Well suppose our alphabet was numbered so that A is 100, B is 101, and C is 102 and so on. Get it?"

"Yes."

Jones wrote the number equivalent under the name HITLER running the alphabet on his fingers to get the numbers.

H=107
I =108
T=119
L=111
E=104
R=117

"Add it up and you get Hitler's geometric number."

He wrote the additions below each column and announced.

"Six hundred and sixty six! The number of the beast. Neat, aye? That's powerful magic."

"Wait, let me see that," Leah grabbed the pen and did the summation herself. "Six… six… six. That's weird."

At that moment Ashby pushed his chair back from the computer, leant back and shook his head. "We can't print this."

"Why not?" asked Leah, utterly disappointed at the lack of enthusiasm she felt her work deserved.

"First they'll think we've all gone bloody mad and second we'd be sued for libel."

"I swear every word is true. You were at the lecture, you saw him."

"It is sensational stuff," mused Ashby hesitantly.

"Isn't it just," said Leah pleased at the recognition. 'The ceremony was something else."

But still Ashby was unsure. "Unfortunately it reads more like a horror novel than a piece of journalism. I don't know."

Leah looked disheartened. Jones held up the front page of his newspaper. "You're not talking about this are you?"

The headline shook Ashby.

'FOUR KILLED IN CAMBRIDGE OCCULT CEREMONY'.

Ashby read on, 'Survivors claim to have seen the resurrected body of their occult leader Aleister Crowley.'

"God! You think..?" Ashby queried.

"Yes. They've got the results but we've got the whole weird explanation."

"The explanation," mused Ashby. "Okay we're going to press but we might just be crucified for this."

"Let's have a gander," said Jones sitting down at the computer.

Ashby leaned over him, "This is going to hit the Nationals," he enthused. "Leah is going to…."

He looked round to see Leah on her way out of the door.

"Hey, where the hell are you going?"

She held up her camera.

"You said you wanted a photo of Crowley didn't you?"

Leah closed the door and left. Ashby turned round to Jones then suddenly turned back to the door.

"Crowley? Crowley? It's Haddo."

In the laboratory Mathers stood at the observation window in the control room looking down at the glass room. He knew behind the glass in the dark, the suit was in there waiting. Nothing made much sense. He pulled out his notebook with the equations and tried to do some calculations but found himself looking at his watch incessantly. He gave up and wandered aimlessly to the Z93 and fired it up. Glancing round the lab he saw on the shelf a file labelled 'Victor Neuman'. He took it down and glanced through articles cut from magazines. He read one.

Ancient Stone Technology

by Will Hart

There are many more significant and pressing questions about human history and the archaeological ruins that litter the planet than have or are being asked. Unfortunately, established scientists do not care or dare to address these issues. This is becoming critical because they are promulgating and protecting false theories and speculations, which could well bury the truth within a generation or two.

It is utterly absurd to claim that the ancients used primitive tools, method and knowledge to produce very sophisticated results that we would have difficulty reproducing today with modern technology

In fact, such tests have been attempted in Egypt several times with disastrous results. Various teams have tried to duplicate what Egyptologists have claimed were the tools and methods at the ancient's disposal without success. The most recent was an effort sponsored by NOVA, filmed and supervized by Mark Lerhner and other prominent Egyptologists. They utterly failed to quarry a rather small 35-ton block of stone intended to be used as an obelisk. The dolerite hammer they say the Egyptian quarry workers used could not do the job. They failed to move the obelisk after calling in a bulldozer to quarry it. They had a truck transport it instead.

Mathers sat trying to get into Victor's mind-set. He turned over another page.

FRED CRISMAN FLYING SAUCERS, THE ASSASSINATION OF PRESIDENT KENNEDY

Michael Riconosciuto was a Wackenhut – CIA employee who said that he had attempted to get a whole helicopter full of documents and evidence detailing illegal biogenetic activities and non-Congressionally sanctioned projects involving 'illegal aliens' out of the Nevada Test Site. The chopper was blown out of the sky, killing all five personnel on board. Michael's father happened to be Marshall Riconosciuto, a fascist and a supporter of Adolph Hitler who was a very close friend of FRED L. CRISMAN. CRISMAN was involved in the Maurey Island incident – the first recorded 'UFO' sighting in 1947 near Tacoma, Washington,' which researcher Anthony Kimory believes involved the test-flight of hybrid CIA–Nazi aerial disks. There are several sources which claim that by the early 1940's the Nazi's had succeeded in test-flying wing-less lenticular craft powered by rotary…

Mathers turned to the next page.

NAVAL INTELLIGENCE and L. RON HUBBARD

The early exploits of L. Ron Hubbard the writer of science fiction and leader of the Scientology movement have been revealed in a series of letters between Jack Parsons the rocket propulsion expert and Aleister Crowley the British occult leader.

L. Ron Hubbard it appears participated with Parsons in Crowley's weird sexual rituals. Leaders of the Scientology movement explained away the embarrassing revelations saying that Hubbard was working for Naval Intelligence and in that capacity keeping an eye on Parsons.

The claims at first sight appear unlikely but certain characteristics in the weird way US Naval Intelligence ran may give credence to the story.

1. L. RON HUBBARD wrote science fiction, was involved

in occult ceremonies and started a semi religious cult. Claimed to be Naval Intelligence.

2. FRED L. CRISMAN claimed to have witnessed the first Flying Saucer incident at Maurey Island as a Naval Captain. Wrote a science fiction story. Involved in Kennedy Assassination. As a Naval Captain if he were in intelligence it would have been Naval Intelligence.

3. GUY BANNISTER. Associate of Fred L Crisman. Wrote a science fiction story. Killed supposedly because he knew too much about the Kennedy Assassination. Was in Naval Intelligence.

4. LEE HARVEY OSWALD. Alleged killer of Kennedy. Served as a Marine. Gave out fake pro Castro pamphlets outside offices of Naval Intelligence in Miami. Remembered by a waitress as a customer in Jack Ruby's club having been picked out to perform by a Stage Hypnotist. If he was a susceptible subject for hypnosis, then as a Marine could have been used as patsy by Naval Intelligence.

5. PHILADELPHIA EXPERIMENT. Naval intelligence would have…

Mathers gave up. It was all too weird. He sat there in silence thinking about Victor. After a moment he turned to the Z93 and typed in 'BAPHOMET'. He let the computer flash through Victor's information watching it dispassionately. Half way through he picked up the phone and got through to the operator.

"Hi, can you put me through to the student newspaper office, Granta?"

The phone rang and Ashby picked it up. It was Mathers asking for Leah.

"Leah? Yes left about nine," replied Ashby. "No she never said...."

"Class? Hang on I'll ask." Ashby turned to Jones. "What time's your first class?"

"Ten in the Cromwell room," said Jones without looking up from the newspaper.

Ashby repeated the information to Mathers. "Ten in the Cromwell room."

Jones leant over and pointed to a small headline in the centre of the Cambridge Chronicle. Ashby glanced as he listened on the phone.

'MASSAGE PARLOUR ATROCITY' Ashby hardly heard Mathers' questions on the phone as he read on. 'Police search for a Mr Crowley after the gruesome murder of Manageress Renee Huston.'

His face paled as he answered Mathers question distractedly.

"Yes, yes. I'm concerned too. Goodbye."

Ashby abruptly put the phone down and took the paper from Jones and read on with a growing trepidation.

Mathers heard the phone go dead. He was disturbed by Ashby's hesitant voice and sudden dismissal. He looked at his watch – 9.50. He grabbed his coat and headed out.

Chattering students filed into the Cromwell Room. Mathers watched and waited. Finally the lecturer appeared, went in and closed the door. Mathers looked through the window in the door at the faces. There was no sign of Leah; he was now seriously concerned.

The storm clouds gathered over the house on the corner of Oak Street. Standing on the opposite side of the road Leah took out the Polaroid camera and shot a photo of the house. It discharged the blank sheet with a whirr. She waved the Polaroid till it revealed the image of the sombre dwelling then blow dried it and slipped it in her back pocket.

Mathers knocked on the door. After a moment a dishevelled

Symons appeared in his dressing gown.

"Well good morning. Do come in. "

Symons stooped down creakily and picked up the morning newspaper.

"I'm sorry, I'm not dressed yet. I worked quite late on the information."

As he straightened he saw Mathers' worried face.

"Is something wrong?"

"I can't find Leah," replied Mathers.

"Oh dear, I did ask you to bring her."

"Why? What is it?"

"Well," Symons paused for a moment as he tried to find a way to express his concerns. "It's her hair."

"Her hair?"

"Let me show you something."

Symons led Mathers through to the hall, which was rich with paintings. He pointed out one. "You see that Raphael. And the Bellini there. And that one. They are all paintings of the Magdalene. Painted centuries apart but do you notice anything similar.

RAPHAEL MAGDELENE ROSSETTI

Mathers looked, "They all wear red."

"Anything else?"

Mathers shook his head.

Symons indicated another one, "It's more obvious in that Rossetti."

It suddenly dawned on Mathers. "They all have red hair."

Symons nodded, "The strong occult power of the scarlet woman is something Crowley always stressed."

Leah's red hair turned as she watched a florist's van pull up outside the house in Oak Street. She lit a cigarette as the van driver took a bouquet of flowers over to Haddo's porch. He rang the bell but there was no answer. He looked around and then placed them behind an ornamental vase and drove off. Leah waited. Nothing. She stubbed out her cigarette and crossed the road to the porch and looked behind the vase at the flowers. There was a card attached. *'The secret truth will be revealed to those who seek and to the blessed Hierodules will be revealed the written language of the Ten Commandments.'* Leah was shocked. That was her fathers point – the language of the Ten Commandments. She read it again then glanced around to see if somebody was playing a sick joke. Nobody appeared to be watching but the feeling of being observed never left her. She turned back to the door took a deep breath and rang the bell. There was no answer. Determined she raised the knocker but the door swung slightly open. She pushed it further. Inside the darkened hallway was a shambles. All the way up the stairs were piles of books. She rung the bell again and called in.

'Hello!"

There was still no answer.

"Anyone there?"

Leah looked round then stepped inside the gloom.

She moved towards the stairs and raised the Polaroid camera and took a photo of the scene. As the camera flashed the door closed with a bang. Startled her heart raced uncontrollably, the primitive reaction in preparation for fight or flight. Looking round and finding no one she regained her composure, pulled the photo out of the camera and waited till it developed. She could see into the door of the first room. There was nothing but a small table in the centre with a half finished game of chess. She went over waving the processing

Polaroid to dry the image before slipping it with the other into her back pocket. She studied the chessboard for a moment then moved the black bishop to take the white queen. "Mate in one."

Symons brought a pot of tea into the gloomy study and poured out a cup each. Mathers took a sip.

"Do you think Haddo is playing out the role?" asked Mathers. "Or is there something else going on here?"

Symons poured the tea. "How can we tell the difference? Haddo knew everything about Crowley; he'd read all his books. So being possessed by the idea of Crowley would not manifest itself any differently from actually being possessed by Crowley."

The metallic voice came from behind Mathers.

"That's nonsense, Symons."

Startled Mathers turned to see someone sitting silhouetted through the open door to the adjoining room.

Symons smiled. "Sorry did we startle you? I'd like you to meet a friend. Mathers, this is Alex."

Mathers got up. Alex wheeled electronically forward. The exuberant student who once stole Crowley's watch back in 1947 was now a face, frozen in a twisted grimace. Saliva dribbled down. He spoke through an amplifier with the same computer generated voice as Stephen Hawking.

"Pleased to meet you Mathers."

"Alex is in your field, theoretical physics. I'm afraid he suffered a stroke. His right side is paralyzed."

The metallic voice added dispassionately. *"He cursed me."*

Symons quickly interjects. "We can't say that for sure, Alex."

Leah came out of Haddo's study carrying the white queen and went warily up the stairs past a rolled up carpet. The hair on the back of her neck began to tingle as the follicular muscles raised them like a cat's. On the landing outside the library door was a large wall clock with no hands. She went into the Library. All the books were gone. The card-boarded windows with their fissures that allowed the streams of light to speckle the chalk circle drawn on the floor and a triangle at the base of the small altar. Between the candles on the altar was the paper with the original runic writing, it had dried wrinkly and next to it a small cat was crucified cruelly on a miniature cross. Leah put the white queen on the altar and raised the Polaroid camera to take another photo. There was a click but no flash. She banged the side of the camera and tried the button again. The camera flashed at the wall. She let the wasted film whirr onto the floor then carefully framed the altar in the camera and squeezed the button again. This time it flashed and out whirred the photo. Suddenly the noise of the front door latch startled her. Then she heard the front door close and voices approach up the stairs. Leah looked round for somewhere to hide. The library door slowly opened and Haddo and Victor entered.

Symons listened sympathetically to Mathers.

"She was at the student newspaper office – left about half an hour ago – hopefully to go home."

"*Ron Hubbard,*" Alex' mechanical voice announced.

"What's that?" asked Mathers.

"*L. Ron Hubbard and Jack Parsons,*" repeated Alex.

"Alex has a theory," expanded Symons. "He's sure you carried something from Cal Tech.

Alex writhed as he struggled to produce his mechanical voice. "*As Crowley died, Jack Parsons and Ron Hubbard were performing Crowley's ritual to produce an elemental.*"

"A moonchild," added Symons. "Crowley was furious. That was the copy of the letter I gave you. Alex believes you brought something, perhaps a virus from Cal Tech and Victor recombined it with Crowley."

"*A moment in time when all conditions entwine,*" toned the mechanical voice.

"Do you believe in destiny?" asked Symons.

But Mathers was distracted. "Can I just try calling Leah's apartment?"

"I'm sorry." apologized Symons. "Here we are theorizing when – yes, of course, by all means."

Mathers picked up the phone and dialled.

"Yes, maybe she's gone home," reassured Symons but then behind Mathers back he looked at Alex and shook his head despairingly.

The phone rang in Leah's apartment. A man's hand picked up the receiver and a gruff voice answered, "Can I help you?"

Mathers was startled, "Hello, who's that....

Symons and Alex watched Mathers as blood drained from his face.

"What? Joshua Mathers....Yes...."

Symons worst fears were etched on his face.

"She's what? – How? – I'm coming now."

Mathers slammed down the phone and grabbed his coat.

"What is it? Leah?" asked Symons.

"There's been – an accident," said Mathers as he headed for the door. Symons looked at Alex then hurried after him. "I'll drive you."

An ambulance was parked haphazardly at the side of the road beside a police car with flashing blue light. As Symons grey Vauxhall turned into the road Mathers saw two ambulance men carrying a stretcher to the terraced house where Leah's second floor apartment was. Symons pulled to a halt and Mathers leapt out and sprinted towards the house. He ran into the open door but at the base of the stairs a police Constable blocked his path. "I'm sorry sir but.."

An Inspector called from upstairs. "Is that Dr. Mathers?"

Mathers looked up. The Inspector was leaning over the banister.

"Yes. I'm Mathers."

He pushed past the policeman and hurried up the stairs. Before he reached the Inspector he saw a pair of feet hanging in the centre of the stairwell. He stopped in fearful anticipation; then slowly walked up the stairs. The naked body swung slowly round blood dripping from between the legs. Mathers circled up the stairs as the face of the white body slowly turned towards him. Hanging from a rope around the neck was Rose.

"I will open my mouth in parables; I will utter things which have been kept secret from the foundation of the world."

Victor stood in the chalked triangle of the bare room reading out loud from the Bible. Haddo was kneeling at the altar.

"Secrets, you see Victor? Now Romans 16:25."

Victor searched for the page. Beneath the altar cloth hiding under the table was Leah.

Victor read, "Now to him that is of power according to the revelation of the mystery, which was kept secret since the world began."

"Ancient secrets," said Haddo getting up.

As he moved Leah suddenly spotted the discarded Polaroid film. It was slowly developing showing that Leah had taken her own image in the wall mirror. Panicked Leah reached for it but Haddo suddenly turned from the altar. She pulled back under.

"I have calculated the position of the planets which dictate that the ceremony must begin at nine two days after the Vigil of Epiphany," said Haddo with total conviction.

"Nine, the number of life and death" added Victor proudly.

"Very good Victor. Then you will witness those secrets hidden from man since the sphinx was aligned to Leo, twelve thousand years ago."

Leah held her breath as Haddo stepped on the Polaroid..

"You've got the Mohel's knife?"

"Yes, it has been kept pure," replied Victor.

"Then let us embark on the greatest event in occult history."

"Will you walk or shall I get the car?"

"Walk, but hurry, I feel a storm coming on."

To Leah's relief they moved out of the library. She listened to them going down the stairs and out the front door.

Symons drove as Mathers sat anxiously rubbing his forehead trying to make sense of it all. The rain began to blur the screen and Symons started the wipers. "So what do they think – the police?"

"They think its suicide," Mathers explained. "Should I have told them?"

"What? About a dream you had?"

"Am I being stupid?"

Symons pointed to the newspaper on the dashboard. "Look at this and tell me I'm being stupid."

Mathers looked at the headline:

'MASSAGE PARLOUR ATROCITY'.

He read rapidly through, "Police search for a Mr Crowley after the gruesome crucifixion of… Haddo! Christ! Do you know where he lives?"

"Oak Street," nodded Symons and spun the car round.

They sped down the main road then after a mile pulled into Oak Street and stopped outside Haddo's house. Mathers ran to the door and rung the bell. There was no answer. Symons followed as Mathers banged on the knocker and tried the handle. Symons looked up through the rain, at the darkened windows. Suddenly there was a crash. Mathers had climbed onto the windowsill and elbowed the glass. Before Symons could say anything, Mathers was in and opening the front door.

Symons stepped in as Mathers checked the ground floor rooms. There was the unfinished game of chess and the stacked books.

Mathers went to the kitchen round the back; nothing, just a mess of opened tins and dirty plates. He ran back and up the stairs and entered the library. Symons followed noticing the large painting of 'Newton' by Blake with its Masonic detail of callipers and angled fingers.

At the top of the stairs was the large grandfather clock with handless face. From the altar in the library Mathers picked up the white queen. Symons saw the discarded Polaroid film on the floor and showed it to Mathers. "She has been here...."

The creased image was of Leah standing before the altar, the bounced flash from the mirror caused a strange triangular flare round her.

"I knew it," said Mathers desperately. "She's in serious trouble, isn't she?"

Symons avoided the answer "I wonder where they might be?"

Mathers stopped. "He said – it's not where we'll find her but when."

"When signifies time." Symons pointed to the wall clock. "Look did you see that?" The pendulum was swinging but there were no hands. Symons shivered and intoned.

"So shalt thou conquer space and lastly climb the walls of time, and by the golden path the great have trod.'

Mathers looked at him, "What's that?"

"Crowley wrote it. He's scared."

"Scared?" queried Mathers.

"Of time."

"Why would he be scared of time?"

"If he's not fixed in this time – maybe he needs to perform the Chemical Wedding."

" What is that, a rite?"

"Yes."

"Where would he do it?"

"I don't know, but there's one person who might."

As she turned into Sion Park Road Leah lifted up the camera and through the eyepiece followed Haddo and Victor as they entered a small Masonic Temple. The shutter closed as she snapped the scene. She let the picture develop then walked to the pillared doorway.

'What the hell are they up to?' she thought. She ran her finger over the crushed wood of the door where the lock had been jemmied.

'They talked about great secrets and portentous moments but here they are breaking in like common criminals.'

She tried the handle. It opened.

Leah entered the hallway where several items of regalia were on a sideboard. She took a photo of them and one of the callipers and setsquare emblem on the wall. She recognized the symbols that gave rise to the expressions 'On the level' and 'On the square.' She walked over to the large bronze doors that had engraved on them the images of the Origin of the World, The Garden of Eden, Noah's Ark and Moses with the Ten Commandments. 'What language are they in?' she reflected with a smile of remembrance. She placed her hand on the central image of the Great Architect and pushed the doors silently open to reveal an interior dimly lit by candles. Leah walked in and moved round the shadowed edge. Suddenly in the dark she noticed a black-cloaked figure sitting in the Eminent Preceptor's chair; so still and silent it could be a statue. She walked along the side aisle to get a better look – just as Professor Brent had done in the interactive suit. The head moved round and light caught Haddo's grinning face.

"The curious cat comes willingly."

Suddenly the bronze door closed behind her with a bang. Leah turned – there was nobody there. Victor jumped out from behind a pillar and grasped her round the throat. She twisted violently, thrusting her knee into his groin. Victor gulped and sunk to the floor.

Leah apologized. "I'm sorry but…"

From behind, Haddo grabbed her round the mouth and thrust

a syringe deep into her neck. She struggled but slowly felt the strength drain from her muscles till she sank to the floor.

A light shone in Professor Brent's frozen eyes. Symons gently moved the reflection from Crowley's old pocket watch from eye to eye as he attempted to induce a hypnotic state. Mathers and Dr Timlet stood by.

"Deep sleep – Deep sleep. Now as you wake you will only hear my voice. Do you understand – only my voice?"

Professor Brent answered mesmerically. "Yes."

Dr Timlet was amazed, he'd never heard of a catatonic being susceptible to hypnosis. This was one strange case.

"We are going back… going back to yesterday morning. You are in the interactive suit… in the suit…. You remember?" asked Symons.

"Yes."

"You see something. An image… What is it you see?"

"An office," croaked Professor Brent.

Symons looked round at Mathers who nodded. Symons turned back and continued. "Then what happened?"

"She showed me a door."

Again Symons checked with Mathers. "He saw something through the door we didn't generate."

Symons continued, "What did you see through the door?"

Professor Brent did not answer.

Symons tried again. "What did you see through the door?"

Brent pursed his lips.

"You will answer me."

Brent shook his head. "We are forbidden to speak."

"Forbidden. Who forbids you?

"No."

"Who forbids you? Haddo?"

"No."

Mathers leaned forward. "Was it Crowley?"

"He can't hear you," interjected Symons. "He can only hear my voice."

Symons turned back to Professor Brent. "Was it Aleister Crowley?"

Professor Brent became agitated. "Thou closes the door of my lips. Thou closes the door of my lips. Thou closes the door of my lips."

Mathers suggested a new track.

"Haddo knew everything about me from the suit. He must know what's going on. Some of that information from Victor's program should still be installed in his brain."

Symons bent down and stared into Professor Brent's eyes.

"What do you need to perform the Chemical Wedding?"

"The relics of Joseph of Arimathea."

Symons turned to Mathers and nodded. "The religious relics associated with Joseph of Arimathea are a knife, a cup to catch the holy blood and a reed."

"Ask him where it's performed."

"Professor, where is it performed?"

"Notre Dame."

"In Paris? He's taken her to Paris?" whispered Mathers.

"No, Crowley told me that's where it was last performed by Abelard and Heloise."

"Wait, Arimathea is legend but Abelard and Eloise are real. I've seen their tomb in Paris, in Pere Lachaise cemetery."

"I would say they are both real. And both must have performed the rite, one in the tomb in Gethsemane in AD 33 and the other in Notre Dame in Eleven seventeen. You know the story."

"Abelard was a monk who was having sex in Notre Dame with Eloise, a nun. Her uncle the Bishop of Notre Dame caught them and in a fit of fury – cut off Abelard's penis.

"And then?" asked Symons.

"She was pregnant and gave birth to a child, Astarte."

"Sounds totally implausible unless there was no angry uncle and what was actually going on in Notre Dame was a rite. A rite which resulted in Abelard becoming a great spiritual leader, and within the year one of the most powerful mystical groups in Europe was formed – the Knights Templar."

"The knife, the cup to catch the blood, what's the reed for?"

"A substitute phallus to perform a non carnal union – a virgin birth."

Dr. Timlet was beginning to think he had another couple of patients ready for the padded cell. But Mathers was equally sceptical.

"That can't be it. Mutilation as a spiritual rite? "

"What do you think circumcision is as performed by a Rabbi?"

"Circumcision is one thing but –"

"Remember castration was still common a hundred years ago. And in the Grail mystery – the Fisher King is injured and his lance is brought into the banquet in a salva bleeding at one end. A salva being a long dish"

"The lance – the amputated penis?" queried Mathers.

"The suggestion is clear enough even in Richard Wagner's 'Parsival' Klingsor amputates his penis to join the knights who guard the Holy Grail."

"She's not going to participate in that."

"She just has to arrive willingly – then.."

Mathers looked horrified; he turned to Professor Brent.

"Where did you see Crowley?"

Brent didn't react.

"He can't hear," said Symons. "Let me hand him over to you,"

He looked closely into Professor Brent's eyes, "The next voice you will hear is Dr. Mathers, only Dr. Mathers. You will answer everything he asks.... Everything he asks."

Mathers lent in. "Where did you see Aleister Crowley?"

Professor Brent looked scared. "High throned between Boaz and – no... no!"

Mathers forcefully "Where – where? What was through the door?"

"Blackness."

"No, you saw something. What did you see?"

Brent's lips are sealed.

Symons interjects. "Was it the ho tekton?"

Brent leapt up. "THE BLACKNESS! THE BLACKNESS!"

He rushed towards the window. Mathers grabbed him and struggled him back to the chair.

Dr. Timlet assisted anxiously. "I'm sorry I can't have you agitating the patient like this. You'll have to bring him out."

We need to know where..?"

"NO! I've said that's enough. I'm grateful that you've opened up a line of diagnosis but I must insist that you bring him out, NOW!"

Leah tried to move her limbs but they felt so tired and heavy. She squeezed open her eyes, the blur of dim pinpoints of light flickered around her but she could not focus the image. Then a dark shadow crossed her sight, as Victor, still in some pain, hobbled round lighting a circle of candles. His eyes watched Haddo sitting in his black cloak snapping open a phial and sucking the contents up into a syringe.

"Brother Omnia Vincarn. You watch me like a hungry dog."

Victor realized and looked away. Haddo held the syringe to the light and flicked it then injected it into his arm. After squeezing out the contents he then pulled blood back into the syringe.

"I've eaten the meal. Do you want the scraps?"

Haddo held up the blood filled syringe. Victor hurried over rolling up his sleeve. Haddo thrust the syringe into Victor's arm and let go.

"By the pricking of my thumbs, something wicked this way comes."

Victor grabbed the dangling syringe and pressed the plunger. His face relaxed with relief.

Haddo looked up to the Gods. "Tis now the very witching time of night, when churchyards yawn and hell itself breathes out."

Haddo noticed Victor's wrist watch.

"And before we get started, Brother Omnia Vincarn – GET THAT FUCKING WATCH OFF!"

Victor jumped and hurriedly un-strapped his watch.

Haddo sat back calmly. "And be a good chap and make sure she's not wearing one. Time is after all, only relative."

Symons' Vauxhall sped down the High Street. Mathers turned questioningly.

"What did you say to him? Hotekon?"

"Ho tekton," corrected Symons. "It's a Greek rendition of the Semitic word naggar, which in the Bible is mistranslated as 'carpenter'."

"Like Jesus' father was a carpenter?" asks Mathers.

"Jesus' father was never a carpenter, especially as it clearly states he was of the Royal line of David. The word actually translates as the Masonic, 'Master of the Craft'. Joseph, Jesus father, is described in the Bible as a Ho Tekton, a Master of the Craft, and nowhere is he said to be a carpenter.

"So who was his father?"

"Well, there is another person - another Joseph - who is described as a Ho tekton in the Bible who it would seem is the father."

"Who?"

"The other Ho tekton is Joseph of Arimathea."

"Joseph of Arimathea!"

"That is why he is able to take charge of events at the crucifixion. Why he can ask for the body from Pilate. Why he can lay it in his tomb without any protest from his mother or anyone else. It also explains why in Bloodline stories like 'The Holy Grail,' Joseph of Arimathia is mentioned as the father of Lancelot and Grandfather of Galahad. And of course it explains the legend of Glastonbury where he brought his son, on a visit to Britain."

"That's extraordinary," said Mathers.

"'And did those feet in ancient time, walk upon England's mountains green'. There are a lot of things that become clearer if you correctly translate the Bible. 'Almah' for instance is the Semitic word translated as 'virgin' but it means no more than a 'young woman'. The actual Hebrew word denoting a physical virgin is 'bethulah'. The 'Red Sea' in the Exodus is a mistranslation. It is actually the 'Sea of Reeds', which was a marshy area on the Mediterranean coast. So a tidal wave from the Thera volcano would explain the sea going out a long way and then returning with amazing force. A tsunami."

Mathers pondered for a moment then anxiously returned to the pressing problem. "Then why did you say 'was it the Ho Tekton' to Professor Brent?"

"He mentioned a couple of Masonic terms so I wondered if it might be some sort of clue. Does it relate to anything you saw when Brent was in the suit?"

The car pulled into the University and round to the Physics block as Mathers explained, "We only saw part of the event that happened in the suit. He disappeared into blackness."

Symons picked up on the idea. "Magic has but one dogma, that the seen is the measure of the unseen. And Crowley said 'Magic is science in posse'."

"Magic is science in posse?" thought Mathers.

"Pythagoras asserted that all mystery arises from the vibration of the spheres. You see?"

Mathers shook his head, "No, what are you driving at?"

Symons pulled the car to a halt and turned to Mathers. "Crowley also wrote, 'All energy implies vibration'."

"Vibration, you mean String Theory?" asked Mathers.

"Isn't that the latest unifying theory?" suggested Symons.

"Ed Witten claimed that vibrating strings predict the existence of extra dimensions and..." Mathers brain sped furiously through all the historical, philosophical and mathematical information stored in his memory, "in Copenhagen, Niels Bohr stunned Schrödinger with proof that his quantum equations, which Schrödinger thought expressed the real world, actually represented a complex form of vibrations in an imaginary mathematical space which Bohrs called 'configuration space'. Worse than that, each particle such as an electron needed its own three dimensions of space. So to describe two electrons requires six dimensions and three electrons nine dimensions. Then Feynman suggested a pion can turn into a neutron and an antiproton for a short time and this can happen to a virtual pion." Mathers was now beginning to lose Symons totally. " In fact mathematically, taking in the uncertainty principal, a proton can explode into a buzzing network of virtual particles all interacting and then subside back into itself before the Universe notices in what Frtjof Capra called 'the cosmic dance'."

Symons interrupted, "The point is, could Brent in his cyberworld have moved into configuration space or even into another dimension?"

"Well yes, but you'd need to produce a graviton to pass between dimensions and nobody has ever produced a graviton – unless..."

"Unless what?"

"If a particle meets its antiparticle it is thought to annihilate. But maybe in cyberia it doesn't. Maybe it just becomes a graviton and... And that would also be the one place to experience what Brent saw. Come on."

Mathers leapt out of the car and hurried towards the Physics block. Symons thought for a moment then realized the implications.

"No!"

Too late Mathers was through the doors of the Lab. Symons followed anxiously. He passed a group of students hanging round a 'Granta' distribution box. The headlines read, 'CROWLEY RETURNS AS CAMBRIDGE LECTURER'

In the laboratory Mathers purposefully started switching on terminals. Panel lights flicked on. Through the window the spotlight picked out the suit. Mathers wrote on a pad: Symons watched him anxiously.

"These are the instructions you type into the computer," said Mathers without looking up, "It's all pretty straightforward."

Symons looked out at the suit. "The last man in there never made it out in one piece."

Mathers finished his notes and handed a disc to Symons.

"This disc is a record of Professor Brent's experience."

"Are you sure about this?"

"What other choice have I got? I do have one trick though; it might just work. If you think I'm in trouble type this."

Mathers pointed to a command in his notes.

Symons read: "Space flight simulator" he looked up. "How does that help?"

"Acceleration changes the speed of time. Einstein," Mathers said as he headed for the door.

"Wait!" Symons pulled out Crowley's pocket watch. "Take this. In demonology if you possess a personal object you have power over that person."

Mathers gingerly took the watch, Symons looked into his eyes.

"Good luck. Uncertainty may be your best chance."

Mathers opened the door. "I feel like Schrodinger's cat."

Symons smiled. "Let's hope God *does* throw dice."

Mathers closed the airlock door. Symons went to the observation window and watched him cross the hangar to the bright glass room where the suit waited. As Mathers opened the glass door Symons whispered to himself. "Lasciate ogni speranza voi ch'entrate." Dante's famous words carved over the entrance to Hell. 'Abandon hope all ye who enter.'

Haddo sat in the chair with his eyes closed. His black cloak was slightly open showing his fatty breasts. He breathed evenly, his nostrils flaring wide. His eyes were rolling under his eyelids, the right cheek trembled with involuntary muscle spasms. There was a sudden crack of lightning and the eyes opened wide to reflect the Temple in the dilated pupils. His lips whispered in Latin.

"Tu Venus orta mari venius tu filia Patris, Exaudi penis carmina, precor, Ne sit culpa nates nobis futuisse viriles, Sed caleat cunnus semper amore meo."

Another flash of lightning illuminated the body of Leah, tied by her foot to the central pillar. Victor was extracting blood through a syringe from her arm. The pillar dropped back into shadow and Victor came out carrying the blood filled syringe. He handed it to Haddo who held it to his lips. With both hands he raised it in the air and shouted.

"MORS JUSTI!"

Then plunged the syringe into his heart.

Symons watched as the computer generated the Japanese office on the monitor. He glanced out at the suit in the bright glass room then back to the monitor where Kieko was sitting at her desk. Symons lent forward and spoke over the intercom.

"Who's that?"

Mathers voice replied over the speaker. "She's computer generated."

Symons lent back and watched the monitor where the image was moving towards Kieko. She rose and smiled.

"I'm pleased to meet you Dr. Mathers. My name is Kieko."

"You know my name?" asked Mathers

"Professor Brent implanted that information as he came through. How can I help you?"

"I would like to follow Professor Brent."

The image turned towards the door. There was just a blank wall.

"Where's the door?" Mathers asked her.

"I'm afraid that was Professor Brent's creation."

"The chaos factor. Symons, feed in Prof Brent's record."

"Are you sure you want to risk that?"

"It's the only way," replied Mathers.

Symons gingerly inserted the disc marked 'Professor Brent' into the computer and fearfully wondered if this information would lead to the imaginary mathematical space where Brent encountered the destructive force? Niels Bohr's infamous 'configuration space'?

Haddo sat with the syringe still in his chest. He looked down and shivered with pleasure. "Now are our brows bound with victorious wreaths. Bring me my crown, I have immortal longings in me."

Haddo reached down and sucked his own blood back into the syringe. He stood up and walked towards the altar. As he knelt he raised the syringe. Through the red liquid the Temple was distorted red. Victor untied Leah and dragged her across the chequered carpet into the chalked circle. Her eyes were half open, but her body was limp.

Haddo stared deep into the syringe where the red blood corpuscles were floating in the plasma. Amongst them black amoeboid structures engulfed platelets.

"And the earth was without form, and void; and darkness was upon the face of the deep."

Symons watched the monitor where Kieko was looking at the blank wall space. Slowly, half transparent at first, the computer generated the missing door.

"It's working," announced Mathers

Symons smiled with satisfaction; Mathers tried the handle of the door. It opened slowly but it revealed nothing but blackness.

"Goddamn it."

"What was there before?" asked Symons.

"I don't know. That's where Professor Brent saw something we didn't. He was mouthing something that sounded like a religious ritual."

Mathers pushed his hand through the door. It disappeared. He withdrew it then tried moving forward but everything just went black. He pulled back.

"Professor Brent's blackness," reminded Symons.

"Something generated an image here - unless it could be.... CDM.

"CDM?" queried Symons.

"Cold dark matter."

Haddo turned towards Leah. She raised her head and saw the blurred dark figure approaching with the infected syringe. Haddo stopped in the triangle before her and raised the syringe again. "Jungitar in vati vates."

Victor fell to his knees and held his knuckles to his mouth in fear.

"I summon thee from the depths of the abyss to enter this Holy Union."

There was a crack of lightning and a window broke overhead. The glass fell gracefully down and finally smashed to tiny pieces on the floor. Suddenly a wind gusted and swirled into the Temple.

Haddo yelled. "CHORONZON."

And the wind grew to a thunderous roar. Victor grasped the foot of the pillar. Haddo's cloak flapped wildly like an enormous bat, his jowls rippled like a jet pilot's, his fists clenched.

In Cyber-world a sudden gust of wind pulled papers off the desk. Kieko grabbed for them but the wind grew, sucking the papers and files through the open door of the office into the blackness. The wild tempest sucked with such force that Kieko was forced to hold onto her desk.

Symons watching on the monitor jumped to his feet.

"What's happening?"

"A singularity!" Mathers yelled. "It's a black hole."

Mathers and Kieko fought the sucking wind that raged to a roar.

Symons watched horrified as the image was sucked violently through the doorway into the black hole. And suddenly – BLACKNESS.

The computer lights flashed. Then silence.

Symons jumped up and looked out at the glass room.

Mathers and the suit had gone. Symons eyes were wide with disbelief. Urgently he turned to the computer and typed. 'SPACE FLIGHT SIMULATION'.

The tornado swirls round the temple. Out of the roaring confusion, Mathers falls onto the chequered carpet. He is not in the suit. He tries to understand his surroundings. A bolt of lightning flashes through the broken window and hits the altar. An energy band zips from the altar to the metal candlesticks on either side and up to the light bulb above. A vibrating electric blue triangle formed with Haddo in the centre. The light bulb bursts and the circle of light forms a permanent after-image, like an eye in the triangle. Haddo steps forward in slow motion. Mathers moves quickly towards Leah but the energy field encompasses the circle and flings him back with a static spark. Haddo moves towards Leah with the syringe. Mathers notices Crowley's watch that has fallen on the floor. The hands are moving quickly.

Haddo grabs Leah by the hair and pulls her head up to face the syringe. Her bleary eyes open passively. She sees Mathers try again to enter the circle but he is zapped back into the puddle from the rain through the open skylight. Mathers points Leah to the large metal candelabra. She makes a last desperate struggle and kicks the candelabra, it tips across the circle into the puddle. There is a sharp electric flash as the power earths for a second and Mathers leaps over the fallen candelabra into the circle. The watch stops in the negative field.

Mathers swings the watch chain round Haddo's throat and yanks him back. Haddo struggles in surprise. Then with surprising strength he yanks Mathers round and turns the syringe on him. Mathers grabs the hand and tries to hold it away. Haddo forces it closer and closer to Mathers throat. Mathers is slowly forced down on to one knee.

Haddo suddenly knees Mathers in the throat and viciously thrusts the syringe deep into Mathers face. Haddo grins as he presses the plunger. Mathers jerks back, the syringe leaves a hole in his cheek. Haddo holds him up by the collar and smiles.

"As above. so below."

Mathers, dazed, grabs onto Haddo's cloak and pulls himself

slowly up. Haddo smiles down at him with the contempt of the conqueror over the vanquished. Mathers rises closer and closer to Haddo's face. Their eyes meet.

"Blood of my blood, body of my body," smirks Haddo.

Mathers purses his lips as if to kiss him then spits out the blood, which had entered his mouth through the cheek. It covers Haddo's face and eyes. Grasping the moment Mathers leaps up and presses the watch to Haddo's face. The watch flashes red and starts to run backwards. Mathers pulls at Haddo's face and opens the mouth. He thrusts the watch into his mouth. Haddo panics, he struggles frantically to get free. The watch is choking him. Haddo sinks to his knees his eyes bulging. As the watch spins backwards the circle also spins and the walls rotate against it. Suddenly the, broken window glass, reforms on the floor and flies up into the air. It replaces itself into the window frame. The reversed crack of lightning in the sky sucks out the blue triangle and flashes blindingly.

A violent blue flash surrounded the computer. Symons jumped back. The lights pulsed off. The blue electric flare ran down the umbilical chord to the glass room and hit it with a blinding spark. Symons shielded his eyes. In the empty glass room the form of the suit suddenly reappeared and fell to the ground. The computer lights died.

Symons clicked on the intercom, "Mathers! MATHERS!"

There was no answer. Symons looked round at the dead computer then back to the window. He hurried to the door, pulled it open and ran into the hangar. The door behind him closed with a thump and the computer suddenly burst back to life. All the lights came on and the tapes ran. The digital time code numbers sped through.

Symons ran along the umbilical chord to the glass room. He entered and turned over the suit and unzipped the back. Then he rolled the limp figure back and unclipped the helmet and pulled it off.

Symons was shocked. "Haddo!"

Haddo's face appeared red and flustered; his hair wet and matted.

"W..w..w..where's that V..V..Victor? M..My t..t..t.," stuttered Haddo.

"Where's Mathers?" asked Simons.

"M..Ma..Mathers? W..w..who's M..Mathers?"

The intercom switched on.

"What's going on down there?"

They looked up at the control room window. Victor was standing there looking down at them.

Haddo stammered in shock. "Y..y..you d..d..damn fool. I could have d..d..died of suffocation."

"After 30 seconds."

"It w..w..was longer th..than th..that."

"You fat idiot, you panicked. A girl came looking for Mathers. I had to get rid of her."

Haddo tried hard to control his breathing. Victor shook his head despairingly.

Symons looked from Victor to Haddo and back to Victor.

CHAPTER 5

DAY TWO

Wednesday 6th January

The globular sun rose and Cambridge awoke and went about its business like any other day.

In the laboratory Mathers knelt over the suit in the glass room. He had spent a bad jet lagged night with sordid dreams about the suit and a girl with red hair.

As he slid open a hatch in the helmet there was a knocking sound. For a moment dreams and reality were confused. A couplet from Shakespeare crossed his mind and unfortunately he murmured it out loud.

"Wake Duncan with thy knocking? I would thou could'st," recalling too late the theatrical superstition that it is very unlucky to quote the 'Scottish Play' at the beginning of any enterprise. The knocking persisted. He looked up to see Leah smile and open the glass door.

"Dr. Mathers."

He took a moment to place her. "I thought I'd dreamt you. Leah yes?"

"Robinson." Leah added.

"From Granta," remembered Mathers.

"You said five but you didn't say where."

"Sorry I was a bit jet lagged.

Behind them Symons entered the hangar. "Thank God you're all right."

"I'm sorry?" queried Mathers.

Symons looked from Mathers to Leah and back to Mathers. It began to dawn on him.

"You don't know me, do you?"

"Should I?"

"No... no," said Symons as he turned slowly to the door.

Mathers watched him then turned to Leah. "The interview."

At the door Symons stopped and watched them.

"I suddenly felt strangely out of place..."

CHAPTER 6

STRING THEORY

The speeding clouds hurry over the ancient buildings. Symons stands at the window as before telling the story.

"...I suddenly felt strangely out of place – as if I was on another planet, in a different time zone...."

He turns to Alex in his wheelchair.

"Not one person seems to have missed those days. Why just me?"

Alex's amplified voice responds. *"You witnessed his death."*

"And so his resurrection. I don't know maybe I just dreamt it all."

"No. Scientific equations are reversible, even those with time. The uncertainty principle almost demands that parallel universes exist. What could have happened is Schrodingers theoretical experiment of the cat in the box. Only when the experimenter opens the lid, or in your case, takes off the helmet, only then does he find out what universe he's in."

"So in some parallel universe Aleister Crowley is wandering about."

"And in that other universe the world is a more evil place. Wars, earthquakes, atrocities, disasters."

"Thank god he's not in ours."

Symons turns and wheels Alex out of the study. He stops in the corridor.

"Hold on, I'll just get my newspaper."

He returns to the study and picks up the newspaper off his desk. He hardly gives a glance at the headline:

'AL GORE IS PRESIDENT AFTER FLORIDA RECOUNT'.

Symons tucks the paper under his arm and walks out into his world.

He pushes Alex down the corridor.

"You won't remember this but you know what your theory was?" muses Symons. "That it was nothing at all to do with Victor's program but Mathers' suit carried a virus of Parsons Moonchild from Cal Tech. Interesting no?"

"Respice finem!"

"Judge the end," translates Symons and walks on thinking he is the only one who remembers those missing days. But.....

Mathers carefully adjusts the suit on Professor Brent. He pays extra attention to the elbow joint which has a small brown blood stain. Professor Brent is a little apprehensive.

"What happened there?"

"I fell. It's sometimes hard to keep your balance in Cyberia.

Victor's voice comes over the intercom.

"Dr Mathers."

Mathers looks up at the window., .

Victor continues, "Could the suit be carrying a virus?"

Mathers shrugs, "I don't see how. Why?"

"Well its weird," says Victor hesitantly, "There's something wrong with the Z93's date time file."

There is a pause as Victor scratches his head trying to understand. "The Z93 is set two days into the future and its not allowing me to correct it"

Mathers looks at Professor Brent blankly.

Victor's voice echoes round the hangar. "Is there a code to access the helmet's computer?"

"Sure, says Mathers, "1, 12, 47 my date of birth," .

Victor mumbles as he types the date into the computer.

"Sagittarius. Deep with hidden.... Wait a minute, the first of December nineteen forty-seven, that's the day Aleister Crowley died..." Victor smiles at the coincidence and presses enter.

The computer screen image blanks as slowly the Z93 puts together all the information and slowly prints out the word....

'MOONCHILD'.

Victor looks from the computer screen to Mathers down in the glass room. He rubs his head as he tries to remember something deep in his subconscious.

Symons and Alex continue their discussion as they approach the lecture theater.

"Symons, there's a couple of details that don't add up."

"For instance?"

"How did Mathers get out of the ceremony when the door was locked? And who killed Rose?"

They pass the blackboard at the door of the Lecture Theater.

'MAUDLYNE CLASSICS LECTURE'

The Psychology of Hamlet by Dr. Oliver Haddo

In the packed theater, Leah is chatting with Jones. Symons watches her then leans over to Alex.

"The time is out of joint. O cursed spite, that ever I was born to set it right."

"You set it right because you had the watch."

"Yes, I suppose. Wait a minute where is the watch?"

Symons feels his empty waistcoat pocket.

Suddenly Haddo appears and walks to the lectern. The porter closes the doors. Haddo coughs and the chatter subsides. Once it is quiet he begins.

"It has become c..c..common practice to describe H..H..Hamlet as a t..t..tragic figure who c..c..could not make his m..m..mind up. But surely th..this is just a sym..symptom of a disease. A diseased m..mind that speaks the w..words, 'O! th..that this too, too sordid flesh would m..melt, Thaw and resolve itself into a dew..."

Haddo's face is back to its soft roundness his mouth a little less firm. But there is something odd about his speech. Behind the sound of his voice, somewhere deep inside, there is a gentle sound of ticking....

'On the seventh day, the old King gave me a
golden medal, bearing on one side the words,
'ART IS THE PRIESTESS OF NATURE
and on the other,
'NATURE IS THE DAUGHTER OF TIME'

The Chymical Wedding (1642)

BIBLIOGRAPHY

Timothy Freke. Peter Gandy *The Jesus Mystery* 1999

Francis King. *The Magical World of Aleister Crowley* 1977

H. Lincoln, M. Baigent & R Leigh. *The Holy Blood & Holy Grail*

Fred Gettings. *The Hidden Art* 1978

David Wood. *Genisis* 1985

Flavius Josephus. *The Antiquity of the Jews* 70

Flavius Josephus. *The War of the Jews* 70

John Gribbin. *In Search of Schrodinger's Cat* 1984

Laurence Gardner. *The Magdalene Legacy* 2005

C. Knight & R. Lomas. *Uriel's Machine* 2000

C. Knight & R. Lomas. *The Hiram Key* 1998

David Rohl. *Test of Time* 1995

Colin Wilson Rand Flem-ath. *The Atlantis Blueprint* 2000

Tacitus. *The Histories* 79

Jim Keith. *Secret and Suppressed* 1993

C. Morton Ceri Louise Thomas. *The Mystery of the Crystal Skulls*

Aleister Crowley (ed. K. Grant & J. Symonds). *Confessions of Aleister Crowley* 1979

Stephen Knight. *The Brotherhood* 1985

Robin Lane Fox. *The Unauthorized Version*

M. Baigent & R. Leigh. *The Dead Sea Scrolls Deception* 1991

Trevor Ravenscroft. *The Spear of Destiny* 1973

Oliver Sachs. *The Man who Mistook his Wife for a Hat* 1985

Peter Berrisford Ellis. *Celtic Inheritance* 1985

Johann Valentin Andreas. *The Chemical Wedding of Christian RosenKreutz* 1616

Sandy Robinson. *The Aleister Crowley Scrapbook* 1988

APPENDIX

Was Joseph of Arimathea Jesus' Father?

The Grand Master, Symons describes the mistranslation of the word 'Ho teckton' in the Bible. This is well known and appears in many books. A modern Greek would even translate Ho Teckton as 'Master of the Craft'. Craft as in witch-craft or as a description of an expert in Masonic ritual. A few books also draw the conclusion that Jesus father, Joseph was unlikely to be a carpenter.

Surely it clearly states in the Bible that the young Jesus was brought up in Nazareth in his father's humble carpentry shop. We have the images in our minds and we know the stories.

But no! These stories are not in the Bible. Nowhere does it tell such a story. And in fact there is even question as to whether the town of Nazareth even existed at that time in Israel.

Samson is described in the Bible as a Nazarene and a Nazorite is someone who lives his life to strict Jewish religious law. In fact the real meaning has slipped through into the Bible. Both in the description of Samson and also when Paul is brought before the Governor Felix, Tertullus accuses Paul:

> 'For we have found this man a pestilent, and a mover of sedition among the Jews throughout the world, and a ringleader of the sect of the Nazarenes.' (*Acts* 24:5)

Nazarene here is clearly a sect that appears to apply to Jesus' group. And perhaps the word's meaning is changed to disassociate Jesus from these Jewish rebels. The Bible often attempts to separate Jesus from his Jewish self. For instance several places in John's Gospel it states 'And the Jews called out to Jesus." Or "Jesus said to the Jews." Quite ridiculous when you consider Jesus is not only a Jew but is actually described in places as a Rabbi!

Mistranslations are common. When Mary and Joseph arrive in Bethlehem and find there is no room at the inn. But the Greek term translated as inn (*kataluma*) had multiple meanings. And Luke uses the term again – at the last supper - this time clarifying his use of the word. *Kataluma,* not as an inn but a furnished large upper story room within a private house.

Jesus may not have been conceived by God, his father was not a carpenter, he didn't live in Nazareth and was not born in a stable.

So Joseph was not a humble carpenter especially as he was from the Royal line of David, of the King line. Blood-line was considered extremely important in Israel. Even the historian Josephus, the only Jewish historian writing at he time of Christ, claims at the beginning of his Histories that he is important because he is from the bloodline of Aaron. And Josephus writes that even King Herod took as his second wife a Blood line Princess to try to gain legitimacy to his king status. This means quite clearly that if Jesus is from the line of David, this humble carpenter's son, is a more legitimate King than Herod.

So what and who was this Joseph who was a Ho tekton – a 'Master of the Craft - who was Jesus' father? If here you say Jesus' father was God – you have to read Jesus genealogy as stated in both Matthew and Luke. Both admit Joseph from the line of David was the father. The idea of Jesus being the Son of God only appears after the Council of Nicaea 300 years after his death where it was established that he was the Son of God, by a vote of Bishops.

The one Joseph in the Bible who fits the description – a Joseph from the line of David; an important person, a Ho Teckton – the probable father of Jesus is – Joseph of Arimathea!

Is this just an unfounded fabrication on my part? Let's look into my research.

Joseph of Arimathea is mentioned in just one event in the Bible, The burying of Jesus in his own tomb. The Gospels tell us (M 27:57-61; P 15:42-47; L 23:50-56; J 19:38-42) that after the death of Jesus, Joseph of Arimathea, a wealthy member of the Council, asked Pilate for the body of Jesus, and buried it in the tomb he had intended for himself. But Joseph of Arimathea might pass through the gospels very briefly, but he enjoyed an incredible role in later legends. According to various accounts, Joseph of Arimathea lived in Egypt, and traveled to England where he founded the first Christian Church. He appears in the legends of the Holy Grail, being the protector of the Holy Grail, and an ancestor of Lancelot, Galahad or even of King Arthur himself.

But could he be Jesus father?

Well just taking the events in the Bible – Joseph goes to Pilate to ask for the body of Christ – surely only a relative would make this plea and could be granted the body. And what does he do with the body. Place it in his family tomb!

But more, Aleister Crowley was born on the same year that the mystic Eliphas Levi died and claimed to be his reincarnation.

Leah quotes one of Levi's statements:

> 'Elders from the Line of David would impregnate a young maiden to preserve the blood-line.'

Could this be what happened especially as in art Joseph is always shown as an older man?

Is there any other synchronicity between Jesus and Joseph? Well after birth Jesus is taken by Mary and Joseph to Egypt. Strangely in legend Joseph of Arimathea is said to spend time in Egypt.

As a bloodline child it would be prudent to leave Israel as it was common for Kings of Israel to kill off any potential competitors. The Bible tells us David did it: as did Solomon. Josephus, the historian tells us that Herod himself killed his sons from his bloodline wife when they showed signs of leading a rebellion

It is said Joseph of Arimathaea derived his wealth from tin mines in Cornwall, which he visited from time to time; and that Jesus as a teen-ager accompanied Joseph on one such visit. This is the background of the poem 'Jerusalem', by William Blake.

> And did those feet in ancient time walk upon England's
> mountains green?
> And was the holy Lamb of God on England's pleasant
> pastures seen?
> And did the countenance divine shine forth upon our
> clouded hills?
> And was Jerusalem builded here, among those dark satanic
> mills?

Legend also has it that Joseph established a community of 12 believers in Glastonbury. He was given 12 hides of land by the King and established there the first Christian Church. Legend? Well in the Doomsday book the 12 hides of land are listed and not taxed because of their religious significance.

Interestingly when Joseph took Jesus to Egypt as a child, the place they would most likely settle – the place where there was a large Jewish community – was Alexandria. And a charismatic sage there called Timotheus fused Osiris and Dionysis to produce a new God for the city called Serapis. Like all the mystery religions at the time the features of this God were.

1. A God made flesh.
2. His father is God his mother a mortal virgin.
3. He is born in a humble cave on 25th December
4. He offers his followers a chance to be born again through the rites of baptism
5. He miraculously turns water into wine at a wedding.
6. He rides triumphantly on a donkey while people wave palms

in his honor.

7. He dies at Easter-time as a sacrifice for the sins of the world.
8. After his death he descends to hell, then on the third day he rises and ascends in triumph. (Note in the film we use the three days to resurrection.)
9. His followers await his return as the judge during the last days.
10. His death and resurrection is celebrated by a ritual meal of bread and wine - symbolizing the body and blood.

Sounds familiar? What about the philosophy of the Mystery religions?

1. Be pure of thought and deed.
2. Have a personal loving relationship with god.
3. Love your neighbour.
4. Love your enemies.
5. Embrace poverty and humility.
6. Believe in one God.
7. Attack idolatry.
8. The Son of God is the embodiment of the logos.
9. Conceived of God as a Holy Trinity.

And when Jesus and Joseph finally returns from Egypt how would they view Him in Israel. Presumably he would have a different accent.

Interestingly the historian Josephus writes of a prophet who he calls the Egyptian. Obviously the Jews would not follow an Egyptian but a Jew with obvious Egyptian characteristics.

> 'There was an Egyptian false prophet that did the Jews more mischief than the former; for he was a cheat, and pretended to be a prophet also, and got together thirty thousand men that were deluded by him; these he led round about from the wilderness to the mount which was

> called the Mount of Olives. He was ready to break into Jerusalem by force from that place; and if he could but once conquer the Roman garrison and the people, Now when Felix heard he ordered his soldiers to take their weapons, and came against them with a great number of horsemen and footmen from Jerusalem, and attacked the Egyptian and the people that were with him. He slew four hundred of them, and took two hundred alive. The Egyptian himself escaped out of the fight, but did not appear any more'. [Flavius Josephus, *Jewish War* 2.261-262]

In Antiquities he also tells the story:

> 'about this time, someone came out of Egypt to Jerusalem, claiming to be a prophet. He advised the crowd to go along with him to the Mount of Olives, as it was called, which lay over against the city, and at the distance of a kilometer. He added that he would show them from hence how the walls of Jerusalem would fall down at his command, and he promised them that he would procure them an entrance into the city through those collapsed walls. Now when Felix was informed of these things, he ordered his soldiers to take their weapons, and came against them with a great number of horsemen and footmen from Jerusalem, and attacked the Egyptian and the people that were with him. He slew four hundred of them, and took two hundred alive. The Egyptian himself escaped out of the fight, but did not appear any more.
> [Flavius Josephus, *Jewish Antiquities* 20.169-171]

Why is this character not related to Jesus when it sounds so much like the event in the Bible? First the fact that he is called the Egyptian and second that it occurred during the time of the Governor Felix. But when Paul is arrested it states in Acts of the Apostles:

> 'And as Paul was to be led into the castle, he said unto the chief captain, May I speak unto thee? Who said, Canst thou speak Greek? Art not thou that Egyptian, which before these days made an uproar, and led out into the wilderness four thousand men that were murderers? But Paul said, I am a man, which am a Jew of Tarsus'. (*Acts* 21–38)

So Paul is accused of being 'The Egyptian' suggesting that the Egyptian was functioning at the time of Christ.

But what about Felix being the Governor and not Pilate? There is in fact strong evidence in the Bible that Felix was the Governor at the time. When Paul is brought to trial before Felix, the Prosecuting Lawyer proclaims:

> 'When Paul was called in, a lawyer named Tertullus presented his case before Felix: "We have enjoyed *a long period of peace under you*, and your foresight has brought about reforms in this nation, everywhere and in every way, most excellent Felix, we acknowledge this with profound gratitude...
> We have found this man to be a troublemaker, stirring up riots among the Jews all over the world. He is a ringleader of the Nazarene sect'.

And Paul answers:

> 'Then Paul, after the governor had beckoned him to speak, answered, Forasmuch as I know that thou *hast been of many years* a judge unto this nation, I do the more cheerfully answer for myself.

So Felix had been Governor of Judea for many years; enough to have brought about reforms. Could the Gospels have made a mistake while Acts is correct?

Possibly, as the Gospels were written about 80 years after Jesus death they could well be historically inaccurate. For instance Herod the Great was supposed to be King at the birth of Jesus but in fact Herod died in 4BC, four years before His birth. So he could not have been the King.

FISHER KING

One day, Perceval comes upon a river and seees two men, richly dressed, who are fishing in a boat. He is, therefore, invited to stay over in their castle, which then appears to Pereval behind a hill.

Nobly accommodated, Perceval dines in the company of the rich Fisher King, who is crippled and cannot rise from his seat. A young man enters, holding between his hands a lance, from the point of which blood runs, drop after drop, towards the arm of him who carries it. Perceval is seized by astonishment, but he does not dare raise questions. A young lady then comes holding in her hands the Grail, which shines like a precious stone. When the Grail passes close to the guests, each one is at once served with meats, varied dishes and drinks, acccording to his most secret desires.

The rich Fisher King, who seems to suffer much, looks at Perceval with sadness, but Perceval, struck dumb by timidity, always postpones the questions which burn on his lips. Led to his room, he falls asleep. The following day, Perceval would really have liked to raise the questions about the Grail and the Lance which bleeds, but he no longer sees anyone.

THE AUTHORS

Collaborating on Iron Maiden Pop Videos, Bruce and Julian found many common interests, including a scientific interpretation of the Ancient Occult world.

JULIAN DOYLE

is one of the world's most versatile Film Makers. He has written, directed, photographed, edited and created Fxs all to the highest standards. He has also written a play 'Twilight of the Gods' and directed award winning pop videos such as Kate Bush's 'Cloudbusting' featuring Donald Sutherland. He is most famous for editing Monty Python's films and shooting the Fx's for Terry Gilliam's 'Brazil'. He has just finished directing the feature film of 'Chemical Wedding' featuring Simon Callow.

BRUCE DICKINSON

is equally versatile. He has already published one comic book 'Lord Iffy Boatrace', he Captains passenger jets round the world and he has his own radio program. But despite all this he is also the lead singer of Iron Maiden, the greatest heavy metal band ever. Not only has Bruce sung on hundreds of multi-selling albums but he can fill stadiums from Rio to Tokyo.

CPSIA information can be obtained at www.ICGtesting.com
Printed in the USA
BVOW07s2229281113

337625BV00001B/54/P

9 781848 761339